D0556981

news from home

stories

sefi atta

Interlink Books

An imprint of Interlink Publishing Group, Inc.
Northampton, Massachusetts

First published 2010 by

INTERLINK BOOKS
An imprint of Interlink Publishing Group, Ltd
46 Crosby Street, Northampton, Massachusetts 01060
www.interlinkbooks.com

Text copyright © Sefi Atta, 2010

Library of Congress Cataloging-in-Publication Data
Atta, Sefi.
News from home / by Sefi Atta.—1st American ed.
    p. cm.
ISBN 978-1-56656-803-6 (pbk.)
1. Nigeria—Fiction. I. Title.
PS3601.T78N49 2010
813'.6—dc22

                    2009048648

Grateful acknowledgment is made to the editors of the following publications, where earlier versions of these stories appeared:
"The Miracle Worker" in *Eclectica Magazine*, 2003 (third prize in the *Zoetrope* Short Fiction Contest, 2002). "Hailstones on Zamfara" in *Carve Magazine* and *Los Angeles Review*, 2003 (winner of the Red Hen Press Short Story Award, 2003). "Spoils" as "Spoils of the Death Road" in *Per Contra*, 2006. "Lawless" in *Carve Magazine* and *African Love Stories* (Ayebia Clarke Publishing, 2006). "Twilight Trek" in *International PEN*, 2006 (winner of the David T.K. Wong Prize, 2005). "Last Trip" in *Chimurenga*, 2005 (short-listed for the Caine Prize for African Writing, 2006). "News from Home" as "A Union on Independence Day" in *Eclectica Magazine*, 2003 (finalist for the *storySouth* Million Writers Award, 2004). "Green" in *storySouth*, 2004, and *X-24: unclassified*, 2007.

Cover image © Ferdinandreus / Dreamstime.com

Book design by Juliana Spear

Printed and bound in the United States of America

for Gboyega and Temi

TABLE OF CONTENTS

THE MIRACLE WORKER

Makinde's only point of contention with his new wife, Bisi, was that she gave too much in tithes to her church. Ten percent was not enough for Bisi. She had to prove just how born-again she was, and each time she visited the Abundant Life Tabernacle, she placed a little extra on the collection tray for the married women's fellowship, a haven for gossips as far as Makinde was concerned.

Makinde was a panel beater. He worked on a lot on the corner of a Lagos street. Bisi sold bread and boiled eggs to bus passengers at a nearby depot. When she abandoned her colorful up-and-downs for black dresses, Makinde didn't object. When she stopped speaking to his non-Christian friends because they were sinners, he didn't say a word. He broke his hand after a motorcycle taxi almost ran over him. (Makinde dived into a nearby gutter and held his head for protection. The slime in the gutter was masking a bed of rocks.) Bisi fasted two weeks for his hand to heal. He ate her share of meals and recovered with his small finger permanently bent at a right angle. Bisi was prone to zeal, he thought, so on that afternoon when she came to the lot with his usual lunch of bread and boiled egg, and she saw the windscreen of an old car that had been sitting there for years, and she fell on her knees saying it was a vision of the Virgin Mary, Makinde barely raised his head from his sandwich to acknowledge her. He had cleaned the windscreen with an oily rag to get rid of some bird droppings that offended him. The rain had fallen lightly that morning, and Bisi wasn't even a Catholic.

She ran to the bus depot to tell passengers she'd seen a vision. About a dozen of them came back to confirm. A few, mostly men, walked away joking about Nigerian women and their pious ways. The rest, mostly women, stayed to stare at the dirty windscreen. They trembled and burst into tears. It was a miracle, they said. There was a clear figure all right: one small circle over a bigger mound and rainbow colors around the small circle. More bus passengers joined the onlookers as word of the vision spread. Soon there were enough to make his work impossible. Makinde drove them away.

All his life he had worked—at least from the time his mother had stopped hand-feeding him. He started off by selling oranges on a tray; he never attended school. At age ten he began his apprenticeship with his father, a self-taught mechanic. Makinde pumped tires, plucked nails from them, and patched them up, before graduating to changing spark plugs.

He was not the best mechanic in Lagos, but he was one of the few that people could leave their vehicles with, without fear that parts would go missing. He was amazed by some of the clients he encountered, Mercedes owners, who had access to his country's elusive oil money. Yet these wealthy people were frugal when it came to paying for work. They handed Makinde small change with soft plump palms, while Makinde couldn't even remember the color of his own fingernails. He had black oil under them and cleaned his hands with petrol dabbed on rags like the one he'd used on the windscreen. He ate zero-one-zero to save money: nothing for breakfast, one big lunch meal, nothing for dinner. This was the real miracle: he was still poor.

"My wife," he said, after the visitors had left, "I don't care if you choose to waste your earnings on your church—actually I do, but nothing I say will change your mind. What I won't tolerate is you having a church service here, on my lot, and getting in the way of my work."

"Why?" Bisi asked.

"Your people will scare my customers away with their wailing and shaking."

"How?" Bisi asked.

This was her style of arguing. She wouldn't challenge him, but she asked enough questions to drive him to distraction and hopefully have her way.

"All I'm saying is that it must never happen again," Makinde answered.

He was known as a patient man, because he didn't like talking; talking took his energy. Bisi called him a stubborn man. He refused to attend church services with her.

The next day when Makinde arrived at work a group of about twenty people were waiting in his lot, men, women and children included. They wore white robes and were barefoot despite the ground, a black surface of oil and dirt.

"We have come to see the vision," an old man said.

"In the name of God," Makinde muttered.

It was about five thirty in the morning. Bisi couldn't have told them. He had not bargained on this, those people from yesterday spreading the news.

"I'm sorry," he said. "I can't have you praying on my lot."

"Unfortunately that is out of your control," the old man said. "Celestial forces have chosen this place. You'd do best to submit to their will, rather than try to stand in the way." The old man was smiling, but Makinde was afraid anyway. He believed in a celestial force. He just didn't believe the celestial force considered him special enough to deliver him.

"Over there," he said.

He pointed at the old car, incidentally a once beige Peugeot 405. Now it resembled a carcass. The seats and steering wheel were gone, removed by robbers. The barefoot group walked towards the windscreen. The old man saw the vision first and fell on his knees. His troupe followed, and then they hummed. Makinde beat a panel loudly enough to drown out their noise. At most, he hoped, five groups might visit his lot. Three that day, and maybe two the next. He'd heard about such visions, on dirty glass in poor districts. He could not read, so he didn't know that, in Lagos, these visions actually drew what newspaper reporters called Throngs, and that these throngs Flocked. *Throngs Flock to Vision of Mary on Latrine Window*. *Throngs Flock to Vision of Mary on Popcorn and Groundnut Seller's Glass Cubicle*. Such were past national headlines.

Makinde's prediction was an underestimate. Two hundred and fifty people visited his lot in the morning. By afternoon, about five hundred had been. Makinde stopped showing them the windscreen of the Peugeot. A tall thin woman stayed from her morning visit to act as a guide. She told the story to a reporter: how Makinde and his wife were newlyweds, Bisi was born-again and Makinde didn't attend church. This vision had occurred on his lot nonetheless, and it was a clear sign that God's mercy could manifest just about anywhere.

Bisi came at lunchtime with Makinde's usual bread and boiled egg. She saw the crowds and immediately denied she was responsible: "It wasn't me!"

"Don't worry, I believe you," Makinde said. The situation was out of her control.

The guide woman approached her. "God's blessings to you, my sister."

"To you, too," Bisi said.

"We've been here all morning, without pay, showing the people where to pray for miracles."

"Yes?"

"Yes, and we are getting quite hungry now, so please can you go back to your stall and get bread and eggs for us to eat?"

The guide was referring to herself alone. The miracle she'd prayed for was for others to stop saying she was insane. She knew her calling was to do God's work. Anywhere else in the world she would be a street preacher. Here, she was sent to a hospital, where the doctors injected her while the nurses held her down and later beat her up.

Makinde told Bisi to get her bread and a boiled egg, and then as both women left to carry out their respective tasks, the thought came to his mind. Without pay, the guide had said. The people were standing on his lot, getting in the way of his work. Why not charge them? They paid to attend church. He calculated his lost earnings, net of transportation. He divided that by the number of visitors who came to the lot. He rounded down, taking poverty into consideration, and ended up with a fee of one naira per person.

In front of his lot was the gutter he had dived into to save his life. There was a wide plank over it, tough enough to support vehicles. He stood on the plank and announced, "Excuse me? I am Makinde. Yes, em, the owner of this lot. I have decided I will not get in the way of your worship today. But... I... I am a man of small means, as you can see, and my business is, em, suffering from the constant traffic in and out. Yes, what I'm suggesting is that... can you... can you please... ?"

Talking was exhausting him. Hardly anyone was listening anyway. They were praying, singing, rocking. Makinde raised his voice. "My name is Makinde. I'm the owner of this lot, and I'm telling you now, if you wish to continue to see your vision,

I suggest you pay me one naira each, or else I will take a rag and wipe the vision off."

A hush fell on his lot. One or two people were asking what he was talking about and why he was getting angry. The guide woman was explaining to them when another visitor appeared. Makinde stretched his hand out without looking at her face.

"It's one naira to enter, please," he said.

"Since when?"

It was Bisi. She had returned with the bread and boiled egg for the guide, and so fast.

Makinde earned money that month from the visitors to his lot. He was even in the Sunday newspapers. *Throngs Flock to Miracle at Mechanic's*. People came to pray for cures, scholarships, school examinations, job applications, job promotions, and money mostly. There were visitors in wheelchairs, on crutches; blind visitors; insane, evicted, heartbroken, abandoned, bitter, barren visitors. Beggars and gossips, too, including the women of his wife's fellowship. Some people complained about the one-naira fee. A few refused and walked away. One was a priest. "H-how can you do this?" he asked Makinde. "C-capitalize on people's s-sorrows and-and woes?" Makinde waived his fee as he secretly did for beggars and sick children. The priest still refused to walk into his lot. "D-did Jesus charge for miracles? How do you sleep at night know-knowing you do this for a living?"

Quite well, when he wasn't making love to Bisi, who was now talking about having a child and perhaps taking a break from her work. She conceived one night during a thunderstorm. Hearing the rain on his roof, Makinde worried about the fate of his Virgin Mary, though he'd protected the

Peugeot's windscreen with a tarpaulin sheet and secured its edges with rocks. Had he known the wind was strong enough to shift one of the rocks, and that the rock would roll off the roof of the Peugeot, free an edge of the tarpaulin, and the tarpaulin would flop over the bonnet of the Peugeot, and the raindrops would fall on the windscreen and wipe the vision away, he would have worried more.

He arrived at work the next morning and there were only two people in his lot. One was a vagrant who normally came to look for scraps of food; the second was the guide woman. "Our vision is no more," she said.

The ground of his lot had turned to mud and the gutter in front was overflowing with slime. Makinde could see only the clean windscreen of the Peugeot. He was thinking about how to get back to panel beating.

The guide continued. "It appears the storm last night is the cause. Our work here is done, then. We don't expect you'll have visitors anymore and, as you know, the Lord giveth and the—"

"Quiet!" Makinde shouted, so loudly she ran out of his lot. What kind of Lord gaveth, and then taketh and taketh and taketh? He kicked the Peugeot, which appeared to be grinning, with enough force to dent it. Then he boxed it with just as much force, and the impact straightened his bent little finger.

He did have one visitor that day. A tax assessor, who seemed to be studying the sweat on his own nose. "Mr. Makinde," he began. "Eh, I read about you in the papers. You've been getting a lot of attention here recently, eh? Since you can't call this a church, nor yourself a priest, it means that you are liable for taxes."

Makinde had not paid taxes before. Taxes were for people who wore shirts and ties, people who received checks regularly. He thought the tax assessor was a con man.

"From where are you?" he asked.

"I represent the government."

"Couldn't they give you a clean shirt?"

"You're practically in tatters yourself. What have you done with your money?"

Makinde stroked his bandaged finger, feeling exhausted. Perhaps the man really was a tax assessor, and if so, why didn't he go back to the people he represented, those who had access to his country's oil money, and assess them?

"This is my lot," he said.

"Where is your title?" the tax assessor asked.

"What?"

"Your title deed. To show that the lot belongs to you."

Makinde trembled with anger. How dare the tax assessor question his ownership of the lot. "My father left me this lot," he said. "My father found this lot. He cleared this lot. He worked on this lot." Long before that part of Lagos had been deemed a slum district.

"So it's yours," the tax assessor said. "Then you must show me evidence, at least, that you've paid ground rent on the property, from the time you inherited it. Don't look so vexed. That is another department's business, but I will make sure I alert them after I have finished my assessment of your taxable earnings, eh?"

Makinde removed his shirt. His earnings were hidden under his mattress at home. He slept on them. He wasn't about to let this messenger of wealthy men have access to them.

"What is this?" the tax assessor asked, expecting a blow.

"Here I am," Makinde said, unzipping his trousers. "Tax

my head, my arms, my broken finger included. Tax my legs. See? My foot is sprained, tax that. Here, tax my balls, and when you finish with them"—he turned his backside to the tax assessor—"tax my ass."

The tax assessor promised he would return with henchmen. "You will pay," he said, "or they will help themselves to your wife."

A wife who wouldn't even allow Makinde access to her. She was nauseous and eating dirt now that she was pregnant. Dirt. "I can't help it," she said. "The sight of it makes me want to touch it. The feel makes me want to sniff it. The smell makes me want to eat it."

Makinde watched as she scooped up soil and licked it. He tried to stop her by reminding her of worm eggs. He couldn't afford to take her to a doctor. He couldn't go to work for fear the tax assessor would return with henchmen. They argued. She eventually packed a portmanteau and said she was going to her mother in the village for a week.

Makinde decided to seek counsel from Rasaki, a local man known as the Duke of Downtown; Rasaki, whose work included playing the pools and brokering assault contracts. People said he was friendly with thugs and armed robbers in Lagos, that he smoked marijuana, and drank *ogogoro*, and called out to Lagos chicks, "Baby, I've got a big one." And they replied, "Bet it's the size of a Bic biro." That sort of duke. But he was also known as a person who helped those who were in trouble with the authorities: the police, the mobile squad known as Kill-and-Go, customs and excise and taxmen. He knew exactly who to bribe.

Rasaki was smoking a Bicycle cigarette as Makinde talked. His fingers were as black as his lips, and his teeth were the color of curry. "My friend," he rasped, "what is wrong with your head? You don't insult a tax assessor."

Makinde mumbled, "It's too late for that advice."

Rasaki scratched his armpit. He had just woken up. On his wall was a calendar. The girl of the month, Miss February, had one breast pointing east, the other pointing west. Her teeth had a center parting. Her name was Dolly. "You should have kept your mouth shut," Rasaki said. "Or else you want to offer your wife?"

"My wife," Makinde said. "She smells of boiled egg most days. Right now she eats dirt. I love her. I would not offer my wife to the president if he wanted her."

Rasaki coughed and smacked his chest. "I thought not, and I'm telling you, these taxmen are not normal human beings. They have a lot of hatred in their hearts, and they are vengeful. It is how they get their jobs in the first place. I suggest—and you don't have to take my advice, I'm only suggesting—that you pay him the money he asked for."

"Pay?"

"Yes, because right now he's offended, humiliated. He's a small man psychologically, and nothing you do will pacify him. From my experience, he may probably ask you to pay enough to buy the whole lot."

"How will I ever do that?"

"How much money do you have now?"

"It's here in my pocket."

"Place it on the table, my friend."

Makinde did.

Rasaki studied the naira notes. He tilted his head to one side and then he smiled. "You got this by duping believers?" Rasaki was a Muslim by birth. The last time he visited a mosque was to marry his only wife, who later divorced him.

"I didn't dupe anyone," Makinde answered. "It was an admission fee."

"Call it whatever you want. You were in the game of chances, and you were master of it. People trusted you and you spat on their faith. I'm not blaming you. They were fucking fanatics and they deserved it. Who knows what Mary looked like? Do you?"

Makinde was getting impatient. Rasaki seemed to have a lot of knowledge, except about how to help him out of paying the taxman.

"What can you do for me?" he asked.

"My friend," Rasaki said. "Do you play the pools?"

He was an expert. How else would he have survived without a job for years? Playing the pools was not a risk, he said, and only those who played the pools long enough knew this. They studied odds and they beat odds. Those who lost were outsiders, like believers looking for miracles in lots. "Give me your money and I will return it tenfold," he said.

"How?" Makinde asked.

"Ah-ah? Will I tell you what has taken me decades to learn?"

"Why should I give you what has taken me a month to earn?"

"It's up to you."

"My choices are limited."

"The possibilities are endless."

"You know a lot. How come you're not a rich man yourself?"

"I choose not to be."

"Why?"

"Where else will I be a duke?"

Makinde had to concede; he did not know one person like

Rasaki, who, despite his appearance, skinny with a rash on his neck, walked around downtown as if he were royalty. He wore trousers that were long and flared. "Keep-Lagos-Clean," that fashion was called. His gray hair was cut high on his crown. "Girls-Follow-Me," that hairstyle was called. His girlfriends were prostitutes, he lived in one room, and people knew his wife had divorced him because he was incapable of fathering children, and yet he was extremely sure of himself.

"I came to you because you're a man with connections," Makinde said. "I was hoping for something not so out of the ordinary. A name to slip a bribe perhaps? Let me think about this."

At home, Makinde considered his options. On the one hand was his lot, and in his hand with the broken finger was the money he hadn't earned from working. Free money. It seemed to him that Rasaki was right. He had become master of a game, unwittingly. Who from his lot left with a miracle? Who walked out with more money in their pockets, except him? Those who came on crutches hobbled away, those who came blind shuffled off without seeing. He had not heard from the guide woman, but he was certain she had found another place to preach. Not one of the visitors to his lot was a Mercedes owner, the big masters in his country—so masterful they were actually called "master" and "madam." They were as huge as gods. No matter how long he worked, circumstances remained according to their design. Never his. Never his.

He sweated and salivated. He drifted into that most powerful of mental states—totally dissatisfied. He went back to Rasaki with the money. Rasaki promised a return within a week.

How did Makinde hear about his money? He kept going to Rasaki's place and Rasaki was not to be found. He asked about Rasaki's whereabouts. People said Rasaki had traveled up North. He hovered around the row of collapsing bungalows in which the duke had a room. No Rasaki. The duke had completely disappeared from downtown.

It wasn't until Bisi returned, full of her mother's vegetable stews and no longer craving dirt, that he heard from her. She'd heard from her friend at her married women's fellowship, who'd heard from her husband, who'd heard from his colleague that Rasaki had taken money from someone to play the pools, lost the money, and this person was unlikely to ask for his money back, because this person was in big trouble with the taxmen, and Rasaki knew exactly who to approach to make sure this person ended up ruined, and this person was Makinde.

"Is it true?" Bisi asked him.

"Apparently," Makinde said.

"In the short time I've been away?"

"Yes."

"How could you?"

"I had little choice."

"Well, I am disgusted."

"Why?" he asked, as she would. After all, it was not his fault. She saw the vision on the dirty windscreen. She told people and they came, and stopped him from doing his work, got his name mentioned in the papers and attracted the taxmen's attention. "This would never have happened," he said, "but for your vision."

"On the contrary," she said, and honestly. "It is you who went wrong, being tempted by a man like Rasaki. We were blessed with that money. You lost it the moment you thought you could multiply it by other means."

"How else could it have been multiplied?"

"You should have taken it to church."

"For what?"

"To give as tithes. Your fruit would have been abundant."

"My dear wife, when has my fruit ever been abundant?"

Bisi had to think. Becoming a father was one blessing, even though Makinde might not want to hear that. She couldn't think of another.

"I give tithes," she said. "My prayers are answered."

"The miracle you prayed for on my lot, was that answered?"

"No."

"Ah, well."

"It will be! I know it will!"

"Tell me when that happens. Me, I feel as if I've been fighting a will stronger than mine. A mischievous will. It wreaks havoc and I'm done fighting it."

She had a solution to their problem meanwhile. She was entitled to support from the Married Women's Crisis Fund. "On condition you join my church family."

Makinde was truly exhausted. "For God's sake…"

"It's stipulated. You want this help or not?"

"It's not as though I have several options."

The following Sunday he attended the Abundant Life Tabernacle with Bisi. There Bisi told him: his presence in her church was the miracle she'd prayed for. "I'm so glad you found your way," she said.

HAILSTONES ON ZAMFARA

On the day I die I will rise up, arms outstretched, magnificent as the mother of the Holy Prophet, then my executioners will be forced to admit, "We were wrong. We should have revered you more."

I am not guilty. I have always preferred men as I make them up in my head; invisible men. Not the kind some women want, those silly fantasy men in foreign romance books. My men are plain—ugly, even—with facial marks, oily skins, dust in their hair. They look like men from Zamfara. They ride motorcycles, take buses and taxis to their places of work. They walk mostly. They never own cars, otherwise they would have to be rich men, the kind who become senators of the Republic of Nigeria, chairmen of federal banks and such. No, my men have spread-out feet from being barefoot as children. They have palms as brown as tobacco leaves. Under their robes their ribs are prominent. Some have had a hand cut off because they stole to eat. Allah forgives them now that they are cripples. After all, my men pray as Muslims should, five times a day, even though they perform ablution in gutters. Plus they are humble before Him, even if capable of going home to beat their wives to deafness.

Did Our Husband think I was pretending the day I stopped hearing him? Had he forgotten he caused the very condition that made him so angry? I tried to help him understand. "You call me, I can't hear. You insult me, I can't hear. You tell me to get out of your house. How can I leave when I can't hear?"

"You witch!" he shouted. "I know you're doing this on purpose!"

"It is not my fault," I said. "My left ear is damaged from the beating you gave me. Sometimes I hear, sometimes I don't, even if I face Mecca."

"I divorce thee!"

"Huh?" I said.

"I divorce thee!"

"You must be asking for food again. I'm off to the market."

Where else would I go so early that morning? The trouble with Our Husband was that his anger was like lightning. Lightning from drinking too much *burukutu*, wasting half the profits from his mechanic's shop on the brew, and not being accountable for his actions afterwards. Lightning loves to show off. "Look at me. See what I do with the night? Let me turn it to day and confuse you." I came home one day, and he would be calm. I came home the next, and he behaved as though I'd insulted his father's lineage. Off and on, that was Our Husband, like lightning before thunder comes along and shows who is in control.

He was angry that day because I was not enthusiastic about his announced betrothal, so he boxed my ears. I showed him thunder—the thunder of no secondary education; of being married to him at fourteen; motherhood three times over. To prove my endurance, I even chaperoned his new bride, a girl the same age as my eldest daughter, Fatima. I called her "Junior Wife," and from then on called him "Our Husband."

"It pains me," Junior Wife said to me, the morning after her wedding night.

"It will eventually stop," I said.

Her eyes were red with tears. She made me so angry. I had raised mine already. I did not want another child around the house.

"I want to go home," she whined.

"You're lazy," I said. "You did not rise early to make Our Husband's tea. You're supposed to make his tea from now on."

She wrapped her headscarf over her mouth. Under the white chiffon her jaw trembled. "You see me crying. You don't even take pity on me."

How could I? This was my only home.

"At least you are old," she said. "You should be like a mother to me."

Her kohl appeared like a bruise.

"I'm thirty-two years," I said.

I was orphaned. Mama was long gone. Baba passed away before her, and while he was alive he had three wives. Mama had only one son. I stopped hearing from him after I left home for marriage, and to be his older sister when he was born was an ousting if ever there was one. My brother, who from age two strutted around with his arms akimbo. If you stared at him, he told Baba. If you ate before him, he told Baba. When I pulled his ears for spitting, he told Baba. Mama gave me a good whipping that one time, so that I would not forget what happened to her, after it had happened to me. I loved my brother nevertheless; his ears especially, because they stuck out. And his nose was so long he could pass for a baby elephant. Whenever I bathed him, I poured water over him, picturing him as one, playing in a fountain. That was how I loved him: for what he wasn't, as I loved Baba. I pictured Baba as Allah. Allah, who was capable of anything. He could be furious, enough to use a horsewhip. He could be strict, enough to demand I did not look at his face. Wise. He alone knew why his daughters needed no secondary education. One day he would be caring, I hoped, and I would gobble up his affection like a delicious cup of sour milk meal, cold as I like it.

Junior Wife ran home that first week. Her parents sent her back with a bundle of kola nuts to appease Our Husband. Her father warned her, before parting, that he would do as *Mallam* Sanusi did, if she ever came home again. *Mallam* Sanusi was a legend in Zamfara. His daughter ran away from her husband's house and *Mallam* Sanusi returned her. She ran away again, and *Mallam* Sanusi returned her. The third time she ran home, he cut off her foot so she would never come home again. *Mallam* Sanusi was a wicked man. Men were not that wicked, which was why *Mallam* Sanusi became a legend. But that idle threat from her father was enough to make Junior Wife stay put. I asked my daughters not to play with her, Fatima especially, who thought she had found a sister. I told her gently, "You're supposed to respect her. She is your father's new wife." Fatima said, "Then I should marry my father's friend, so that we can play." I laughed. Fatima's mouth was too sharp. "You're going to finish secondary school before you marry," I said. "I will suffer anything for that right."

Junior Wife cried. She said she had always dreamed of finishing secondary school; she was particularly good at multiplication. She was always feeling sorry for herself, and if I was ever like that, I did not care to be reminded by her sad presence. Plus, she was lax with personal hygiene. Sometimes I passed her and I could smell stale urine on her. "Didn't your mother teach you how to douche?" I once asked. That was when she began rolling her eyes at me. What, she imagined I was jealous? I was glad her father forced her to stay. From then on Our Husband left me alone at night. I told her to relax when he got on top of her, think of his manhood as a cucumber.

I would be fair to her, I promised, so long as she performed her wifely duties and relieved me of mine. Then I gave her extra advice. "Get fat as fast as I did, and he will surely marry someone else."

Our Husband was partial to bones; the bones of girls in particular. To get such bones, he could spend fifty years' savings on a dowry; a hundred years' savings even. In Zamfara, men split young bones on their wedding nights. By the time their brides were as old as me, their wombs were rotten.

Junior Wife came to me. "I'm pregnant."

"That's very good," I said.

"I vomited all morning."

"It's a girl, then."

"Why?" she asked.

"If it's a boy you would vomit all day."

She rolled her eyes. "I don't believe in that."

"Ask your mother. Didn't she teach you anything before you left?"

"It's not a girl. I know."

I had not thought of that. I was so happy Our Husband left me alone at night I was lulled into a stupid state. I was even singing while I cooked. A boy? What would happen to the rest of Fatima's secondary education? I was staring at Junior Wife's face. She had such a haughty expression. Pregnancy had made her stronger, as if she'd found a new companion I could not separate her from.

She actually refused to bed Our Husband. "I have my limits," she said. "You were naive when this happened to you. You didn't know how to trick him. I've told him that if he touches me, his son will be miscarried instantly."

He was dumb enough to swallow that fib? Ah, yes, of course, he knew how to find a young girl's passage, but he didn't care what was going on in her passage.

"I should cook you a meal," I said. "To celebrate."

I wanted my hands to be busy. I did not want to hear about the possibility of a son.

"Many thanks," Junior Wife said, "but I only eat what I myself have cooked from now on. My mother taught me that, at least."

What a cheek for her to assume I would be so malicious as to poison her.

As she grew bigger, the changes began in Zamfara. The state government was building Sharia courts, appointing *Alkalis* to preside over them. A contractor laid the foundation for a court in our town center. The earth cracked during the dry season, sandstorms came and went, hailstones followed and dented the finished aluminum roof of the court. I thought it was a divine sign. That was the first time I heard that the Quran forbade women and men from traveling in the same buses, girls and boys from attending the same schools. Fatima and other final-year girls were transferred to an afternoon session. The boys had the morning sessions. By the afternoons, most teachers were tired and went home anyway, because the girl students were not many. Fatima's school marks remained high throughout. She even won a trip to a television station, after writing an essay about Heaven. She came back with her eyes so big: "Mama, I met Miriam Maliki. She reads the news on television. She says I could train with the station after I leave school."

I looked at my beautiful daughter, jumping up and down. Would anyone care what knowledge she had in her head? And if she ever were on television, how would I see her? "We don't own a television," I said, to be the first to disappoint her.

But she would not stop talking about her Miriam Maliki. Oh, Miriam Maliki had such a pretty smile. Oh, Miriam Maliki wore gold bangles and covered her hair to read the news, because her husband's family disapproved of her exposing herself. And oh, Miriam Maliki had been on Hajj to Mecca.

I thought, what a dimwit of a woman. To care about work when she came from a home with money. She could afford a trip to Mecca? And back? That was typical of the rich; nothing better to worry about. I thought I would tell her off, this Miriam Maliki, if ever I saw her. She had let women like me down.

Then before the end of school term Fatima's favorite teacher, her English teacher, was fined for braiding her hair with extensions. Allah—I don't tell a lie. The *Alkali* presiding over the poor woman's case warned her that she would spend time in jail if she didn't stop being fashionable. Hair perms were not allowed anymore. Hair dye was not allowed, except dark brown and black. We heard of a thief in another town who had his hand cut off by a surgeon at the general hospital. The nurses there buried the hand instead of throwing it away. Our Husband came home complaining that people who drank *burukutu* were being flogged publicly. We got word of the student in another school far from Fatima's. She too was to be flogged, because she was pregnant. Thirteen years old, and she said a madman had raped her. Unfortunately, the *Alkali* told her, as she was a woman, her testimony was not so important.

Our Husband came to my room at night. His breath reeked of *burukutu*. He fell over me and I gasped in the dark. "Spread," he said, fumbling between my thighs.

"I have no juices."

"I'll use my spit," he said.

I struggled under him. "Please, I'm not supposed to lie with you. It's not my turn today. I'm not supposed to."

That was the night Junior Wife gave birth to a baby boy. Our Husband named him Abu. He announced that Abu was going to university and the rest of us would have to make sacrifices. I wandered around the whole day after Abu's naming ceremony, thinking of Fatima. I went to the tailor's to order a dress for her. I passed the Quranic lessons where young boys chanted verses. I stopped for cattle rearers. I smelled fresh blood in the abattoir. It made me sick. I heaved by the wood carvers' sheds and there he was. He had the facial marks of a peasant, my invisible man.

"What happened to your hand?" I asked.

"It got cut off," he said.

"What did you do to get it cut off?"

"I stole."

"Did you ask for penance?"

"This is my penance." He waved his stump at me. His extra skin was folded neatly at his wrist like a belly button. He was smiling.

"How do you carve?" I asked.

"With my one arm."

"How do you pray?"

"With my one arm."

"How do you love?"

It could have been that I found my partial hearing in his missing hand. You know how people find others in life to compensate, especially in difficult times? Why else would I ask? He pointed to his temple. "Love is here."

"I'm a married woman," I said, in case he suspected me of flirting.

"You have a rather sad face," he said.

He laughed and it scared me. If a man laughed in Zamfara these days, a woman could be in trouble. I drew closer to my invisible man and he smelled of wood dust and cracked earth. The mixture cured my nausea instantly.

"Let me see your carvings."

I took the one with the biggest head and traced her broad nostrils, then behind her neck. Then her lips. I was thinking of Miriam Maliki.

"I like you," I heard my invisible man murmur.

"What do you like about me?"

"Your breasts. I would like to suck them hard."

"Let me feel," I said, meaning his carving.

In his shed, among the carvings and wood dust. We were standing.

"When did you become a bad woman?" he asked as I unzipped his trousers.

"Today, I am not so well," I said.

He was like a rod of warm iron. He said he didn't mean to insult me, he just wanted to know. Women in Zamfara could consent and then act as if they were raped. I let him suck my nipples. I felt fear for Fatima's education like a tremor between my legs. He said I reminded him of his first cousin, one he almost married. He said this was not an abomination. In his village, people married within their families, but most of them were deformed people, so he refused, because he never thought he would be one himself. He stole a transistor radio. It belonged to another cousin who died, but a half-brother claimed it. It was a property dispute. He just wanted to listen to the news, he said. The whole world could be explained by listening to the news. "You see what is happening in Zamfara? It has nothing to do with Sharia law... You are exciting me... It has nothing to do with Islam. It has nothing to do with the

Quran. It doesn't even have anything to do with Arabs... who come here to preach against infidels... You're making me excited! Slow down!"

It was a property dispute, he said. All the madness and the sadness in the world, from war to starvation, came down to property disputes.

"Except my ear," I said, fastening my brassiere. My hands were wet.

"That, too," he said, zipping up his trousers. "Your husband believes he owns you."

"Not his drinking," I said. "That is no property dispute."

"That, too. He drinks to appease himself. If a rich man drinks, who flogs him? Ah, you are like sweet mango to taste. I could lick you all over."

"I feel sick," I said.

Truly, to think Our Husband and I were part of the same sorry group. Who forced his hand in marriage twice? Who led him to his beloved *burukutu*? I pulled my panties up.

"You are going?" my invisible man asked.

His nose was as broad as his carving's, and his eyes were a shade of light brown.

"It seems unreasonable," I said, "to cut off a hand for stealing a transistor radio. For the sin of drinking, they really should cut a throat."

He frowned at that. "You are quite a harsh woman."

I was pregnant by the end of that month. I had not been as sick as I normally was. I was sicker; sick all day. It made me thin. I was worrying about Fatima's schooling. I was running around for Junior Wife's newborn, Abu. She was refusing to touch him. She said he might as well have been born a stone. She cursed her parents who gave her to Our Husband in exchange for a dowry. She said marriage was like slavery.

"But you're a miserable one," I told her. Everyone was quick to compare themselves to slaves. What slave had the power to tell Our Husband to let her sleep separately? I had to fake typhoid so that he would not come to me at night. My temperatures were easy; I was making his morning teas again. My nausea was convenient.

Junior Wife told me one evening, "You're hiding something from me. You seem one way while you are the other. You say one thing and mean the other. Our husband says you do this to drive people to madness."

Her eyes were red, not from crying but from lack of sleep.

"Have you fed your son?" I asked.

"See?" she said. "You're doing it again."

"Your son needs to be fed," I said, sharply. Doing what?

"My son is like you," she said. "A snake hidden in the grass. He does not cry so that I will worry about him. That is why I no longer sleep at night."

"He's an innocent child."

"No, he isn't. His big head almost killed me."

She turned her face away from me. I moved my hand to check her head for fever. She slapped it. "Don't touch!"

By the end of the week she was rocking herself. Her hair was falling out, her breath stank, she'd stopped douching. Her baby was shrieking now, and it was I who was acting like his mother. I, who was carrying him and attending to his mess.

Our Husband was furious. "This household is cursed from top to bottom. One really has to be sure where one picks his brides. Everything is falling apart since she arrived. If she doesn't take heed, I will send her back to that father of hers, so that he can do as *Mallam* Sanusi did and cut off her foot."

Threats. He was trying to outshriek his own son.

"What will happen to the baby?"

"He will stay here. My son will not be deserted. If his own mother won't care for him, I will accept the next best mother."

"Who?"

"Who else? You, of course. And he will attend university. And he will become a doctor. And he will be rich. Then he can be president of Nigeria—"

"*Bismillah*," I said. "I'm sure he will, since he resembles you."

"Oh, shut up."

To him, that was an invitation to come to my bed again. Not because we'd exchanged pleasantries, mind you. He said that since I was up to my usual tricky ways, my typhoid must have cleared. This time I was prepared for his entry.

"I'm pregnant," I said.

"How?"

"By the grace of Allah, as usual, and it is a boy, and if you lie with me, your son will instantly be miscarried."

"Spread your legs," he said.

He was rubbing spit inside me. I was writhing not from pain, but from the thought of *burukutu* in my passage.

"I'm—" I said.

He collapsed on top of me.

"Will you shut up? Now see what you've done. Only you are capable of doing this to me. Never, ever, has this happened..."

His manhood was like water on my belly. His chest hairs were in my nostrils.

"I can't breathe," I said.

Junior Wife had strayed into the room without a knock. She stood there with her hair looking like a mongrel's; her eyes were redder than ever.

"Something terrible has come to pass," she said in a soft voice.

"What?"

It was I who asked. A mother knows. She senses danger. She senses it in silence, a silence that is connected to her womb.

"Have I married a couple of witches or what?" Our Husband asked, staggering out of my bed. "Why do you barge in like this?"

"Unfortunately, he is dead," Junior Wife said.

"Who?"

"Abu."

I heard the ceiling collapse. You know how coincidences happen? A whole section of the ceiling just caved in behind me. It made such a noise I was sure it had pounded the floor to pieces. I turned to check. The ceiling was intact. It was Our Husband lying on the floor. He had fallen down in grief.

I could have pitied him the way he mourned. He embalmed the body. He wrapped the body in white cloth. He dug a hole and placed it gently in. He covered the hole up. He even ordered a tombstone. One morning I heard him weeping like a woman, "Abu, Abu." I asked, "Would you like some tea?" His eyes widened as if he'd seen a witch. He ran away from me.

That same week he sent Junior Wife packing, back to her parents. He said she should be prepared for her foot to be cut off, after the way she neglected his son. Neglected? But he was always dumb for her sad face. I was happy to see that murderer out of the house. To kill her own child; there was no excuse, not even motherly madness. I told Fatima when she started lamenting how two losses in one week were impossible to bear, "Save your upsets. Save them for times that are worth it. They will come."

Our Husband was drinking *burukutu* like water now. He'd stopped going to work at his shop. He would leave home early in the mornings to do the work of drunkards. Meanwhile, his mechanics were pilfering from him. I was thinking, how did they dare in this new climate? The situation was so tense that Christians and Muslims were coming to blows on the streets, burning each other's houses, taking daggers to each other's throats. One Christian in the marketplace, a Muslim ripped a cross pendant from his neck. It wasn't even real gold. They fought until the Muslim died, and then a group of Muslims retaliated with bows and arrows on a Christian settlement. These were the stories we were hearing, and Our Husband's mechanics were pilfering? That was some poverty. I would rather beg knowing I had two hands to show for myself.

We did not hear a word from Junior Wife who had returned to her father's house. We never even asked, so we did not know her father finally begged her forgiveness for abandoning her. He said he did it to make her strong, so that she would not be homesick and run away. She told him of the threat Our Husband made. Her father said, "Come on, I'm not as wicked as *Mallam* Sanusi." She told him also of Our Husband's drinking, and her father exclaimed, "He drinks? You never said!"

That was it. They came for Our Husband while he was doing the work of drunkards. They dragged him out of the shack. They took him to court. The *Alkali* presiding over his case ordered fifty strokes. I did not know any of this until his friends brought him home, whimpering like a baby. They could find no trousers soft enough to cover his buttocks, so he was naked except for a dirty shirt. Fatima cried the most, of my daughters, as we lay him face down on his bed.

"There must be a reasonable explanation for this," I said.

He cursed Junior Wife and her father, and told me what happened.

"I am so forlorn!" he wailed, louder than a muezzin. "Heaven awaits me! I've always been humble. Leave me to die. Let my sores fester…"

"I've heard alcohol helps," I said.

He wept silently now, into his mattress, gibbering something about me never changing my tricky ways and his friends coming back to save him. I used warm water and a boiled towel to cleanse his skin. The job took a long time. His buttocks looked like shredded cloth and he had urinated on himself. Shit was hanging out of him. I took Vaseline and slid it over each of the fifty welts while he sobbed on. He cursed the day this and that. He really was like a baby with all that complaining, and as I reached his anus with the Vaseline he farted.

"Hm," I said, holding my nose. "Men really should douche."

"You can't even say sorry!" he shrieked.

I was laughing. Not because of what he said, or what I saw, but because of what I'd said: "Men really should douche." It came out of my mouth like a bullet, without me thinking. I laughed so hard tears poured from my eyes and burned them. This house of ours, what else could go wrong?

"You evil woman," Our Husband said. "You will pay for this. You think it's funny? You will pay. Just wait. I will get better, and I will do something that will make you want to die." I stopped immediately and held my chest. "Fatima?"

His voice became shaky. He'd reached the stage of uncontrollable lips with his crying. "W-what did Fatima ever do to me? It was you. Y-you and this horrible behavior of yours since you lost your hearing. P-punishing me, punishing me, for what was m-merely an accident. Did you think I made you h-half deaf on purpose? C-curse you..."

I nodded. So long as it was me.

The day Our Husband was able to walk straight he went immediately back to court and told them he had an accusation to make. The *Alkali*, knowing his face, asked him to make it concise. Our Husband declared that it was his wife. She was pregnant, by another man. She had committed adultery and that was why he'd been drinking *burukutu*: his wife was a very loose woman.

They came for me in the afternoon. What was I doing at the time? Dyeing my hair. My real hairs were so white for a woman who had turned thirty-three years. They told me of Our Husband's accusation in court. They took me into custody. "Who will look after my children?" I asked. One of them answered, "Why are you bothering to ask?" I said, "I shall be away several days." He said, "Your pregnant belly is evidence, if ever I saw any. I warrant you will be away longer than that."

That was when I met Miriam Maliki. She came to visit me in custody. I'll never forget the way she commanded the guards, "Let her out of there. She's pregnant and she's no danger to anyone." The doors miraculously opened for me. Allah. In all my life, I'd not seen such a delicate woman with power. She was as tiny as Fatima. Her head was covered with a black scarf and her eyes were big and sparkly. I saw her thin wrists and fingers without knuckles. I thought, this one, she hasn't suffered a second in her life.

"I'm Miriam Maliki. Have you heard of me?"

"My daughter said she met you."

"Your daughter?"

"Fatima."

"Fat?"

"Ima."

"What?"

"That is her name. Fatima. You said you would train her, and she would be on the news. She was jumping up and down, and she even said——"

She nodded. "Listen, it's you I'm worried about. Do you know I heard your story and immediately came out here? I could not believe what they were telling me. You were taken from your home? Like a mere criminal? To this mud dungeon with nothing but a bucket? And your own husband accused you? What did you tell them when they came for you?"

"Who will look after my daughters?"

"Did you tell them you were innocent?"

"Did they ask?"

For the first time she seemed to see my face. "I'm sorry," she said. "I am so angry about this. Forgive me. I heard your trial is tomorrow. I'm disgusted by the prospects of such a case in Zamfara. I will be there at your side."

"My side?"

"Do not be afraid. Look at me. I know you're innocent. You will not be put to death."

"Death?" I said. "For what?"

She said, "Don't you know? Don't you know how these courts intend to punish married women who have committed adultery?"

How, I asked.

"Death by stoning," she said. "Have you not heard? You are the first."

Indeed she was with me during my trial. Not by my side, but she was sitting with others who were allowed in the court. If she had been by my side, I might have been able to answer the questions better.

"Why didn't you tell your husband earlier that you were pregnant?"

"I just didn't."

"How do you lie with a man who doesn't exist?"

"I just did."

Miriam came to spend time with me after my sentencing. She said all her life she never imagined this would happen in a place she lived, that a woman would be stoned to death for adultery. She said I was maligned, or raped. I told her imagination was a dangerous exploit.

"You're brave," she said. "You're like a mountain."

"See me as I am instead."

"The court was unfair to you."

"You can't fault Islam."

Her voice rose. "It has nothing to do with Islam!"

"A property dispute?" I asked.

She began to pace. "The state cannot sanction such courts. The federal government won't allow it. You know what this is really about? People wanting to break our country apart. Not about declaring Zamfara an Islamic state. Not even about the Islamic fundamentalism that people say is sweeping the world." People said that?

"I've fought for the rights of women…"

What about children? What about men who had one hand cut off?

"I'm against underage marriages. The psychological effects alone are bad enough. Some women develop cancer of the cervix…"

My mother died of a rotten womb.

"And God only knows why, when Muslim men want to get closer to Him, they look for Muslim women to pick on."

"I'm going to die," I said.

She took my hand. "I will make sure. I will so make sure people hear of you. Others have taken an interest, not just me. Elsewhere in the country they are writing about you in newspapers, calling this a barbaric injustice. Foreign papers are hearing about your case as we speak. Once they carry your story, there will be activists involved. They will petition our president. Very soon, our little court in Zamfara will be the focus of the world. A world that is worried about the spread of Islamic fundamentalism. You understand? It is very likely that your life will be saved because of this. Have hope. You are a symbol."

Fatima came to visit while Miriam was still with me. She brought me sour milk meal and mangoes. She hardly spoke when Miriam said to her, "I remember your lovely face." And the way Fatima could not meet her eyes, I knew my daughter had found a love on which to base all others. She would love women, and her love would be unrequited. She told me her sisters were doing well, considering. She told me Our Husband was fasting and growing a beard for religious purposes.

I told her, "Tell your father Allah has his reward." Was he allowing her to continue her secondary education nevertheless?

She said he was.

"Make sure you get your education," I said. "Make sure it's

in your hands, then you can frame it and hang it on the wall, and when you go to your husband's house, carry it with you."

"I don't think that's what education is," she said, "something to hang on a wall."

"Listen," I said, "I know what I'm saying. What is in your head might not save you. Hang your education on the wall of your husband's house, so that whatever happens you can say to yourself, 'This is my education,' and no one can take it away from you."

She left only after I ordered her. She wanted to stay, but I did not like her seeing me in custody. "Did you include me in your essay of Heaven?" I asked. She said no. I said, "Therefore don't worry about me going there."

"Are you being sarcastic most times?" Miriam asked, after Fatima left.

"Me?" I answered.

"I notice," she said. "The way you talk. You say one thing and mean the other. I don't mean to be rude, but it's like I hardly know you."

She hardly didn't.

"Sometimes, I wonder if, forgive me, you are crazy."

I was thinking of Junior Wife. Could I be, if I saw madness in others?

She rubbed her pretty lips. "You and I, I feel for you so strongly, as though you matter more than my mother. Can I be bold? There is nothing to lose. I want to show you something."

She unwrapped her scarf from her head. Underneath was a rainbow. Red, orange, yellow, green, blue, indigo—stripes all over. Her hidden hair.

"It's prettier in the sky," I said.

"My husband says it's ugly. He says I've lost my head. He calls it my lost head, but he says it as a joke, mind you. I have two girls by him, you know. He loves them as boys. You will call me lucky to have such a man, but really, he should love them as girls. He also thinks he was my first. I married him when I was twenty-three, after I graduated from university. He was not my first. I lied that I was stretched by riding horses. I hope I'm not overwhelming you."

"A little." The rich again. Why would she tell me now I was about to die? Would she tell me if I were not about to die?

"What are you thinking?" she asked.

I was looking at her gold bangles.

"Does your husband have a lot of money?" I asked.

"No. We are what you call comfortable. A lot? Not at all. Do you consider me spoiled?"

I thought hard about that. In our country, Sharia was a poor person's law.

"Yes," I said.

"Are you scared to die?"

"Yes."

She drew closer. "You're carrying a child. That will give you time. They will not stone you until your child is born."

"It's a nothing," I said. "It is nothingness within me."

"Why didn't you answer the questions you were asked in court?"

"I just didn't."

"What really happened to make you pregnant?"

"What difference would it have made?"

I didn't have to think a moment about this. Sometimes I was confused, often afraid. To answer correctly was to give in most days. But so what if my reason was one or the other? I had a lover; a man who became invisible in court. There was no evidence against him, the *Alkali* said. I needed three independent witnesses to prove his guilt. Our Husband's testimony, anyway, was greater than mine.

Miriam was crying. "You shall not be forsaken."

When stones were hurled at me, they would be hailstones on my head; hailstones on Zamfara.

"In the name of Allah," I said, "the Beneficent, the Merciful."

SPOILS

Lubna is waiting for me under the old acacia in town. We bet with pebbles over there. I always win. She is smarter in school because she has a longer memory. Allah, she can even remember what happened to her ten years ago when she was a baby, but she loses our pebble bets every time because I am much faster at thinking ahead.

I stand in a gap between the shadows of the tree branches and shield my eyes from the sunlight. Anyone looking at me might think I'm crying.

"There was a bus crash last night."

"Allah?" she says.

"Allah."

"Where?"

"By Gandu Biyu."

Gandu Biyu is Settlement Two. Our town is Settlement Five. We are small settlement towns in this part of Nigeria. The capital city is miles away.

The ground is covered with flattened cardboard boxes on which the taxi drivers have taken naps in the shade. Now, the drivers are gathered around the community tap by the mosque on the other side of the street. They fill their plastic kettles to perform ablution and leave wet patches in the soil. Soon it will be time for afternoon prayers. Men can attend, and boys, too. Women have their own separate section to share with girls, but we are not allowed to participate in Friday prayers, not since our *sarki barraki* banned us.

"Did you bring any *kilishi?*" Lubna asks.

She is sitting on a hump of tree root. Her hair is covered with a scarf, as mine is. She wears a nose ring, but I don't care for them because whenever I sneeze they get sticky with mucus.

I raise my hand. "Are you listening? I said there was another crash on the expressway. A bus overturned, people perished, and all you can think of at a time like this is *kilishi?*"

Sometimes I have to wonder. This is precisely why she always needs to take rests, and why she uses double the cloth I use when our tailor sews her up-and-downs. Lubna eats too much. *Kilishi* is delicious with Coca-Cola. Chewy. The strips burn your tongue, work your back gums and scrape off your inner cheeks.

"I'm just asking," she says.

"You, you're never satisfied."

"I can't help feeling hungry."

"Well, food is not always the answer."

"Was anyone in our town on the bus?"

"No."

Not one. Still, it is her lack of respect for the dead that I cannot tolerate. She ought to know. We are not that young. Last year, my husband was killed on the expressway. He and I had been betrothed for several years. He was forty-two and prosperous with older wives. Mama was bereft. His surviving brother was a drunk. I should have been passed on to him as part of my husband's inheritance, but Baba refused. "That useless one with his breath always stinking of *burukutu?*" he said. "I would rather give my daughter away to a goat."

"They say the driver's head rolled into a ditch," I explain to Lubna. "They say he wasn't properly secured. They say he will be buried tomorrow, and once he is wrapped up in cloth, no one will know the difference."

I overheard that from Mama. She sent me out to play. She thought I would be too scared to listen. I wasn't scared. This is not the first crash we have had on the expressway to the capital. We call it the Death Road around here, and anyway, there was the Christian woman who was burned this year. She refused to step aside for a group of men walking into the mosque for Friday prayers. They asked her nicely and she made the sign of the cross. That wasn't necessary, but I agree with Mama that the men went too far. They needn't have set her on fire. They could simply have beaten her up. Baba said she was being unreasonable. She should have stepped aside.

"Remember the Christian woman?" I ask Lubna.

She nods. Everyone remembers the Christian woman, even though we'd rather not talk about her.

"Binta's seen a body burned before," she says. "Her math teacher at Government College. He was an Indian man from Calcutta, and when he died, his family burned him to ashes on the school grounds and the senior prefects were allowed to watch."

"Allah?"

"Allah."

I doubt that. Binta is her elder sister by her father's junior wife, major trouble if you ask me. She was supposed to be betrothed to my brother Hassan, the firstborn of my father's senior wife. Our families agreed to the union but Binta refused. She said Hassan's head was shaped like a cashew nut. She was about our age when she ran off to Sokoto and stayed with a guardian there. After her secondary education at Government College, she escaped to a teachers' training college in Zaria. Did Binta end up teaching? No, she got a job with a non-governmental in the capital that stops girls from marrying and gives them scholarships. A woman like her from a respectable family. It was a scandal.

"Here," Lubna says. "She's sent me another newspaper cutting."

"Give me that," I say, snatching it from her. "Why didn't you tell me before?"

Allah, whenever Binta sends her newspaper cuttings I could screw them up and throw them as far away as possible, but my curiosity always gets the better of me. They are always about one so-called heroic Hausa girl or another. This one is about a girl with polio who walked eight miles to Binta's non-governmental to escape from her husband. She almost collapsed from thirst along the way. Now she is posing for a photograph, standing there with her little leg and holding up a certificate. She has such huge teeth. I have to smile at the sight of her. Twit, I think. Why did she have to walk all that way? Why couldn't she just hitch a ride?

"They gave this one a scholarship?" I ask, handing the newspaper cutting back to Lubna.

"She will be going to secondary school next year."

"Well, I am disgusted."

"Why?"

"Because I am."

"But why?"

"Because it's not right."

Doesn't she know? What further education does a woman need? Can education push a baby out? When Binta is crying out from labor pains, how perfect will her English be?

The muezzin begins to call men and boys to afternoon prayers. They are like a herd of cattle walking into the mosque. Their heads are bowed and their feet scrape the ground. Lubna slaps sandflies away from her legs. They always suck on her blood because hers is sweet. They keep well away from mine because I have a bad temper and my blood is sour.

"Binta's going to arrange for them to give me a scholarship," she says.

What is she talking about? She is not even betrothed yet. She won't be until she sees her period. How can she qualify for a scholarship?

"On what basis?"

"My schoolwork. Binta says they will take that into consideration."

I sniff. "I'm sure they will, since they can give a scholarship to a girl who ran away from her husband."

I am not jealous. The standards of Binta's non-governmental are well beneath me, and their patron is a wrinkled old white woman with two big balloons in her breasts. She lives in Hollywood, she and her dog.

"I want to apply," Lubna says. "I want to move to the capital."

I stamp my foot. "What is wrong with our town?"

"It's boring over here."

"But there is so much to do!"

"Like what?"

"Spending time with Farouk."

"Farouk? All we ever do is spend time with Farouk."

Farouk is a street hawker. We help him to sell his wares. His mother raised him as a *yan dauda*: he speaks in a high voice like a woman. He wears headscarves, paints henna on his hands and pencils his eyes with kohl. Our tailor sews him the loveliest up-and-downs. Farouk is a lot of fun.

"Come," I say. "Let's go and help Farouk."

Lubna shakes her head. "I'm tired of helping Farouk."

"He'll give you a Bazooka Joe."

"OK," she says, stretching her hand upwards so that I can pull her up.

She will do anything for food this girl, or perhaps it's the story about the other girl who walked eight miles that I find upsetting. I don't know what comes over me.

"No," I say, backing away. "You're a lefty. I don't touch lefties."

"But I never use my left hand to go," she says.

I cross my arms. "I can't hold hands with a lefty. I don't know where that hand of yours has been."

I shouldn't have said that, but she squeezes up her face and begins to yell as if she's possessed or something: "Go! Go wherever you want! You're bossy! You've always been bossy and you have a bad mouth to boot! I'll be glad when I'm finally rid of you!"

My best friend I have known all my life. I leave her under the acacia tree to think about what she has done.

Afternoon prayers have begun. The men and boys are already in the mosque. I can recite some of the *suwar* by heart: Al-Fatiha, Al-Lahab and An-Nas. I cross the exact spot where the Christian woman was burned, pass the shed where boys write Arabic alphabets on their *allo* boards, run past the hut where the *lailai* woman paints henna patterns for brides on their wedding eves. The ground is too hot to meander and I have to hold on to my scarf to make sure it doesn't slip off. Farouk is where he always is, on the corner of the road by the millet farm.

"*Hajiya*," he says, lifting his cigarette.

He addresses me as a married woman because he knows I'm mature for my age, unlike some I no longer care to mention. Farouk is pretty for a man. He has pointed cheeks and his eyes slant upwards. He is seated behind his stall with his legs crossed.

"Good day to you," I say.

"And to you, too," he says. "Where is your friend, Lubna?"

"Please don't talk to me about that girl."

He laughs. "What happened?"

I, too, start to yell: "It's her elder sister! She leads Lubna astray! She's planning to sneak her off to the capital to further her education and Lubna won't listen to me!"

"Allah *sarki?*" Farouk says.

"Allah, and look at their father, a man of such a high standing in society, he cannot even hold his head up in this town again."

"Now where did you hear that?"

"Everyone knows."

That was Binta's doing. She was like a sandstorm flattening everything in her path when she got her education. She once opened her mouth to say that women should be permitted to lead prayers. She blasphemes regularly like that. Now she's making my voice hoarse. I cough hard.

"Hassan... says she needs a husband to manhandle her..."

Farouk beckons me to sit. His feet are clean in his flip-flops. Mine are covered in soil. Whenever a car takes the corner too fast over here it raises a cloud of dust. Farouk covers his stall with a cloth until the cloud subsides. He is finicky about tidiness. We have that in common.

"*Bismillah,*" he says, rubbing my shoulder. "No woman needs to be manhandled and that is good news about your friend. I hear you too have good news in your family. Hassan's wife had a baby boy?"

"Last week."

"What is his name?"

"Osama."

"Hm. Every baby boy in this town is called Osama."

"What's wrong with Osama?"

"Nothing, but you would think the man is our *sarki barraki* the way we carry on."

He smokes his cigarette. People name their boys Osama to make sure they will grow up fearless. The real Osama is more revered than our *sarki barraki*. He is so popular here you can't find an Osama poster to buy anymore. They're sold out. What did know-it-all Binta have to say about that? That a thousand Osama posters cannot beautify our mud walls.

Farouk arranges his wares with his free hand. His henna patterns are dark against his fair skin. He sells cigarettes, Bazooka Joe chewing gum, kola nuts and aspirin. He always smells fresh, no matter how hot it gets. In the mornings, he dabs a little perfumed oil behind his ears. He keeps himself cool with a raffia fan. It's funny about him; he has no hairs on his chin or his chest. I have heard that his mother was a witch because she stank of urine. She is dead now and Mama said she stank of urine only because she had an ailment from giving birth to Farouk too young.

The millet farm seems to be whispering to us. We are lucky in these parts. Our crops are safe from desert locusts. They swarm farms further up north and eat up their crops.

A car horn interrupts our silence; it's a white Peugeot creeping around the corner. The passenger door is dented and a rope keeps it from swinging open. The driver calls out from his window, "Farouk, you're an abomination for a man!"

Farouk spreads his fingers. "Me? Curses on you, worthless thief bastard!"

I have never heard him sound so shrill. The Peugeot leaves fumes in the air.

"Why did he say that?" I ask.

Farouk hisses. "Don't mind him. He's a lout. He has no job. He's just come from the Death Road. He heard of the bus crash and rushed over there to look for spoils."

I recognized the driver. He was one of those who burned the body of the Christian woman. I thought they were devout. So he is a looter? He is not originally from here. He has the facial marks of the Kanuri people. But why call Farouk an abomination? Everyone knows about Farouk. We love Farouk as he is and trust him. Apart from the men in my family, he is the only man I am allowed to be with unaccompanied.

"Here," he says, handing me a Bazooka Joe. "Now what happened between you and your friend?"

I tear the wrapper open and put the gum into my mouth. I don't bother with the cartoon inside. It is hard enough to chew and look angry at the same time.

"Oh, her... She told me... she wants to leave town... after I told her... about the bus crash last night. The driver lost his head. That's all I'm saying. I'm not predicting the same fate will befall Lubna. Allah will always protect her, but that is what can happen when you go traveling up and down the Death Road willy-nilly."

Farouk blows out smoke. "Yes, yes, but don't you yourself want to leave this place?"

"Do you?"

"Only on a day like this when I encounter a lout like that."

He smokes. My gum is much softer now and is sweetening my temper.

"I just wish people would be more obedient."

"Like who?"

"Lubna for a start."

"What else has she done wrong?"

"She is left-handed."

"She's always been."

"It's most unsanitary. She should have been corrected."

Farouk smiles. "You two are like husband and wife. Me? I don't blame her. If I had the opportunity I would want to leave this town. Things are changing too much around here."

I push the chewing gum to the side of my mouth. "It's the Americans, you know."

"Which Americans?"

"The woman with balloons in her breasts."

He pats his flat chest. "I wouldn't mind having those."

"She's ruining everything. She keeps giving out scholarships."

Hassan said she used to get attention because of the balloons, then her skin got shriveled up and the balloons began to leak. After that, no one would give her work to do in Hollywood, so she tries to get attention by saving African girls. It is either wild animals, or us, Hassan said.

"The Americans indeed," Farouk says.

"It's true. They're to blame. Hassan watches cable television whenever he goes to the capital. He says they are debauched and greedy. They want to take over all the oil in the world and kill Muslims."

Farouk tilts his head. "Is it Muslim blood or oil they're after?"

"I'm not playing. They won't stop until they succeed, and once they finish with the Arabs they will turn their attention to us. You'll see."

Farouk puts his cigarette on the edge of his stall. "But look around you. Who stops you from going to Friday prayers? The Americans? Who makes it a crime to walk around with your hair uncovered? The Americans?"

"I want to cover my hair."

"What if you don't? And remember the Christian woman? Who killed her? The Americans?"

"She was being unreasonable."

"Our *sarki barraki* should be ashamed for letting that happen over here."

"She should have stepped aside."

"But should the men have killed her? And what about the woman in that other town, the one the Sharia court sentenced to death, did the Americans do that, too?"

"No one would have stoned that silly woman."

"How would you know?"

"Hassan told me."

"But did the court have to sentence her? Was that just?"

"They just wanted to scare her. They only wanted her to serve as an example for other women who are unfaithful. They wouldn't have followed through with the sentence. Hassan said the Americans blew it out of proportion. They do that to make themselves look superior."

"*Haba.*"

"But it's true. They are infidels, the lot of them. They worship anyone. They have this black woman on television, Okra. All the housewives in America have fallen under her spell. She gives them gifts and they follow her commands. If she tells them to lose weight, they lose weight. If she tells them to leave their husbands, they will. When she asked them to write letters to protest against the sentence, they did."

None of them knew exactly what they were protesting against, Hassan said, but they felt better for writing their letters, and in no time they were back to accepting expensive free gifts from her.

"*Haba,*" Farouk says. "You're a clever girl, but I've never thought what your family teaches is right. Look around and see for yourself who we follow around here, the Arabs or the Americans. I worry for us, really I do, the direction in which we are heading."

"Fine."

At least I don't think I know it all. The business about the Christian woman confused me, to be honest, so did the stoning sentence, and I couldn't understand when our *sarki barraki* announced that women could not attend Friday prayers. I once asked Baba, "What does our *sarki barraki* do?" Baba said, "He passes edicts." "What are edicts?" I asked. "Edicts are what our *sarki barraki* passes," he said. "Why?" I asked. "He passes edicts," Baba yelled. "I've told you already. Why do you persist in asking what he passes edicts for?" Then Mama said, "That man confuses me with his edicts."

I'm also a bit puzzled by Farouk. His boyfriend is our tailor, and yet our tailor is married. Who will eventually marry Farouk, and can our tailor be sentenced to death for being unfaithful to his wife? How will education help me to make sense of all this when education only made Binta more spiteful?

On the day I met my husband I was as pleasant as possible. I was grateful to be betrothed to him. He kept rubbing my shoulders. He even wanted to take me away right then and there, but Mama said he couldn't until I had seen my period.

"I can never leave town," I confess to Farouk. "I would miss my mother too much."

"I know."

"She's kind and loving."

"I know," he says, turning his mouth downward.

I forgot about his own mother. I change the topic to cheer him up. "My ambition is to become a housewife."

"But you are already a widow," he says.

I forgot that, too. My memory is terrible.

"Who will marry you now?" he asks.

"I don't know."

He strokes his smooth chin. "Will your father promise you to someone else?"

"I don't know."

"But you can't stay a widow forever. Don't you think it might be better to further your education?"

"*Kai!*" I exclaim and spit out the Bazooka Joe on the ground.

"What's wrong?" he asks.

"I bit my tongue..."

"The pain will pass."

"I can't talk again."

"Is it that bad?"

I cover my face with my hands. How can Farouk do this to me? He merely pretends to be a woman. He doesn't know what it means to be one. He will never know what it means to be promised. "My husband died."

"Are you upset over that?"

"Very."

"But you never knew him."

"Still." At least I have respect for the dead. I get up and tighten my scarf. I can't spend time with him today or ever.

"Where are you going?" he asks.

Where does he think? When certain friends go running off to capitals and certain sisters can't keep their big mouths shut, and certain chaperones, who ought to know better, try and lead you astray, where else can you go?

"Home," I say politely. I don't look left or right as I approach the road. Farouk has warned me several times not to do that.

"Be careful," he calls out. "This is a dangerous curve we're on and there's no telling what can come out of nowhere and knock you over."

Some people think he has the gift of prophecy. The way I see it, I'm no longer sure he does. The man does not even know what is happening now.

LAWLESS

We were third-year theater arts students due to graduate in the summer of 1994 when the Abacha regime closed down our university, just two weeks before our convocation ceremony. They announced the closure was for public safety, but who didn't know they were punishing our students' union? That hapless body of enthusiasts, still hoarse from screaming "no" to the IMF, had organized a peaceful protest in support of the National Democratic Coalition. All they succeeded in rallying were a few area boys, who marched to our chancellor's office, threw petrol bombs through his window, set a couple of lecturers' cars on fire, assaulted the cooks in the canteen, while chanting, "Sufferin' rights for de masses."

This was just after our president-elect was detained, way before his wife was assassinated. Anyone who dared to disagree with the regime's constitutional conference was being spirited off by State Security for questioning. Those who could, and would, had fled overseas to claim political asylum. Lagos was not exactly a peaceful paradise when the Lawless was formed. We were not a band of armed robbers, or some student cult. We certainly had no intention of adding to the bloodshed around. I, for one, feared barbarism and guns more than I did the student unionists with their placards and self-righteousness.

The founding members of the group were Crazehead, Professor, Fineboy, Shango and I, Ogun. They were out-of-town friends who asked if they could stay with me until our university reopened, and I said yes. It was the middle of the rainy season, no time to be looking for a place to bunk.

Fineboy was from the Niger Delta, thick-chested, and he had all that Norwegian ancestry working for him. He'd slept with girls from all faculties. The rich ones wouldn't speak to him after they'd used him. They said he was a bushman: he couldn't use a fork and knife properly.

Professor was another who had good reasons to begrudge women: his small hands, small feet. Add to that, his back was crooked from scoliosis, so he panicked when he got undressed and couldn't successfully get laid. To save himself, he wrote poetry. His tributes to Biafra were so masterful they drove a literature lecturer to accuse him of plagiarism. I told the Professor I wasn't taking any of that tribal bullshit from him. The Civil War ended decades ago and Nigeria was one nation now, united in its mess. He said, "But you don't know what I witnessed as a boy. My father got shot in the head. My family almost starved. My whole town was razed…" He went on and on until I apologized for my insensitivity and stupidity. The little liar! His family was in France throughout the war. True, true, he was a poet.

Crazehead, now, he had spent more time in Fela's Shrine than he had on campus. He mixed up his H's like a typical Ibadan man, had these crowded teeth covered in plaque, and his eyes were perpetually red and swollen. At one point he said he was giving up theater arts to be in an Afro-juju band. "Doing what?" I asked him. "Shaking the *shekere?*" Crazehead had no musical talent whatsoever, except for singing off-key after he'd smoked a joint. He said the purity of his falsetto intimidated the other band members, so they were jealous and they dropped him. Perhaps it was Crazehead's belches that overpowered the band. "What the hell did you eat, man?" I once asked when he let out a combination of fried fish, boiled eggs and mango. He rubbed his belly and explained that hactually, 'emp made him 'ungry, and he had inherited a susceptibility to food allergies, 'ence he experienced occasional bloating. I asked him to clean himself up, from all orifices. The guy was a bloody mess. He was the one who asked me to consider using real guns on our opening night as the Lawless. "That's the trouble with you," I said. "Too many drugs in your blood. Too many *Rambo* movies in your head."

Shango was my right-hand man. We named him after the god of thunder and lightning whom he played in the one-act, written by him and me, though I did most of the creative work because Shango wasn't exactly what you call "that bright." The Goethe Institut in Lagos agreed to sponsor us. Shango received a standing ovation for his suicide scene, during which he pretended to hang himself. He was over six foot tall with deep dimples, the darling of our drama association in university. Women trusted him. He and I were roommates in our first year and, I swear, he had lace curtains hanging from our barred windows, a jar of hibiscus on the floor next to his semen-stained mattress. For a while there he was a Buddhist, then a Seventh-day Adventist. Shango was just big for nothing, really. He couldn't swipe a mosquito without feeling guilty. He wouldn't even squash the cockroaches that sauntered into our kitchen, snatched bits of bread, and strutted out. Crazehead chased them around and tried to pound them to pulp with his heels. "Leave them alone," Shango always pleaded. Cock-roaches were just trying to survive, like us, he said.

We lived in the two-story house my father had designed in Shapati Town, his hometown. We had a plot number, not a street number, and the street had no telephone lines. My father had had a brick wall built so high that armed robbers would need pole vaults to catapult themselves into the grounds. He must have envisaged them trying despite the odds; on top of his wall were broken bottle pieces, like jewels on the crest of his architectural crown. In our garden was his one concession to my mother, a now empty swimming pool, shaded by her favorite jacaranda and flame-of-the-forest trees. The pool was four feet at its deepest. My father, God rest his soul, could not swim. He had nightmares of dying by drowning, not by the bullet. That fate he never expected in the fortress that was our home.

The garden all but blossomed into a bush after my family was killed. That happened one night while I was accepting my runner-up award for "Mr. Caveman" on campus. I was also in the process of failing my first year in engineering. I came home the next morning with my inscribed "Mr. Caveman" club and found them dead in the dining room. I broke all the windows in the house so that the whole of Shapati Town could hear me crying for them to come back to life, then crawled into the garden and sniffed the grass and earth until I wet myself. Shango found me out there and almost developed a hernia from trying to pull me away. I was clutching the grass and would not let go. Strangely, the blades did not break; they came out by their roots and I believe that was when I kind of lost my mind.

From then on, as a tribute to my family, I placed candles on the pool steps whenever the Lawless performed in the shallow end of the swimming pool. They also served as stage lights in the evenings, unless the rain unleashed on us. Our stage, of course, was missing tiles, and our backstage was a thatched gazebo. Our audience sat on the veranda of the house. They clapped during scenes, oftentimes jeered and shouted out warnings like, "He's after you," or "He's plotting your demise." One deaf man, who had a wandering eye, sounded a broken gong at the point of Shango's suicide. A more hilarious death knell I'd not heard. Some audience members, who couldn't help themselves, ran into the swimming pool and yanked off Professor's wig, or snatched his wrapper to see what he was wearing underneath. He played the goddess Oya, Shango's beloved wife, complete with red lipstick and thick Charlie Chaplin-like eyebrows.

Our audiences were people from the neighborhood. They doubled as extras, stagehands, and sound technicians. They improvised. They wanted us to ad-lib. There was no dividing line between them and us, but this wasn't Wole Soyinka's intellectual mythology or street-level guerrilla theater. This was theater of the basest kind, theater as it was performed in the villages of old, theater as it was meant to be performed, or so we thought after enough bottles of Star beer. The point was, who said theater was dead in Nigeria?

Toyosi joined the group when we were tired of getting constipated from the roasted plantains and groundnuts we bought from local food hawkers. I was becoming more and more sluggish, particularly doing the acrobatic scenes in which I wrestled with Shango. One night, I tumbled on stage and couldn't get up again, and there I was, playing Ogun, the god of iron and war.

Toyosi was an actress in a soap opera. Her part had been discontinued due to "lack of funding"—she refused to sleep with the producer. She came to see us after a show, with her plump daughter clamped to her hip.

"I'll cook for you," she said, "if you let me stay."

"No space for you," Professor said, shooing her away. "I play the women here."

"Did I say I was looking for a part?" she asked.

"What did you come here for then?" he said, removing his

glasses to eye her up and down, as if she was sent to poison us.

Fineboy stepped forward, sticking out his massive chest. "Beautiful lady, we go by aliases in this place. What shall we call you? Nefertiti? Queen Amina of Zaria?"

I couldn't believe what the bobo was saying.

"Call me whatever you want," Toyosi said. "Just give me a place to stay."

"I thought we were friends here," I said. "I thought we treated people with respect."

I wanted her to like me more than the rest, even though I was about to let her down. We had no room for one more, let alone a woman with a child. She had cropped natural hair, bleached gold. It made her skin look darker. Her legs were a little bandy, and her expression was, well, sort of bored. I winked at her daughter.

"Hey," I said.

The little so-and-so began to howl. She bucked and threw her head back. Toyosi tried to hush her. The more she did, the louder the child cried. Then Toyosi unbuttoned her blouse and released the tiniest breasts I'd ever seen on a woman. None of us knew where to look, except Crazehead.

Toyosi eased her nipple into her daughter's mouth. "You guys should really consider taking me in, you know. I'm writing a play and from what I've seen, you need better material."

"Are you also a Broadway critic?" Professor snapped.

Toyosi smiled. She could have been teasing him.

"I've seen what *you* do," she said.

Professor's voice became shrill. "So say thanks then! Isn't it for free you entered?"

"Enough," I said.

Sometimes I wondered about him. Why was he so

effeminate? Toyosi shifted her daughter higher up her hip. She might as well have yawned. Her daughter was sucking away. She was such a pretty child.

"Em, what do you mean, 'better material'?" I asked, trying to focus on Toyosi's face.

"Come on," she said. "A play about warring Yoruba deities? It's like drama society in secondary school, not even original. Haven't you just copied Duro Ladipo's *Oba Koso*?"

"*Oba Koso* is based on the story of Shango. The story of Shango belongs to everyone."

"Yeah, an old folktale."

"Not a folktale. Shango is part of the Yoruba religion, like Adam and Eve in the Bible. You see? That is the problem with we Africans. We disrespect ourselves…"

She rolled her eyes. "Oh, here we go again. Who cares? The story is so parochial and not relevant today. Then you wonder why no one will sponsor you and you have to end up performing in an empty swimming pool."

"We had the Goethe."

"They must have pitied you."

"The British Council is considering."

"You won't be lucky twice."

"The Americans—"

"Who?" She laughed as if I'd cracked a joke.

"Listen," I said. "Don't come here and insult us. It's bad enough everyone thinks our years of studying drama were a waste of time. Anyone who produces relevant plays in Nigeria today will be locked up. You of all people should understand."

She hissed. "You're not acting. You're messing around over here, and you might impress a few expats, who are always suckers for an authentic cultural display so steeped in native metaphor that the average Nigerian can't digest it, or thrill a few locals who can't tell the difference between a drama performance and a wrestling match, but don't expect me to be singing your praises after I leave this place."

"At least we have formal training," I said. "At least we didn't get our training in a dubious local soap."

"Theater arts grads?" she said. "You're right there at the bottom of the manure heap, next to the agriculture students. Tell me something, with no bio to speak of, who will employ you when you finally graduate?"

That led to us faking coughs and covering our crotches.

"Excuse me," I said. "I have to talk to my friends."

"No," Professor said. "I don't want her here. You heard how she insulted us. She'll come here and ruin everything."

Everything. We were in what my mother would have called the parlor. I was on my father's faded reclining chair, the rest were sitting on sofas with pockmarks. The white paint on the wall was peeling, the carpet had missing patches, and the windows had wooden bars. I'd nailed the bars in myself after I'd smashed the panes. So many mornings, after overnight rains, we'd wake up to find puddles on the floor.

"She didn't go for my line," Fineboy murmured. "Nefertiti, Queen Amina of Zaria. Why didn't she go for my line?"

"Crazehead?" I asked, ignoring him.

Crazehead was scratching his head. Did he have ringworm?

"Shango," I said, hoping he might have something useful to add.

"You're the owner of the house," he said, shrugging. "It's your decision. Although, I don't know why she needs a place to stay. The way she speaks and behaves, she's an elite, definitely a pepperless chick. She even sounds like an away Nigerian. She probably went to school in England, probably has an old man somewhere with a house twice as big as this..."

I'd almost forgotten his inability to stick to issues, any issue at hand. There was agreement all around; Toyosi was definitely an away Nigerian, a pepperless Nigerian, an assorted chick, an *aje* butter.

"So why is she an actress?" Professor asked. "Shouldn't she be working in a bank or in Daddy's law firm or medical practice?"

"Perhaps she's been thrown out of home," I said. "She has the baby girl and no ring on her finger. You know the elite: their children must carry on their shenanigans within wedlock, or else—"

"Or else it's instant disownment," Fineboy said, as though I'd reminded him of an incident in his past.

I had to ask Toyosi, since she had so many answers. "I don't understand. A woman like you—why do you want to cook for a group of guys?"

She frowned. "I beg your pardon?"

"Aren't you for the liberation of women?"

Her daughter was sleeping face up on the mattress that was my sister's. I couldn't confirm the mattress was free of bugs. My sister's photograph was in a square-shaped frame on her dresser. Sweet troublemaker, she had been fourteen at the time, and was always harassing me for fifty naira to buy fruit-flavored lip gloss.

Toyosi shrugged. "Why should I be for women's liberation? The person who chased my father and broke up my family is a woman. My mother herself, who threw me out of home, is a woman. Plus, what other skills do I have to offer a group of hungry guys?"

Her lips were so thin I could gobble them up with one parting of my mouth, or at least nibble on her lower one, I thought.

I sat on the mattress. "Em, what about this play you're writing?"

"What about it?"

"Title?"

"The Lawless."

"Premise?"

"The breakdown of society."

That was huge. "How many players?"

"I haven't written it yet. Don't keep hounding me."

"Who's hounding you?"

She wagged her forefinger. "Yes, you were. Yes, you were, just now. Stop it, you hear?"

Why did I still want her to like me? I kept trying: "I suppose you must be fed up with the kind of material for women, em, actors..."

I'd read that in a magazine passed around the Theater Arts department for so long that it had more palm-oil stains than print. It came from a Hollywood actress with skin as delicate as crêpe. She was half starved, yet she wanted to be taken seriously. We looked to America for slang and elements of craft, and to our budding local Nollywood video and stage productions—not to the British; they were inaccessible, like their Queen's English.

"Poor parts for women," Toyosi said, stroking her daughter's legs. "That's a good reason to quit acting, not to pick up a pen."

"I can never give up acting, *sha*."

"You probably can't do anything else."

"Not since I caught the bug."

"It's more like a terminal disease to me. Me, I'm through with it."

"How come you're so cold?" I asked.

She tucked her chin in. "How come you're trying to sleep with me?"

If she didn't work miracles with beans and palm oil, I would have asked her to leave. Immediately. I would have told her, "Look here, you're harsh, snobbish and not that attractive."

I never once saw her write, but she could cook, and she had our scenes moving again. That, and the other good reason for having her around was that every girlfriend I'd ever had had looked endearing, even the campus sluts and sugar-daddy types I ended up with. Whatever their conduct in private, they were the sort of women my mother would have approved of, because they had the same wash-and-set hairdo that was popular in Lagos, and they slept with pink foam rollers to maintain that look.

"How can we ever have decent sex with rollers?" I'd asked my last girlfriend. "I mean, can't I ruffle up your hair once in a while?" She said, as an African woman, she didn't appreciate her hair being ruffled up. I complained and complained until she agreed, "OK, I'll take them out, but after sex, I'm rolling my hair up again."

For that alone I broke up with her, so Toyosi was right, and I was surprised she knew me that well from the start. Whenever I saw a woman who was different from the norm, all I wanted—all I'd ever wanted—was to sleep with her.

Toyosi occupied my sister's room. Sometimes, I'd see her snoring with her mouth open and her daughter's head in her armpit, and I suppose that was when I loved her, or perhaps it was later. Who knows? I let her share my parents' bathroom, scrubbed the tub daily so she could wash her daughter in the evenings. She never once said thank you.

I noticed how she spent more time with Professor than with any of us. She smiled at him and let him bounce her daughter on his knee. One morning, I heard him singing a special anthem he'd made for her: "Pretty girl, pretty girl, who is your daddy? I'm your daddy." I could have kicked the door down.

"He's trying to chase you," I whispered in Toyosi's ear. "He's even using your daughter. How come you treat him better than me?"

"Prof?" she said. "He likes women?"

Prof. "Of course he does."

"*Na wa*. I could have sworn he wasn't that way inclined. He told me he lost his father in the Civil War."

"He's a poet and a liar."

Professor and his sisters were raised by their mother. Their father was so devastated when Biafra lost the war, he stayed in France.

As soon as I had the opportunity, I made sure I tripped him up. He was coming out of her room with a soiled nappy. The nappy went flying, followed by his glasses.

"Ah-ah, see what you made me do?" he whined, picking himself off the floor.

"Ehen?" I said. "So what are you going to do about it?"

The water shortage in Shapati Town changed our friendship in that house. Every tap in the town center dried up after the rainy season, right through the beginning of the harmattan season, so we had the usual dusty winds in the mornings and evenings. During the hot afternoons, the townspeople disappeared into their cement brick bungalows, under the shelter of their corrugated-iron roofs, just waiting.

Our local council couldn't tell us when they would "recutify de problem." A water tanker came round every other day. We had to be on the lookout for the driver, because two honks and that man was off. When he arrived, we ran outside with our aluminum buckets, shouting, "We're here, oh. We're here, oh." Then he'd grab his big hose between his legs and drench us until he'd filled our buckets, then we'd hobble back into the house.

We boiled some of the water to drink and brush our teeth. The rest was for bathing, flushing and Toyosi's cooking. After about three weeks of this, we were exhausted in the evenings, and not prepared for our performances. People in our audience, who couldn't afford tanker water, were fetching polluted water from Lagos Lagoon and Five Cowrie Creek. When they showed up, they crossed their arms and expected us to bring not just entertainment, but some frigging joy into their lives. Shango did his usual fire-breathing trick, spitting kerosene from his mouth onto the flame of a hidden lighter. They hissed and called us useless; our story about Yoruba gods was no longer relevant.

We stopped putting on our free show. I went to the British Council to see how far our script had gone there. They said they were still considering us. Shango went to the Americans. Some asshole there told him they only sponsored talented people. Back at the house, my friends were beginning to smell as guys do when they stay together too long: of rivalry and unsatisfied desires, and sheer bad manners.

One evening, Crazehead let out one of his belches. Normally, I would hold my nose until the mist subsided, but I was too tired. I was lying on a sofa. We were in the parlor again. We'd had a power cut and there were shadows dancing on the ceiling from the light of our kerosene lanterns. Shango was studying a journey of ants to and from a bit of bread. "Can't you even say excuse me?" he said. "Hexcuse," Crazehead said. Professor hissed. "You this boy, you have no manners." Toyosi was in the kitchen, boiling water to make her daughter a bottle of milk. She was trying to wean her—not that this was the right time to introduce any child to Lagos water, but the girl was almost one year old and biting hard.

"No consid'ration," Fineboy said.

"Ah-ah?" Crazehead said, smiling as if he were made popular by our criticisms. "Why is everyone picking on me tonight?" He shuffled across the room and dived by my feet, and then he let out another belch. I smelled it first: bushmeat and orange peel.

"What the hell did you eat, man?" I asked.

The parlor already stank of mosquito repellent.

"Shit," Fineboy said, burying his face in a cushion.

"One more coming up," Crazehead said.

Fineboy sprang from his chair. "I swear to God if you…" He reached for Crazehead's feet.

Crazehead sat up: "It's not my fault! It's not my fault!"

"Out of this place," Fineboy ordered. "Are you an animal or what?"

Fineboy—and I suppose this tallied with his good looks—was particular about personal hygiene. He insisted on shaving despite the water shortage. I'd caught him, numerous times, glaring at Crazehead, who walked around with patches of beard on his chin and dried-up sleep in his eyes.

I heard Toyosi's daughter crying. Toyosi was checking her boiling water. I turned around again and Fineboy and Crazehead were on the floor, wrestling. Crazehead was on top.

"What are you fighting for?" I asked.

Toyosi hurried into the parlor with her daughter on her hip. Shango dragged Crazehead and Fineboy apart. They were breathing through their mouths. Shango grabbed Crazehead's shoulders and lifted him. I thought he was about to throw Crazehead across the room. Crazehead kicked his shins. He looked like a puppet with entangled strings.

"Shangooo!"

Toyosi's shriek so reminded me of my mother's that I sat up straight. Shango lowered Crazehead to the floor and went back to studying ants, as if he'd never moved from there. Crazehead was grinning. "What's wrong with 'im?"

I walked over to Shango as he crouched by the wall. "Hope nothing," I said.

He was watching the ants crawl up and down. "Everyone thinks I'm soft. I'm not that soft."

"Why did you do that to Crazehead? You know his head is not correct."

"Are we really useless and untalented?"

"We're extremely talented, in fact."

"Then why will no one sponsor us?"

"Because theater is dead, art is——"

I had to stop myself; I was sounding like the student unionists, specialists in screaming about how they were voiceless victims. But who were we to feel sorry for ourselves because a few foreign embassies wouldn't give us attention? And why did we have to depend on their charity anyway? Not one stinking rich Nigerian was willing to support us?

I slapped Shango's back. "What do you expect, *jo?*" After all, if I allowed myself to address the issue at hand—the real issue: what was the state of art under a dictatorship? Where was the state of art under a dictatorship?

My house was one state. Here, we were so free we deserved to fly our own flag. For this, we had to be grateful, at least.

Shango let an ant crawl onto the tip of his forefinger. "You know the people I feel sorry for most in the whole wide world?"

"Who?" I asked.

"Ants," he said. "Because all they ever do is live for their work and see how we trample on them."

I placed my hand on his shoulder. Shango wasn't soft; he was as thick as a tree trunk.

"Why are your friends such morons?" Toyosi asked, as she bathed her daughter that evening. Her hair was tied up in a turban and she carried the girl in the crook of her arm.

"They're not so bad," I said, meaning it.

"Why can't they just go home to their parents?"

"They don't have homes they can 'go' to."

On campus, I'd dreaded being on my own in the house. The thought had had me sitting up at nights with a dry throat. Now, I wondered if I should brave it. Toyosi wiped her daughter's cheeks with a washcloth.

"Are they orphans or what?" she asked.

"Their families can't afford them."

"Can you?"

I was broke from paying for water, food and baby milk. What little funds I had left would cover my electricity bills. I remembered the smartest statement Shango ever made. "You'll spend your inheritance," he said, "until pain is all you have to live on."

"What happened to your parents?" Toyosi asked.

"Killed."

"Eh? How?"

"Armed robbers."

"*Kai.* Where?"

"Here. Gateman took a bribe and let them in."

She looked around the bathroom as if she could feel their ghosts watching us. The windowpane over the bathtub was smashed; I could hear crickets outside.

"My sister, too," I said.

"When?"

"Remember when there were so many raids?"

There were riots after the Abacha regime announced their constitutional conference. The mobile police squad promptly quashed them. Armed robbers took over Lagos streets at night. They attacked homes with machetes and guns. People swore some of them were university students—they spoke so well. The raids were a social revolution, I'd bragged at the time, not knowing I would be personally affected. Meanwhile, the Abacha regime was passing decrees to muzzle dissidents. Lagos State set up a special squad to combat armed robberies, and the rumor was that the squad was selling arms to the robbers.

Toyosi pulled her wrapper up her thigh and trickled water over her daughter's belly. "What's Shango's own story?"

"His parents had twelve kids. They gave him away. My parents were his guardians. He got me involved in drama, saved me from insanity."

"Crazehead?"

"*Ogogoro* and hemp. His father is a trumpeter, drinks *ogogoro* like water. Crazehead himself started smoking hemp at the age of ten."

"Professor?"

"Premature ejaculation."

"Fineboy?"

"He made a pass at you. How come you don't shun him?"

She shook her head. "I don't understand. You're not from the same background as any of your friends."

"What do you mean?"

"You're... you know."

"'You know,' what?"

"Posh," she said, but I was the son of an architect who'd inherited an estate, and the middle class were as nonexistent as theater was dead.

Her daughter took ill with malaria, or bad water; we were not sure. At first she was refusing to take her bottle, then her temperature spiked in the evenings, and her little eyeballs sank. At night we could hear her gibbering in baby language. Toyosi got up every hour to sponge her. I gave up asking if I could help. She wouldn't even let Professor near the child, only during the day, when her temperature subsided. Then we would take turns to place her on our chests and feel her tiny heart pumping and her fingers grasping at our sleeves. She scratched us with her fingernails, wet us with the sweat from her head, and left us smelling of milk and medicine. Professor, Fineboy, Shango, Crazehead, we were all involved in administering her chloroquine and antibiotic drops that Toyosi bought from Hausa street hawkers, knowing they could well be fake.

After a week, she was not getting better, so, regardless of my fatherly feelings, I told Toyosi, "You have to take her to a doctor."

We were in my sister's room. Toyosi smoothed the mattress with such diligence I knew she was scared. The child kicked weakly. I'd never seen a baby with cheekbones before.

"I can't afford to," Toyosi said.

"A pharmacist then," I said.

"I can't afford that either."

"This child will dehydrate. You want her to? *Abi*, is that it?"

She didn't answer.

"Toyosi," I said.

"What?" she said, wagging her forefinger at me. "You can nag somebody like an old woman. Leave me alone."

"At least get her a proper diagnosis."

"How?"

"You know what I mean. Go home. Apologize to your people if necessary. Lagos without family? You're not that rugged. It's over now. This is our reality not yours. You can't romanticize slumming."

She hissed. "Who is romanticizing? You think living in a dilapidated mansion is slumming?"

"Go home."

"No. I'm not going back. They suffered me. 'Toyosi, don't say such things. Toyosi, Uncle would never do that to you.'"

"Who is Uncle?"

"My mother's I-don't-know-what."

"What did he do to you?"

"This is his daughter. Is that not enough?"

Her own story was as byzantine as our national politics, the stuff of Lagos suburban life, as debauched as it was hidden. I understood that her mother, having divorced her philandering father, was now the outside woman in a polygamous union with this Uncle, and this Uncle thought he'd help himself to Toyosi.

"He denied it. My mother tells everyone I slept with the houseboy. My father says I'm unnatural for sleeping with a houseboy, worse than unnatural. I'm dead to him. Now, I'm kicked out of home. That's fine, but nobody should tell me about violation of rights, or censorship, or persecution in this country. These things have been going on in homes for years and I don't see anyone fighting for freedom in that realm."

"But what can we actually do for you here?" I asked, hoping she would find practical ways for us to support her. So we were both without families, slightly unbalanced, and far removed from the struggle for democracy, but I was going back to university. She couldn't stay in the house forever.

"Steal," she said.

I thought she was joking.

"We're not thieves," I said. The last time I stole was from Duro Ladipo's *Oba Koso* and I didn't even do that properly.

"You've played gods," she said. "Can't you play thieves for a night?"

I stood up. "You're the one playing here."

She carried her daughter. "I know someone. Someone with money. Someone you can get money from. Easily."

"Didn't I just tell you what armed robbers did to my family?"

"What will I do? My child is sick. You're running out of money. We're your family. Me, you, her and the village idiots downstairs. You're lord of the mansion. You want to be with me? Save us, instead of sniffing around me like a dog in heat."

She beckoned with one hand, as if she was looking for a fight rather than love. I was done for, I thought, and warped. How could I still be attracted to her?

"Who is this someone?"

Yes, that was the moment I loved Toyosi.

"My sister. She's a banker. She won't speak to me now I've been disowned. Just because she is my father's favorite. Just because she doesn't want to fall out of favor. She goes around calling me a liar, the selfish, spoiled..."

"Toyosi, the men in your life have some responsibility to bear."

"I trusted the women."

"OK," I said.

"Speak to your friends," she said. "I beg you."

"What if she's setting us up?" Professor asked. "I don't know. I just don't."

He was hugging himself and rocking. The rest had said yes. I was waiting for one more voice.

"Shango?" I asked.

He pursed his lips. "Well... at least it's a real gig."

"She lives on Victoria Island. She works for a merchant

bank there. She makes stupid money doing foreign exchange deals."

"Which kin'?" Crazehead asked.

"It's too complex to explain."

"Fraud?" Professor asked.

"Probably," I said.

"I don't pity her, then," Fineboy said. "Let's do it. I'm in."

"All right?" I asked.

The rest nodded; they were in. We'd taken greater risks in life anyway: pursuing careers in theater arts for a start, condoms we should have used for another.

We set off at night in my mother's Volkswagen Beetle, because the gear stick of my father's Peugeot got stuck. I was driving, Shango was by my side, Crazehead and Fineboy were behind with the Professor between them. We backed out of the gates and Crazehead said, "'Alt!"

"What for?" I asked.

"Let us pray," he said.

I pleaded with my palms pressed together. "I know your head is not normally correct, but please, let it be correct tonight, OK?" We'd bathed, shaved, washed and pressed our clothes. Crazehead was carrying two blunt daggers.

The road to Victoria Island was an expressway that ran through market towns and fishing villages. We passed hamlets, which had red flags to show the incumbents were cherubim and seraphim worshippers, Lekki and Eleko beaches, oil-palm clusters and bushes. There was a plot for Lagos Business School, a satellite center for the University of Calabar, Victoria Court Cemetery where I'd buried my family. The sky was indigo and the air smelled of dust and salt. Billboards advertised the usual cigarettes, beer, medicine, born-again churches and toothpaste. Towards the island were villas with terra-cotta roofs and balconies. Victoria Island was meant to be a residential district; it was a commercial one now, bright with the neon lights of banks and finance houses. It was also a red-light district; prostitutes flagged us down near the diplomatic section, at the junction of a street named after Louis Farrakhan, to spite the Americans.

The block of flats Toyosi's sister lived in was one of those built to capitalize on the commercial growth on the island. It was converted from someone's knocked-down home, had no uniformed security guards, mirrors for windows and a cemented yard. Expatriates wouldn't rent a flat here. The gateman, a Fulani man in a black tunic and embroidered skullcap, let us in. He took a bribe, as Toyosi said he would, holding his prayer beads in his other hand. Fineboy, Crazehead and I got out of the Beetle. Shango and Professor waited as our lookout and backup.

I knocked on the door; no bell, no peephole.

"Ye-es?" I heard her say.

I breathed in. "Daddy says you should come downstairs."

She hesitated. "My father?"

"Yes. Daddy is downstairs and he says you should come down right now."

She muttered, "Again? For goodness' sake."

My heart scrambled around my chest. I glanced at Fineboy who was bowing his head, preparing himself to waylay her. Crazehead was behind me. We heard footsteps then clicks in her keyhole. Security was generally tight in Lagos. How did robberies happen? Because, sometimes, robbers had inside information.

Toyosi's father had forbidden her sister to leave home and move into a flat of her own. She was an unmarried woman and it was not done in society, but she was also making enough money to disobey him. It was Toyosi's mother, feeling bitter about the divorce, who had given her daughter permission to leave home, and her father paid unexpected visits, on his way from Island Club, or from his girlfriend's, to check that his own daughter wasn't entertaining men. He was a lawyer for an oil company, too fat and important to get out of his car. His chauffeurs called him Daddy. Everyone who worked for him called him Daddy.

Toyosi's sister opened her door with a wig on her head and one brow raised.

"So how many of you does it take to drive my father's Merc?" she asked.

Fineboy ushered her back into her flat.

"Inside," he said. "And don't make a sound."

"Yeah," Crazehead said, "or else we'll fug you hup."

I raised my eyes. Was this what we had agreed on? No one forced me, though. I walked in with my own two legs.

Her eyes puffed up from crying. She was sweating in her black skirt suit. Her wig was askew and her mouth was shaped as though a chicken bone was wedged in sideways. Her flat was done up in matching purple tie-and-dye sofas and chairs with ruffles. Toyosi had said a well-known Lagos interior decorator was responsible for the mess. Her sister was a smoker, stank of tobacco and perfume, and in her living room was a crystal ashtray of lipstick-stained cigarette butts. Crazehead and I searched the wardrobe in her bedroom where she said her money would be. Bruno Magli and Ferragamo were the shoes she favored. Her bags were Louis Vuitton and Fendi.

The money was in a mesh bag of dirty underwear. I handed it to Crazehead, who dug his hand inside and pulled out a bra.

"La Perla," he said. "Dis one be African Jackie Onassis. Are Ferragamo and Fendi your mother and father?"

He rolled the bra into a ball and sniffed it, then cast it on the floor and pulled out a thong.

I winced.

He sniffed that, too.

"The money," I said, feeling nauseous, yet strangely intrigued.

Toyosi's sister was crying again. Crazehead found the wad of dollars.

"Is this all?" he asked.

She nodded. Mucus trailed from her nostrils into her mouth.

"Let's fade," I said, overwhelmed with shame.

"No," Fineboy said. "Let her do one more thing for us."

I frowned. "Like what?"

"Call Daddy," he said.

The woman herself looked bemused. She had to know we were fakes now. No armed robbers could be this stupid.

"Call Daddy for what?" I asked.

"Let her call him and you'll see," he said.

"Now!" Crazehead barked so loudly I jumped.

I promised myself that I would one day have to think about why my friends were such morons. Toyosi's sister dropped her mobile phone three times, she was trembling so much as she called her father.

"H-hello? D-daddy?"

"Tell him you like sex," Fineboy whispered. "Don't start crying wah-wah."

She clutched the phone. "It's me, Daddy. I like... sex."

"Tell him," Fineboy said, "you have a boyfriend who is not from a good family."

She shut her eyes. "Daddy, my boyfriend is not from a good family."

"But," Fineboy said, "he gives it to you hard."

She shook her head. Crazehead was giggling. He raised his dagger and bit the edge. "Real 'ard," he whispered.

Toyosi's sister placed her hand on her chest. She was gasping for air. Her skin was fair, probably from chemical bleaching.

"Daddy," she said, "my boyfriend… gives it to me… hard."

As soon as my shoes touched the ground outside, I smacked Fineboy's big chest.

"You're a bastard," I said.

"*Yei*," he said and ducked.

"And you," I said, pointing at Crazehead. "Your head is not correct. Why did you do that to her? Was that our plan?"

They were raising their fists. Shango and Professor were leaning on the bonnet of the Beetle. I tossed the mobile phone on the driver's seat, unable to bear what had passed between father and daughter. Wasn't our population over a hundred million when last I checked, give or take ten million for census fudging? And fewer than ten people in Nigeria, I was sure, would admit to their parents that they'd had sex, let alone enjoyed it. We didn't even have to lock her up in her bedroom; she collapsed on the floor after her phone call to Daddy.

"Let's go," I said.

"What happened?" Shango asked.

I pointed at Crazehead and Fineboy. "Ask them."

Crazehead was calling the gateman. "Tss, *Mallam*, you get kola nut?"

The gateman was standing at attention by the cement column of the gates with his wife by his side. She was a street hawker. They were nomadic people, sort of permanently stuck in the city. They'd come from the North, with robes as colorful as petals and feet as filthy as roots. The woman had a pink chiffon scarf covering her head. Her husband shoved her and she immediately squatted over her tray of Bicycle cigarettes, Trebor mints and Bazooka Joe chewing gum.

Professor hissed. "Why did he push her like that?"

"Blame Crazehead," I said. "Is it now he's asking for kola nuts?"

I yanked the door of the Beetle open. Shango went round to the other side. Fineboy was coming towards us. I noticed Professor waddling over to the gateman.

"Prof," I called. "What happuns? I said, we're leaving."

Professor placed his hand on his crooked back like someone's grandmother and began to berate the gateman: "Why did you push her? Did you have to push her? Isn't she your wife? Couldn't you say common please?"

The gateman backed away, gabbling in his language.

"Ignorant Northerners," Professor said. "All of you are the same."

I shook my head. He was being a tribalist at this late hour?

"Misogynist," he said. "You have no respect for women."

No, he was being a feminist. I knocked my head against the Beetle.

"Prof," I whispered. "Why?"

He waved his arms like a traffic warden: "*Alla Wakuba. That's all you know. Alla Wakuba.*"

The gateman, who couldn't understand a word of English, understood Professor's attempt at Arabic. He was gobbling like a turkey now. I was sure he was calling Professor an infidel. He snatched Professor's arm and twisted so hard that Professor was off balance and flat on the gravel in one second. His glasses went flying, followed by his confidence.

"*Chineke*, hellep me, oh," he yelped.

The gateman reached into his robe and pulled out a

scabbard longer than Crazehead's puny daggers placed together.

"Shango," I said. "Save the bobo."

Shango ran across the gravel. He grabbed the gateman's shoulders, lifted him, and threw him against the cement column. The gateman slumped at the foot. His wife screamed, "*Barawo! Barawo!*" Thieves.

I sped out of the gates. My mother's Beetle protested with a screech. I tried to straighten the wheel, but my hands were shaking too much.

"D-did we kill him?" Professor was asking. He was squinting. We'd left his glasses on the gravel when we fled.

"We injured 'im," Crazehead said. "There was blood everywhere."

His voice was loaded with an accusation. Shango stared out of the window. Fineboy leaned forward and squeezed my shoulder. "Steady on, o-boy. At least let's get home. Drive safely and all that, eh?"

"I'm trying," I said. I was so ashamed: I had a hard-on.

When we reached the mansion, I snatched the wad of dollars from Crazehead and delivered it to the real lord—Toyosi.

"Here," I said. "Are you satisfied?"

She glanced at the notes in her usual manner, as if they were inevitable circumstances in her life, but she wouldn't move, so I threw the notes on my sister's bed where her daughter was sleeping. I didn't even care if she hated me. I was fed up with her lack of gratitude.

"Thank you," she mumbled.

"We almost killed a man for this."

"Thank you. You've been so kind to me."

"Make sure you get her to a doctor and buy her the right medicines."

She reached for me and I pushed her away. What if Shango had killed the gateman?

"Did you hurt my sister?" she asked.

I rolled my fist against my mouth. "I can't say."

"Ogun, answer me."

"I cannot."

"Ogun, tell me. Did you hurt my sister?"

Ogun had several translations depending on how it was pronounced. It could mean sweat, poison, medicine, inheritance, an army, a battle, the number twenty, or the god of iron and war. With Toyosi's appalling Yoruba intonation, Ogun was a basket for catching shrimps, but she gripped my wrist and her eyes watered, so I told her about Fineboy's inferiority complex, Shango's hidden rage, Professor's over-identification with women and my desperation to avenge my family. I also told her about her sister's forced confession, and she smirked.

"Serves her right."

"We were not acting. We were just being ourselves and yet..."

Was that redemption I felt? That rush of potency and sense of possibility? I leaned against Toyosi. Who was I to think theater could save us? Who was I to think art could save anyone in Lagos?

She stroked my forehead. "See? See why I had to give up? There's enough drama in our lives. We must be supernatural to survive here. Why bother with any myth about gods?"

We heard a giggle as heartening as rainbow-colored bubbles popping. It was her daughter. She'd woken up and found the dollar bills.

"Hrscht," she said. "Hrsch-tup."

Her first words. Shut up, she was trying to say, and she was absolutely justified. There was no need for her mother to pontificate, not at that stage.

At first we were a little shy of one another in that house. We were not sure how to regard each other, as actors or armed robbers. Then, the haze of harmattan lifted and it became clear that we were brothers.

The Abacha regime announced they were reopening our university. We knew we would not be returning to graduate. We heard from the British Council and I asked them to save their patronage for a more deserving theater group.

One surprise: as we prepared for our next night as the Lawless, it was Crazehead who became the most solemn in our group, Crazehead who made us promise to stick to our plans and vow never to spill blood again.

As for Toyosi, and this was way before she christened me Lord of the Lawless, way before we became lovers, her daughter got better, plumper than the day she arrived, and Toyosi began to write her play. Just like that. She didn't know how the story would end, but I had a clue how it began. She claimed that she'd unblocked us and now we were unblocking her. I told her she'd invented a new form of plagiarism. As we went out to perform in homes throughout Lagos, the woman just wrote and wrote, and wrote.

Twilight Trek

Gao. An agent hands me a fake passport—my name is not Jean-Luc, I'm not from Mali and I'm definitely no Francophone African.

I'm fluent in English though, and luckily the agent can communicate in pidgin. He leads me through a haze of smoke to a mud hut where I will hide until nightfall. The smoke is coming from the compound where a group of old Malian women are cooking a midday meal. The women are shrouded in robes. Being such good Muslims, you'd think they would invite a stranger to eat. Anyway, I'm happy to go indoors, instead of sweltering in the heat like them. I don't care to know the town of Gao. The further north I am in Africa, the more one place begins to resemble another.

Like me, other travelers in Gao have come from some-where south. We will cross the Sahara to get to Morocco, and from there cross the Mediterranean to get into Spain. We are illegals. It's not that we don't have enough money to fly overseas; it's just that the foreign embassies don't grant Africans like us visas. Half my fare is hidden in my sneakers. To raise the full amount, I sold marijuana. I wasn't making much of a cut, so I duped my boss. He threatened to send a gang to slit my throat, after they'd raped me. I knew I had to leave town immediately. Death I could live with, but I couldn't afford to be tampered with like that, against my will.

When I was young, my mother used to smear lipstick all over my face. "Keep still," she would order as I struggled. "See how pretty you look." She oiled my hair with pomade and braided it into cornrows like a girl's. In the afternoons, after school, I'd beg her to let me play football with other boys in our neighborhood; she'd make me sit on a stool and watch her roasting groundnuts. She'd be singing that awful nursery rhyme:

> The birds have come home
> *Tolongo*
> One black, one red
> *Tolongo*
> Their tails are touching the ground
> Sho

Instead of clapping, I'd be frowning at her huge crusty feet. Even with those feet, my mother managed to walk the streets in high heels and solicit all sorts of men: rich, married, handsome, fat—white sailors like my father. One day she introduced me to a saggy-ass Lebanese who was known for liking light-skinned boys. "He'll only touch," she promised. I ran away from home after that, lived on the streets, played football with a group of louts and discovered just how professional I was at the sport. In fact, for a while, before I warned them to stop understating my talent, my football friends were calling me... what's-his-name? Pele?

In the hut there's a prayer mat. I fall asleep on it. In my dream, my mother's face appears as I remember: two thick penciled-in lines for brows, a chip in her front tooth, and pink rouge on her cheeks. Her feet are the roots of a tree, with dry bark for skin. She can't move, and yet she is able to hunt me down and find me, wherever I am, even here in Gao.

She tells me that, all things considered, to trek overseas is reasonable. A man she knew hid himself in the wheel well of an airplane that flew overnight to London. It could have been the low temperature or high altitude that finished him. Immigration officers discovered his body two days later. By the end of the month, they'd deported him back to his family for his burial.

She says the lesson to learn is that the world is round, which means that if I run too fast I might end up chasing the very homeland I am running from. She lectures me even in my dreams, my mother. She is the daughter of a schoolteacher, lest anyone forget.

When it is dark enough, I come out of the hut. My stomach is so fed up with grumbling for attention it's in a silent sulk. I buy myself bread and sardines to eat, enough to last the journey. I buy drinking water, bottles of it. I meet a pretty chick called Patience at the depot where the agent instructed me to wait with other travelers for our transportation out of Gao.

Patience is skinny with a bit of a butt. Her trousers are too tight. Her hair is curly and greased back. She wears a silver hoop in her nostril. She claims to be from Mali, but she has been living in the capital city, Bamako. She says this as if it is some sort of achievement, as if it separates her from villagers who are happy to stay in Africa herding their cattle, hoeing their land or whatever.

"You have a man in Bamako?" I ask her.

"Do you know how old I am?"

"Sweet sixteen at most?"

"You small boy! Don't cheek me! How old are you yourself?"

She laughs and swings slaps at me. I'm a year older than I was on the day I left home, is all she needs to know. African chicks are proud of their ages. I bet Patience is taken by my looks. I bet she's taken shit from men not nearly as good-looking as me. I bet she's used to taking shit. Plenty of it. In my old neighborhood, a pretty chick like her would have been beaten up several times by her man.

Our trucks arrive while she is still busy trying to snub me. They are small trucks with tarpaulin covers. We don't scramble for them. We all believe we'll get in one way or another. Our guides are Tuaregs with indigo cloths wrapped around their heads. They know the desert routes. They will drive us through Mali, Algeria, and beyond. There is talk that travelers are sometimes attacked by bearded Muslims and bandits, that trucks often break down and there is no guarantee the gendarmes on patrol will arrive in time to rescue us. This makes a few women turn around at the last moment, especially those with children. I hop into the same truck as Patience and sit by her.

"You again?" she says.

I wink. "I'm just here to protect you."

There are seven of us under the tarpaulin. I check out the others while cracking my knuckles: passenger one, tattered shoes; two, greasy skullcap; three, lopsided headscarf; four, chapped lips; five, gold chain and red eyes. Nothing new.

How long can I bear this godforsaken place? We can only travel at night when cold winds blow. During the day, the sand—you can't understand—it's like needles in my eyes, ants in my nostrils, cobwebs in my chest. It's everywhere. I eat bread and crunch on grains. I gulp down water and grit gets stuck in my throat. I cough so hard my head could detonate.

I'm telling you, in the most crowded cities, I have ridden in taxis with wobbly wheels and no doors, hitched rides on highways in lorries that bounce from one pothole to the other. I have slept in villages where dogs won't stop to take a piss, had bouts of diarrhea, fever, to get to Gao. I can't understand these Tuaregs. Only camels are meant to survive in the Sahara.

At first, Patience would say, "Mr. Protector, how now?" and I would mumble, "Cool." Then I couldn't be bothered to answer because my tongue started to swell. Then she stopped teasing me, perhaps because she realized that joking around might eventually exhaust her.

Now, even she is choking away like everyone else in our truck. We spit where we crouch. We reek of fart. Our legs are cramped. The man with the skullcap says he's suffering from piles because of the constant jolts. His wheezy wife complains that she can't breathe. "Shut up," I want to shout.

Day two. We stop for a rest, finally. I fall out of the truck and roll underneath to avoid the afternoon sun. Shit, there's sand even in my ass.

Patience slides next to me. "Are you all right?"

"Yes."

"Sorry I teased you earlier."

"Don't worry."

"It's just that, to me, you're young. Too young to be on your own, crossing the desert." Her breath smells of sardines.

"I'm not that young."

She stretches. "You know, in Bamako, I heard that this is the same route the Arabs used to traffic African slaves in the olden days."

Who cares?

"Do you have someone to meet you overseas?" she asks.

"Nope."

"What will you do when you get there?"

"Play football."

"Yes?"

"Yeah, and I'll be famous, then I'll get a white woman. I hear they're less trouble."

She sucks her teeth. "You're still very confident, aren't you?"

"Sure."

Sometimes I'm too afraid to think, especially about my mother and that Lebanese. Perhaps that's why I am this way: braggadocios. Perhaps that's why it's impossible for me to worry about where I will end up. Right now, here, under the truck, I'd do *it* with Patience to prove my manhood, but she pulls a white Bible out of her pocket and begins to tell me about Moses who led the Israelites. It's a good story. It puts me straight to sleep.

Again, my mother finds me. This time, she wants to know if my little girlfriend is aware that she's reading a testimony passed from generation to generation. She says if only we Africans took time to compile our stories in a holy book, we might just learn from our past. How many of us have sought the Promised Land and ended up driving taxi cabs, guarding buildings at night, washing dirty plates and toilet seats, sleeping in cold ghettos and on streets?

She says she knows of African women overseas who are recruited as domestics and service their masters in bed. She says she's heard of African men who will marry any sort of woman for the sake of being right with immigration. These men call their wives darling, eat their bland stews, father their children. Yet they can't open their mouths to talk because their wives are liberated. Their children have rights, too, so if a father dares to raise his hand to discipline his son, he might find himself sleeping in jail. She says she hopes I will not become that kind of African man, a whitewashed African, the kind that even she will not lower herself to sleep with.

I wake up so fast Patience says my eyes look like they're about to pop.

That fucking Tuareg is making us pay him extra. I can't believe the lunatic. He beckons that he is about to drive off. He pats his palms, all dried up like beef jerky. He wants more dollars or else he's leaving us here, stranded in the fucking desert. He is yelling in bloody Berber or whatever. The wheezy woman is pleading that she's suffocating and can't he take pity on us. Her husband with the piles begins to weep. I could punch him. Why do we Africans make spectacles instead of fighting for ourselves?

Patience says, "Look here, Mama and Papa, I want to get to Morocco. I don't want to die in the desert. Pay the man, you hear?"

The Tuareg pipes down when we give him an extra $100 each to continue our journey. How I wish I could curse him to his face, but his eyes never seem to blink, asshole.

As we set off, I see the sun setting through a tear in the tarpaulin. It is orange and sliced in half by the horizon. We pass two trucks almost buried under the sand, like giant carcasses. I shiver, not because of the evening wind. For the first time, I think we might not make it to Morocco after all.

Two birds, I keep humming. One black. One red. Their tails are touching the ground. Their tails are...

Tangier. Well, almost. The Tuareg drops us at the foot of a mountain. It is the end of his own journey. He has driven us hundreds of miles and none of us is thankful to him, the cheat. We have prayed, cursed, and crossed the border with our fake passports. Our feet are numb, and now we have to walk to a camp in a forest on the mountain where travelers stop.

Patience says it's unfair. Climbing up a mountain is not what she bargained for. She is meant to be in a guesthouse some-where in Tangier, overlooking the Mediterranean. "I'm not doing it," she says, bursting into tears. "I didn't leave Bamako to sleep in a bush like a common villager."

Three women surround her. The wheezy one rubs her back whispering, "Shh, is OK, is OK." Patience gasps as if she's expelling something bitter. "All right," she says, wiping her tears with her thumbs. "I'm ready now."

Her trouser seams have burst; her hair is so covered in sand she resembles an old woman. I'm surprised she's capable of crying. Every drop of water I've drunk is dried up after the desert. My brain is like fried gizzards at this point. It's almost evening and I think I might have forgotten how to fall asleep. My legs have taken charge. If someone shows me the sea and says, "Here, walk over it," I will. Still, I want to give Patience some assurance, so I reach for her hand.

"No, no," she says and eases mine away.

She hobbles up the mountain like the rest of us.

Honestly, it is like finding an open sewer when we reach the camp. People sure can stink whenever we're like this: in deep shit. I fit in well, me in my shirt that hasn't seen soap since before I got to Gao. The people here are not like any villagers; they're like refugees on television, squatting under plastic sheets: men, women and children, mothers nursing their babies. They are coughing, scratching, and slapping their arms and legs.

"I can't," Patience whispers, and collapses by the root of a tree. She begins to sob again. This time she says that fleas are biting her all over. She gets on my nerves. While she sits there with her head in her hands, I build a tent for the two of us. One good thing: the others are willing to help. They give me a plastic sheet and show me how to tie it to a tree. They tell me to be prepared for thieves, the Moroccan security forces, and to look out for con men who will take my money. Even the air we breathe may carry plagues.

All they want to do is work. They'd work in their countries if they could; they'll work overseas. They've worked in Casablanca, in Tangier. It's easier for me to venture to the port, they say, because I'm—you know—a mulatto. No one will suspect I'm from *pays-z'amis*—you know—black Africa.

I lie under my new tent and catch what conversations I can in English: who has reached Ceuta, who was caught by the *Guardia Civil* and sent back before they could make it to Ceuta. Before I can find out where Ceuta is, I fall asleep with my sneakers on, just in case they get stolen.

This place is no stop, my mother says; it is the anteroom to Hell. It is where spirits wait to pass to the other world. It is the only time left for those who have stopped living and are yet to be pronounced dead; the ground between madness and reason; the Mountain of Babel, where Africans speak in foreign tongues and nothing they say makes sense, so I need not listen.

TWILIGHT TREK

How is it possible, she asks, that I can be denied asylum in Spain, when this place resembles the aftermath of a war zone?

Patience is under the tent with me when I open my eyes. Miraculously, she has magicked a tin pot and is cooking over burning sticks.

"What are you making?" I ask, stretching.

"Chicken," she murmurs.

Four feet. They are boiling in a sort of frothy broth. My stomach groans.

"That's why I like my women African," I say. "A white one would be of no use here."

"I'm almost old enough to have given birth to you," she mutters.

So much for my kindness. She brings up my mother.

"I'm not that young," I whine like a girl.

"Sorry I lost my nerve earlier," she says after a while.

"It's all right," I say. "I suppose you're used to the good life."

She shakes her head. "In Bamako, I was a prostitute."

I don't know what to say to that. I remove my sneakers to air my blisters. She stirs the chicken feet.

There is a Nigerian here called Obazee. I think he fancies himself some kind of a village chief. He has a university degree. He lays down the laws of the forest, he and his cronies. Patience won't go to consult him, though. She says it's only God that can save us now. She's reading her Bible again.

Nigerians are an arrogant lot. This Obazee, all I do is call his name without adding a Mr., and he comes so close to me, with his chest hairs all matted like dead flies.

"*Mr.* Obazee to you," he says. "Who's asking?"

"Me, Jean-Luc."

"Don't you know how to respect your elders?"

"I've crossed a desert."

He could give me that, at least.

There are tribal marks on his cheeks and sores have eaten up the corners of his lips. "*Parlez-vous Français?*" he asks, tilting his head.

"Wee?"

He laughs. "You're no Jean-Luc, but whoever you are, just be careful how you mention my name next time. None of this shouting Obazee, Obazee, all over the place, or I'll conk your little head."

I've decided. I hate him.

"How long have you been here?" I ask.

"Six years."

"Six," I yell.

He frowns. "What? People have been around longer, for over ten years, even. Time is not the object."

"Why don't you just cross to Spain?"

"You think it's as easy as that?"

"I have to cross."

"You think you're the only one?"

"Then why do you stay?"

"Come," he says, beckoning. "Come before the sun goes down, and see for yourself, since you think we're all fools here."

Again my legs carry me, snapping twigs and stamping them into the mud. Obazee walks too fast. I follow him through the camp, past a group of people singing, "When shall I see my home? When shall I see my native land? I will never forget my home…"

"When I first came," he says, "I used to stay in Tangier, in a guesthouse near Petit Socco. It's not easy like that anymore. The security forces, if they find you, they will deal with you; then they'll send you back to Algeria. You'll die before you ever see Gao. I moved here to avoid them. I'm trying to sneak overland into Ceuta. It's what all of us are waiting for. They have a center there. You'll get meals. They will decide if you deserve asylum. The trouble is, they have barbed wire around the place, and the *Guardia Civil* patrol it. They keep catching me. The last time they beat me up well, well."

He stops and lifts his shirt. There are scars on his back.

"I swear," he says. "I would have died if not for Médecins Sans Frontières."

He takes me to a cliff. From there we can see Spain. The lights on the coast are so bright; the houses in the port of Tangier are pure white. The sea that stretches between—it is all I can do to stop myself from leaping over the cliff and getting crushed to a pulp.

"See?" he says. "It's tempting, isn't it? Twenty miles only. El Dorado. You can cross anytime if you have enough to pay a *samsara* to take you. The *pateras* carry more passengers. The dinghies are cheaper, but they capsize. People have drowned."

I can barely hear my own voice. "Which way is better, Ceuta or sea?"

"I've given you the options," he says. "Take your pick."

I take a shit in the dark to clear my thoughts and wipe with a leaf. When I return to our tent, Patience is still reading her Bible. I want to tell her all I've found out from Obazee. I want to find out if she has enough to pay a *samsara*.

"Bad news," I announce.

She shines her flashlight on a page and says, "Listen. 'I have heard the complaints of the Israelites. Tell them that at twilight they will have meat to eat, and in the morning they will have all the bread they want . . .'"

"I'm tired," I say.

Fairy tales can't save us.

So, my mother says, my girlfriend turns out to be just another woman of the night. Why then is she reading her Bible and going on about the Israelites of the past?

Here are real stories from a modern African exodus, she says.

One man from Mali, he couldn't afford his fare. He crossed the Sahara on foot. It took him several years. The Moroccan security forces got hold of him when he reached Tangier. They repatriated him straight back to the border of Algeria and told him to find his way to Gao. Yes, with the same two legs that brought him to their country.

Another man, from Rwanda, came by truck with his family. This was long before the barbed wire was erected around Ceuta. The family got into Ceuta all right; then they were kept in detention for months, waiting for their lawyer to prove that they really were from Rwanda.

What about the Sierra Leonean who, shortly after the barbed wire went up, tried to scale it several times, until his skin was practically shredded? He decided to swim the sea to get to Spain. He had only one hand, by the way. The salt water stung his skin; he still made it to the shore. His missing hand was there to prove that he was fleeing a civil war.

What about the Nigerian who secretly regretted that her own homeland was not war-torn, and hoped that the baby in her belly would be considered worthy of asylum? The baby came out two months too early, right here in the forest. Mother and child never made it to the next day.

Then there was the Senegalese. She couldn't swim. She found a *samsara* to carry her by dinghy, and it wasn't that the dinghy leaked or capsized. It was the *samsara*: he said he could not get too close to the shore; the *Guardia Civil* might catch him, so he ordered her to jump out of his dinghy into the sea and find her way somehow.

Perhaps Africans shouldn't compile these stories in any book, my mother says. Who wants to save such stories for posterity? No, she says, these stories are worse than any nightmares, so considering what may lie ahead, it is better that I continue to sleep for the rest of my journey.

The night is so chilly we sleep curled up like a couple of crayfish. We wake up to the sound of thuds, shouting, pots clanging, babies crying. It is dawn and the sun has not yet dried up the dew.

The commotion is over Obazee and his Nigerian cronies. They've decided to move the camp further into the bush, to hide from the security forces. Some people are protesting that they don't want to move—actually protesting over their little hovels. They follow Obazee as he marches ahead of them saying, "I've given you the options. Take your pick."

Patience and I watch those who are already untying their tents. I have no doubt how we must leave the camp now.

"Do you have money left?" I ask.

"For food," she slurs.

She is sluggish. She took painkillers. I run my tongue over my teeth and spit. My mouth tastes bitter.

"It's five hundred dollars each to go by dinghy and one thousand dollars each to go by *pateras*."

She slaps sand out of her hair. "Who said?"

"Obazee. You should have come. Yesterday. He showed me the shore. He said we can go by sea or wait for months to sneak into Ceuta like people around here."

I tell her what I know. I know exactly what she's thinking. She's put her trust in the Lord.

"Do you at least have enough to get to Tangier?" I ask.

She pushes out her bottom lip. "Mm-mm."

"How did you intend to get to Spain without money?"

"I don't know."

Perhaps she's waiting for a hand to come down from Heaven and part the sea for her. "Where are you heading for after Spain?" I ask.

"Rome."

"What will you do when you get to Rome?"

"Work."

"What work?"

"Jean-Luc, not this morning."

"Tell me."

She waves her arms. "I said not this morning! You see what's ahead of us, eh! We have to pack up and move. All my body is paining me, eh!"

"I told you mine."

She sighs. "When will you learn that you and I are not mates? They recruited me in Bamako. Hear? I'm supposed to be in Tangier right now, working. Understand? When I get to Rome, I'll continue to work. It's bondage. Intercontinental. White men, African women. See?"

Does she think my eyes are the color of weak tea for some other reason? What I see is myself playing football overseas, and Patience not having to sleep her way to Europe. I think about what she told me about the Israelites, and that their main problem was that they didn't have enough faith. Maybe they wouldn't have needed to if they'd had enough sense to stick together.

"I have enough for both of us," I venture.

"Enough what?"

"Cash. To cross by dinghy."

She snorts. "I'm sure."

"It's true. I'm not bragging. It's right here. I'll share with you." I pat my left sneaker.

For a moment she purses her lips. Perhaps she's worried about our dinghy capsizing.

"What?" I ask.

She turns away. "Oh, you're young. What am I doing?"

I poke her in the ribs to force her to smile. "Come on."

The woman pulls my face right into her armpit. "So," she says, "just like that, for no reason, you will help me cross the sea?"

So long as the sea doesn't rise up against us. I hold my breath as if I'm about to dive. Her armpit stinks to high heaven.

She says she'll go to Tangier and find a *samsara* there. She travels with another woman who is going there to buy chicken feet.

Morning. I begin to untie our tent. Obazee is busy organizing the move to another part of the forest. Almost everyone has agreed to go, which means that everyone must. This is the way it is around here, all together, through the forest, up the mountain, hup, two, three. One day, I fear they might move so far they will reach the cliff and fall off. Obazee makes his rounds and guides them like Moses.

"You," he says, snapping his fingers when he passes by me.

"When is your mummy coming back?"

"She is not my mother."

"Well, remember that by evening, we're leaving this place."

I fold the tent as he walks on. The ground is bare except for our footprints, Patience's and mine.

Noon. Most people have moved to the new site. Those who remain gather clothes, pick up pots, and search for what is lost. I sit on the tent as if it's a mat and lean against a tree trunk. Obazee comes by again.

"She's not back yet?"

"It takes long."

"Not this long," he says, checking his watch. This time, he doesn't even stop to look at my face.

I spread my toes. There is space in my sneakers now; too much space since Patience took my money.

Dusk. I can count the people left in the camp: five, besides me. One of them is the woman who left with Patience. They've cleared up everything except for a sandal, a bucket handle and a red rag. Obazee startles me.

"You're still waiting?"

"Yes."

"You don't think you should come at this rate?"

"No." I can spare him only one word at a time.

He contemplates the little I've said and then bends to wipe his forehead with his shirt. "Don't worry," he says. "Maybe she got stuck. Whenever she appears, follow the way to the cliff. You'll find us there." He points to the others.

I would prefer that he tells me to take my pick.

After they leave, I turn on Patience's flashlight and flick through her Bible: Genesis, Exodus, Leviticus. I can't find the story. I reach Revelation and still can't find the stupid story she told me, but you won't catch me running off like some girl. I'll wait until morning if necessary. If I shiver it's because of the winds. They come from the desert and the sea. They carry sand and salt. They clash right here in the forest and can pierce to the bones no matter how well you're prepared for them. It's funny how. I hope she drowns.

A TEMPORARY POSITION

For about four, five months before I began my accountancy training at Price Waterhouse in London, I had a temporary job as a receptionist at the head office of a company I'm not going to name, because I was not legally allowed to work there. The visitor's visa in my Nigerian passport clearly stated this: *Leave to enter the United Kingdom for six months. Employment prohibited*. Luckily, I was living in my parents' flat in Pimlico rent-free. They paid all the bills and had also offered to give me "a little something," as my father would say, until I joined Price Waterhouse and was able to apply for a work permit.

I had told him no thanks. At twenty-two years old, with a degree from the London School of Economics and one year's national service, which I'd spent working at the Nigerian Stock Exchange, I really didn't think I ought to be getting pocket money anymore, and it wasn't just that my pride came before English immigration laws. I planned to eat out as often as I could in London, shop, go to the cinema and to nightclubs and perhaps travel within Europe. This was in the mid-1990s and my father's "a little something" turned out to be just fifty quid a week. I was part of a group—huge community, really—of Nigerian graduates living in London. Some of us were getting financial support from our parents, some were working illegally—as I intended to do—and others were collecting dole checks, somehow. We used fake national insurance numbers. No one was getting caught.

The office I worked in was off Oxford Street, which wasn't a bad commute from Pimlico on a daily basis by tube; I didn't have to change lines. During the morning rush hour there wasn't much of a crowd either, which was just as well, what with people thinking they could get away with not bathing. It was the end of spring and the beginning of summer. Occasionally, the sun shone and I'd shut my eyes imagining I was somewhere else in Europe, somewhere more exciting and beautiful, like Barcelona. I would forget the Thames looked like tepid tea and the pavements were splattered with saliva, chewing gum and pigeon droppings, except when the rain poured so heavily that they oozed a brown muck.

The office itself was rather un-English, I thought. It had none of that dark depressing wood furniture or those intimidating bronze relics. Instead, there was steel, glass and a maze of compartments made of a light wood—very Ikea-ish— and the island of gray carpet in the reception area reeked of an addictive chemical.

Cath, the head secretary, escorted me to my workstation on my first day and I felt so bad because, whatever she said, she reminded me of Pepé Le Pew, the cartoon skunk. Her hair was black and pulled into a ponytail with a single curl. Her suit was cream-colored, made of crêpe, and her voice was full of mucus. Cath was a smoker.

She explained that the department dealt with in-house publications and, looking around, I spotted a few PR-types, with their tans, blue-striped shirts and general busyness. They exchanged praises like "brilliant," "great," and "excellent." I guessed that they were well-paid English graduates, and experts at pretending to be keen.

I did not tell Cath I had a degree in economics. In my CV I'd written that I had five O levels instead of ten and one A level instead of three, so she wouldn't consider me overqualified for the job. I was glad my home address could pass for a council flat's, and even though my name and features betrayed me, I did not reveal that I was a Nigerian, in order to keep my background story simple. I spoke to Cath in the accent I'd acquired in my first year at boarding school when I got tired of my English schoolmates asking, "You what?" as if they couldn't understand a word I was saying. So, I was speaking in my fake English accent—phonetics, as we Nigerians would call it—to Cath who really couldn't be bothered to enunciate herself. She dropped most of her H's and called herself "Caff."

Cath wanted me to be professional at all times. Clients visited the department and sometimes journalists. She whispered the word "journalists" as if I ought to be wary of them. Within an hour, she'd taught me how to answer the telephone, put callers through or on hold, make announcements and buzz the door open, after checking the security screen. By the switchboard was a crystal vase, shaped like a womb, and I had to make sure it was rinsed out and topped up regularly.

She took her flowers seriously, Cath. She favored orchids and spaced out their stems. I was to pluck off their leaves if they looked as though they were dying, and I wasn't allowed to let them touch the water, otherwise the water would end up stinking. That week, as she occasionally stopped by to ask, "All right?" in a voice so cheerful that my heart would skip a beat, I observed her flower rules and other rules, like no eating and no personal phone calls. My friend Remi called to say, "What's up?" and I answered, "Certainly, I'll put you through," and immediately disconnected her. The no-eating rule troubled me more. At lunchtime I had to go to the snack room to eat my roast beef on rye sandwich, with horseradish so strong it burned the roof of my mouth. The snack room was not as clean as the rest of the office. The table had greasy fingerprints and rings of sticky soft-drink sediment.

Cath said I was doing really well, and I could have been any black receptionist to her, any in London, until the afternoon that Raj, an editor in the department, not bad-looking with rockabilly sideburns, was on his way out and asked what time it was. I told him and he pointed at me as if he were shooting.

"Are you Nigerian?" he asked.

Cath had stopped by my station again to make sure her orchids were prim. She separated their stems and her lips were pursed from concentrating on her task.

"Em," I said. "Yeah?"

"I know that accent," he said. "I have Nigerian friends."

Foreigners, I thought, why did we always have to stick together? He slapped the pockets of his leather jacket and was out of the door before I could rebut, and then I had to answer the phone again.

"Good afternoon," I said, rounding my vowels even more.

"I didn't know you were Nigerian," Cath said, when I finished transferring the call.

"Yeah," I said. "But it's not like I've been back there in a while. I really don't identify. I was quite young when we left. My parents came over..."

Her smile was sympathetic and mine, I hoped, came across as grateful for English citizenship.

"So sweet, Raj," she said, plucking a leaf. "Really, really sweet, and he's just got married, you know."

"Yeah?"

All I knew was that he wore leather well.

She nodded. "Mm. I was at his wedding last month. Lovely, and I like Indian food—popadoms and samosas."

From then on I was more relaxed around her, and by the end of my second week, my colleagues were appearing less slick. I noticed crusty eyes in the mornings, laddered tights at the end of the day and dandruff on shoulders. They were exactly like me. Exactly, exactly. I was seeing a trichologist on South Molton Street for my dandruff, which I had initially thought was caused by stress. Misuse of chemicals, he said. That was from my national service year in Nigeria. Scrunched was the best way to describe the texture of my hair now, and my hairline was also receding from plaiting with extensions. I looked like a skinny sumo wrestler, even though I secretly held an image of myself as being very attractive and highly intelligent.

Before my various interviews at accountancy firms with names like Stuck-Updale and Hoity-Toityheim, I had taken the Victoria line south to Brixton to buy a wig and found one imported from America, a pageboy style in off-black. I looked like a Supreme when I slipped it on and practiced how to walk through a door with confidence, give a firm handshake and answer positively without discussing salaries. I was still sporting the wig for the receptionist job. Cath thought it was my real hair.

Through her, I got to hear about Graham, who was the head of the department. He was short with a bald patch, and was always hidden in his office, but he knew exactly what was going on. I could barely hear what Graham said, because his lips hardly moved and they were inverted. His secretary, Moira, complained all day about drafts in the office. "Oh, this place is too cold for me," she would say, or "Oh, this place is making me sick." I thought Moira was West Indian, but she claimed to be South American.

There was Neil, who had represented England in past Olympics. He came from the mailroom a couple of times a day, winked and called me "love." I didn't mind that he expected me to be flattered. How like England, I thought, for someone to represent the country and end up in a mailroom. Now, there he was, and his only consolation was chatting up Trish, the general secretary of the department, the one with the ladder in her tights and crescent of cubic zirconia studs in one ear.

When the word spread that I was a Nigerian, Rupert, a senior editor who called himself "Woopert," told me he grew up in Rhodesia.

"Ah, Zimbabwe," I said, raising my forefinger, in case he had forgotten about their independence.

"No," he said. "Wodesia."

I could have resented him for that, but I suspected that, like me, Rupert had secrets to hide. He talked a lot about his roommate, Sebastian, and I noticed how much he laughed around Steve, a manager from another department.

Steve actually looked like Steve McQueen, except his teeth were more even, like a row of Tic Tacs. "Finally," he said, flashing them at me when we first met, "some class around here." I too was reduced to laughs. He was Irish, engaged to Penny, a manager in my department; Penny, who tossed her blonde hair this way and that as she walked up and down the corridor, clip, clop, in her navy pumps. She was an Oxford graduate. She spoke French and German. She never spoke to me. I eavesdropped whenever she talked to Cath about her wedding plans. She and Steve were getting married in St. Lucia in six weeks and she was on a diet until then. To me she was slim enough, even though her calves were a little bit thick like an English girl's.

It took me about a month to get fed up of buzzing the door open for these people and connecting their phone calls. I was not qualified for the job. I yawned too much and forgot to tend Cath's orchids. Once, the water in the vase developed an odor, like socks soaked for a week. More than once, I was about to make an announcement and had to think twice because I couldn't remember what to say. Whenever clients came in, I gave them fake smiles. I couldn't be bothered to offer tea or coffee. It wasn't just the job that bored me; it was the whole experience of working in London, the whole one. I couldn't quite explain, but if life after graduation was the old conveyor belt, then every day in London seemed built to specification.

Not that London was perfect. One morning on the Victoria line, someone abandoned a parcel and the line was shut down. The tubes and stations were evacuated for bomb experts. Commuters had to find alternative routes. An American executive flung his leather portfolio on the platform and cried out, "Aw, for fawk's sake!" No one paid him any mind. The IRA was suspected; they had detonated a bomb at Victoria station before. This time, no explosives were found. The Victoria line was reopened.

In Lagos, a bomb would have to explode in people's faces before they changed their daily itineraries. The normal routine was chaos: no light, no water and no use complaining. We'd had three military coups in seven years; one of them had failed. Our latest dictator was calling himself president of Nigeria and our constitution was not yet in place. That never stopped the people. They had just come out in thousands to vote in the local elections.

Every day in Lagos was defective. When I worked for the Nigerian Stock Exchange, a simple task like leaving the house became a nightmare because some taxi driver would have

A TEMPORARY POSITION

parked his car across the entrance of my parents' driveway. My mother would say, "*Kai*, these people, always one thing or another with them." My father would thank God he had retired. I would have to beg the taxi driver to give me my right of way. On my way to work, there was always a breakdown on the bridge to Lagos Island, or on the narrow streets in the city center. Cars would maneuver around the broken-down *molue*, or *danfo*, or *kabukabu*, whether or not it meant running street hawkers off the roadside and crushing their feet.

In London, even my beef on rye sandwiches were regular. I knew exactly how much change I would get after I'd paid for them. I expected the beef to be a bit wiry and was already used to the sting of the horseradish in my sinuses. In Lagos, the restaurant I ate lunch in had a menu with dishes like beef stroganoff and shepherd's pie. It was the same dish, bits of beef drowning in peppery stew. I wouldn't even have minded had their prices not kept going up. I'd challenge the waiters each time, "This is not a stroganoff." "This is not shepherd's pie." They'd shrug and answer, "Sistah, that is how it is in Lagos, oh."

London was predictable in a different way, in a ding-dong sort of way, like Big Ben making all that noise that impressed hardly anyone but tourists; a way that was causing me to spend the money I was earning as a receptionist. For instance, I would walk into Selfridges at lunchtime, like a zombie, and emerge with shopping bags, just like that. That was London's fault. London also made me call Remi after work, at home, and spend so long chatting to her that I tore up my parents' telephone bill—rather than hide it—after I'd paid it. London made me go to nightclubs and dance until I was almost deaf, and I couldn't even leave London to travel within Europe, because without a work permit, not one embassy would grant me a visa, not even the Belgians.

"It's rubbish here," I told my father during a half-hour international call that I made home. "I don't think I can survive more than three years of working in this place."

I was thinking about returning to Nigeria after my accountancy training. How interesting would accounting be anyway? Debit this, credit that. I wanted to have a profession, but Thatcher had buggered up the economy before she resigned. I would probably be laid off as soon as I qualified. Management had no obligation to retain trainees. They had a bottom-heavy corporate structure. Only the best and blue-eyed would rise up their precious pyramid towards partnership heaven.

"That's the trouble with you," my father said, meaning my entire generation of Nigerians. "You're shallow. Everything has to be fast, fast, easy, easy. In my day, I got to London and there was no question of coming and going."

There was no means. He had left Nigeria at the end of the 1950s, wearing what he called his coat and trousers and carrying a portmanteau. He boarded a cargo ship that sailed to Liverpool. The journey lasted two weeks. Rain met him at Liverpool docks and then he took a train to London to find his elder brother in the fog.

"At least," I said, "you had a country to go back to."

Nigeria was independent by the time he had graduated. BOAC was already flying to and fro. He came home in the 1960s with a law degree. The colonialists were leaving the civil service and the Ministry of Justice offered him a job that came with housing, servants' quarters and a car. Before the Civil War he was already working as a federal judge. Now, an oil boom and recession later, Nigeria was being structurally adjusted and instead of being concerned, our president was busy bragging that Nigeria defied the laws of supply and demand, because there was no logical reason why the economy hadn't collapsed.

"But you had a normal job here, didn't you?" my father countered. "With a normal salary, and you ran right back to England, didn't you?"

He wouldn't let me forget. I had landed the job at the Stock Exchange because he knew the director. My duties had entailed taking minutes. I took them on the trading floor, which was basically a boardroom where stockbrokers, all men in suits, shouted out their bids. In a busy trading session there were two dozen brokers tops.

The market was small. Investors did not speculate or buy and sell. They held on to their stocks and shares for dear life. I also took minutes at the annual general meetings of multinational companies, and at every meeting I could guarantee the directors would be expatriates, the chairman would be a Nigerian—Chief Baba So-and-So—wearing a lavish brocade *agbada*. He would have no dividends to declare and there would be one shareholder, a Nigerian known as Prof, who would stand up to object, waving the scrap of paper on which he'd scribbled his calculation of the company's price-earnings ratio.

With the salary I'd earned at the Stock Exchange I had three choices: live with my parents, live in a hovel, or find a sugar daddy. Of course I chose to return to London. Of course I did.

"It's rubbish here," I repeated.

"You can't just say it's rubbish," my father said. "You have to give things time. Stick with that job, you hear me? Take pride in it. Develop a work ethic."

I asked to speak to my mother. The receptionist job was a temporary-to-permanent one. I had no intention of leaving it until I joined Price Waterhouse. At the current exchange rate of the pound to the naira, I was earning more than I ever had in my life.

One afternoon like so, I thought sod it, I will eat my roast beef on rye sandwich at my workstation for a change. Cath was off sick. She'd coughed so hard the day before her eyes filled with tears and her face turned red. "I'm coming down with something," she'd kept whispering into her handkerchief. To me, it sounded like a smoker's cough.

I smuggled my sandwich bag into my satchel and positioned my satchel on the carpet between my legs where I could easily reach for it. Somehow, my sandwich, now illicit, was much tastier. Perhaps that was the secret to Lagos life after all: the general unlawfulness of the place. I'd barely taken two nibbles from the corner of my rye bread when Steve McQueen came along. I sat up and buzzed him through the door. He smiled and really, for an Irish lad, his teeth were most African.

"Have you seen Penny?" he asked.

She was clip-clopping in the direction of the loos when last I saw her. Steve waited as I chewed under my palm. I'd lowered my sandwich as soon as I saw him. Now, I was diving and feeling around for my satchel so I could slip the sandwich back inside, at the same time rubbing my lips in case there was a trace of horseradish.

Penelope appeared. Her natural expression was a stare because she wore contact lenses. I imagined her taking a crap, as you're supposed to in interview situations to calm your nerves.

"Ready?" she said to him.

"I was just asking about you," he said.

He opened the door for her and she flung her hair over each shoulder, as if to declare, "He's my fiancé. I'm his fiancée."

It crossed my mind that she might have mistaken my furtive posture for a sexy one, which made me furious because I did fancy her fiancé, but I would never, ever flirt with him. I had my own boyfriend, sort of—Akin, who was an engineer. I'd known him when he was at Imperial College and now he was busy whining about the pittance he earned and living in Maida Vale. But I was not sure where our relationship was going because he had a tendency to be taciturn and he slept too much. Akin could sleep until noon, until a winter day turned dark. One Sunday, he slept until the Tate Gallery closed. The Saturday after, he slept until it was too late to catch a flick at Leicester Square. A Spike Lee Joint, too. I was still furious about that, but I called him anyway, when I finished my sandwich, to complain about Penny.

"As if I would ever fancy her foolish fiancé," I whispered.

"Hm," he answered.

He was at work. I would have preferred to speak to Remi, but she was at home. If my call were traced to a private residence with a Nigerian name, I couldn't lie my way out of that.

"I mean, you know these *oyinbo* guys and their bad teeth."

"Hm."

"I mean, bloody hell, it was obvious I was eating, not trying to seduce the geezer."

"Hm."

"Can't you say something?"

"I told you," he said stifling a yawn. "When you start working for them you will find out how crazy these *oyinbos* are."

"Extremely," I said.

That was the first time I broke the personal-calls rule and the next day, when Cath wanted to have a word with me—

"Just a quick one," she said—my heart did a somersault.

"Sure," I said.

She was still coughing and had the same Pepé Le Pew ponytail, but she looked a little pale. I wondered if she was about to tell me she had a serious illness.

"Em," she said. "I've only been away a day, and in my absence, it has been brought to my attention…"

I kept glancing at the switchboard, expecting the incoming-call lights to blink, hoping that she would note how efficient I was being.

"Look," she said breaking into a smile. "I hear you've been having lunch at the switchboard, and I'm not trying to be funny or anything, but clients come in here, and it doesn't look right, and we have journalists…"

Again she whispered the word "journalists," and I had on what I hoped was a desperate expression now. I was sure she was about to sack me.

"And," she said, pointing at the vase, "these are in such a sorry state."

The orchids slumped over. I could have swiped them.

"I'm sorry," I said.

"I'm not trying to be funny or anything. It's just that—"

"It won't happen again, Cath. I promise."

Stupid orchids. I yanked them out of the vase by their necks and dumped them into the dustbin in the snack room. Then I ordered more loyal flowers: lilies. There were no smiles for the people at the office for the rest of the day—not for Neil when he called me "love," and not a blink for Penny, or that Steve. He was probably IRA.

Again, I broke the personal-calls rule and telephoned Akin later in the day. He sounded as if I'd just woken him up, though he denied it.

"It's that Penelope woman," I ranted. "It must be her. She talks to Cath. She went behind my back, the sneaky…"

He sighed, and I imagined he was stretching.

"I thought you said you are not tired," I said.

"I'm not."

"But you're yawning again."

"I'm not."

"Yes, you are!"

"No, I'm not."

I went all quiet, just to make him nervous.

"I've told you," he mumbled, "*oyinbos* are crazy."

"Bloody bonkers," I yelled.

On my way home the tube reeked of damp hair and an odor I could only describe as suppressed disdain for others. It reminded me of Bovril and my boarding school days in Tunbridge Wells, with those oil heaters, boiled-wool blankets, and schoolgirls huddled together and smoking fags in the toilets, like little tarts, or college freshers puking up beer and lager mixed with cheese and onion, or salt and vinegar crisps. I was the only one screwing up my nose in that tube. The rest stared ahead as if we were in a ski lift somewhere on the Alps. At Green Park, one poor West Indian bloke rushed out of the tube singing "*Un bel di.*" His Walkman headphones pulled his dreadlocks back. His voice swelled and cracked, vying with the screeching wheels of a departing train.

I shifted to the spot where he had stood and eyed my fellow commuters: a woman with shadows under her eyes, a man with hairs growing out of his ears, his son who was picking snot from a nostril. Would I eventually go crazy working in London? English people could do that to a person, the way they were so two-faced. I'd seen them sneaking into Graham's office to tell tales. The tits. What bugged me most was the way they ended up talking about their commutes in the present tense, as if they were commuting right there in his office: "So, I'm driving down the M1, right, and this Renault 5 swerves across and cuts me off…"

"Come to Lagos," I would want to shout. "I'll show you a commute."

She kept trying to provoke me—Penelope. I swear. One morning, I was eating a jam doughnut for breakfast in the snack room before the switchboard opened. She walked in carrying a mug with a smiley and stood by the percolator. The percolator was gurgling and spitting. She sniffed with an air of superiority. It was hard to eat my doughnut with dignity. When I finished, I dusted the sugar from the corners of my mouth, and then she said to me, "That looked good." I said, "Yeah," and threw the doughnut bag into the dustbin. She ducked as if I'd aimed for her, even though she was not near the bin. "Funny," she said. "For someone who eats so much, there's nothing of you." As if I'd begged her to go on her diet. She gave me such bad indigestion.

Another afternoon, I'd just come back from shopping. So what? And Cath, who usually stood in for me at the switchboard, was with guess who, and they went all quiet the way English people went all quiet after gossiping. "Is that from Hobbs?" Penny asked. "No," I said, steering my shopping bag away from her, even though it was from Hobbs.

Penny thumbed Cath. "She's always shopping, this one."

Cath seemed distracted. "Just a mo," she said. "I've got one last thing to do, then we can go."

She went off to Graham's office with telephone messages. I was left with Penny, who crossed her arms while I sat in my chair. Her diamond engagement ring sparkled. It was about half a carat. Wasn't she satisfied? She also had Steve.

Presumably, she and Cath were going to talk about the wedding again, over lunch.

"Where d'you live?" she asked.

"Pimlico," I said.

"Ooh," she said.

That threw me. She had not automatically assumed I lived in a council flat, but I thought of my parents' flat, with the stained carpet and velvet sofas my father had refused to replace since the seventies because he was so miserly. The place wasn't "ooh."

"It must be hard trying to save, working so near Oxford Street," she said.

"Depends if you're trying," I said.

"You've been here a month, haven't you?" she asked.

"Yes."

"Think you'll stay on?"

"No, I'm joining an accountancy firm soon."

"Really, which one?"

"PW."

"Ooh. As a receptionist?"

"Audit trainee."

"Don't you need a degree for that?"

"I have a degree."

"What in?"

"Economics."

"Really?"

"Really."

"From?"

"LSE."

An incoming line was blinking. I answered the call as Cath returned and they left for lunch. After I'd connected the call, I hung my head over the switchboard, feeling spent and not so intelligent anymore.

From then on I expected Cath to have a word with me over the lies I'd told on my CV. I also worried about the Home Office deporting me and a journalist finding out I was working in England illegally—only a bit. The thought of having no money to spend scared me more.

Then this. No, wait. This was the most important part. There were dozens of newspapers and magazines in our department available for the staff, in addition to a few in the reception area for guests, and I had to ensure they were in tidy piles. I was getting ready to leave work the following Friday. The switch-board was closed, but most of the department was still around, pretending to work as usual. I slipped on my new jacket from Hobbs and was wrapping my M&S scarf around my neck when Penny passed by. She was holding a copy of the *Mail*, which, to me, carried trashy celebrity news, but for some reason it was considered posher than the *Sun*.

"Have you seen this?" she asked. The article was about a group of Nigerian graduates in London, children of high-ranking government officials.

They were living in a flat in Knightsbridge and had been arrested for dole fraud. Some nosy parker who lived next door to them had reported them. She'd noticed that they were receiving unemployment checks and coming home every day with Harrods shopping bags. After the story was a quote by a Nigerian lawyer in London: "It's a legacy of the corruption in our governments. For years, government officials have enriched themselves unlawfully and they are never held accountable. The result is that Nigerians don't consider it wrong to steal public funds, and internationally, we're gaining a reputation for fraud…"

"Thought you might be interested," Penny said.

Cow. My friend Remi, too, thought she did that to spite

me. I called Remi from the switchboard before I left. I no longer cared about the personal-calls rule and Akin would be tired of hearing about Penny.

"Hey, hey, she's trying to sabotage your career!" Remi said. "She's marking her territory in that office!"

"She's got it in for me," I whispered. "I can't kid myself anymore."

"No, seriously," Remi said. "Can't you see? They can't stand it. To see us. Over here. On par."

She was nibbling on a carrot and I could just see her in her latest fluorescent number from Fenwick's. Like me, she had a degree in economics from LSE, but the only trends she ever followed were in fashion. I was sticking to basic black that season, even if it showed up my dandruff.

"Cath's all right, though," I said.

"Caff's naff," she said. "And I mean seeing us like this. They want us back to colonial days, or so desperate that Sting can come and save us."

"That's Geldof," I said.

"Oh, yeah, Sting is the rainforests."

I fancied Sting, even though I suspected he was a big fat liar. He was quite fit for a forty-year-old.

"God, I hate that Bob Geldof," Remi said.

We were not Nigeria's brightest, but we were her most privileged. We had learned how to laugh at lower-class Brits and knew how to tick off the higher-ups. We loathed the liberal types who wanted to lay claim to saving our sorry African arses. Some of us, like Remi, had come over to England via cold audit trails. Her parents had a huge place in St. John's Wood. With pillars. They were staying there and driving her crazy. No guys were allowed on the premises after certain hours. Her father was a lawyer for an oil company and he couldn't go back to Nigeria for a while because he feared for his life. Akin's was a former senator, and my mother always had this to say about him: "He's a tricky fellow, that fellow."

Listening to Remi go on about how the fraud story was embarrassing because normally, only Nigerians who lived in places like Neasden, Hackney and Balham were on the dole, it occurred to me that even though I was shallow—as shallow, as if I'd jumped into a pool of my concerns and found myself ankle deep in the deepest of them—I did not share her sense of entitlement.

"But don't you feel one kind when you read a story like that?" I asked.

"For what?" she said.

"I feel one kind."

"Why?"

"But why are Nigerians so corrupt?"

"Who is corrupt?" she said. "Are you corrupt?"

"No, listen. I feel one kind."

"Which kind?" she asked, in the bullying manner she assumed whenever she was trying to be nice.

"I think Akin is smoking hemp," I said, to change our conversation.

"Oh my *gersch*," she said. "That is so Brixton of him."

She didn't understand, and not until I left work and got to Pimlico station and walked up the escalator, past posters of West End shows I would never see, and came out of the underground and caught a whiff of stale urine by the newsagent, did I find the word I was searching for: sullied. Where had I learned that it was all right to break laws? Probably from my father, going on about a work ethic, when he knew he could not have bought a flat in Pimlico on his miserable government salary. Yes, I thought, hobbling over the cobblestones dividing the underground station from the council flats on the other side of the street, I'd definitely learned that from my father, even though his flat wasn't ooh.

That week was the week before Penny's wedding. I'd totally forgotten, and details of the event permeated the office as if they were seeping through our heating ducts. They were making me nauseous, really: the sister who wasn't taking her bridesmaid duties seriously, the guest with the broken ankle who had canceled at the last moment, the mother-in-law who wanted a proper church wedding, the seamstress who messed up Penny's white chiffon. The beading on it. Whether or not anyone in our department cared to know, Penny was her own herald, crying out that her plans were in shambles, and she had a small entourage, whose mouths rang like bells whenever they saw her, "Here comes the bride," including Cath, who organized a collection for a wedding gift.

"No pressure," she said, with a tremor in her voice that made me panic. "Give what you want."

I gave five pounds. She had also bought a card for Penny and everyone in the department signed it and passed it on. When the card reached my workstation, there was barely any space. I read what the others had to say: *Best wishes, Graham. Hugs from Trish. Cheers, Ian. Congratulations, Rupert. PS: We're both legal now, Raj. PPS: Weddings on Caribbean beaches are not legal, Moira.* I squeezed in a narrow *Good luck.*

Cath had decided on a gold bikini for Penny's wedding gift, one of those expensive ones, full of strings, and she thought Penny deserved it because she had worked hard on her diet. They both walked around the office and Penny thanked everyone, including me.

"You're so evil," she said. "How will I ever fit into something this tiny?"

"Enjoy," I said.

"Taking if off an' all," Cath said, nudging her.

"Will you be here when I get back?" Penny asked.

"Where's she going?" Cath squawked.

Penny smiled. "Don't you know? She's joining an accounting firm soon, this one. She's going to be a chartered accountant."

She said the word "chartered" as if it were to be knighted, and she might as well have shoved my head under a guillotine. I wished her extreme bad luck in her marriage.

"You're leaving us?" Cath asked.

"Not yet, Cath. Hope you don't mind. I was going to tell you. I know you were looking for a temp-to-perm."

She waved. "Of course I don't. Just make sure you give us a couple of weeks' notice and remember that if accounting doesn't work out, you can always come back."

"Catherine," Penny yelled.

She laughed and tossed her hair: fiancé, fiancée. She'd never respected Cathy as far as I was concerned, but I, too, laughed because I was relieved. I cleared my throat.

"Thanks, Cath. That's so nice of you. I'll bear that in mind."

"Really," she said, squeezing my shoulder. "I'll miss you. I hate to lose a good receptionist."

I had tears. I would have given her a hug if that were professional. From then on, no personal phone calls for me, no eating at my workstation. I separated her orchid stems, spaced them out so they were at equal distance, eased them down so that they were of equal height, filled the crystal vase with water, refilled whenever necessary, stroked every petal, plucked every dry leaf.

Madness in the Family

One Saturday afternoon your daughter Biola called from London to say she had changed her mind, she no longer wanted to go to university. It was the summer of 1982 and everyone in the family but Biola was in Lagos on vacation. At first you thought she was playing a prank. Stories were circulating about Nigerian students overseas who were going wild without their parents to monitor them. They were smoking marijuana, drinking and driving, crashing cars, getting pregnant and having abortions, but they always, always attended university.

Biola had taken her A levels at Cheltenham Ladies' College in Gloucestershire. She had been accepted at King's College London, to study law. She was meanwhile staying at your house on The Bishops Avenue, "running up bills" as your husband would say. He was a Senior Advocate of Nigeria, a Cambridge alumnus, and would have preferred that Biola sit the Oxbridge exams, but he had to admit that she had done well. She had passed with two As in history and economics and a B in English literature. So, whenever you complained that she was not calling home regularly, or worried that she was going to parties and nightclubs every weekend, he would say, "Remi, relax, let the girl enjoy herself."

"What do you mean you don't want to go to university?" you asked, realizing Biola was serious.

It was about four thirty in Lagos, the same time in London. You and your husband were in his study. There was a family photograph on the wall. In the photograph, your husband was wearing an *agbada* and you were in an *iro* and *buba* of the same white lace. The children, who were not yet teenagers then, were in their church clothes, which you had bought from Marks and Spencer.

Today, your husband was in a blue brocade *agbada* and you were in a matching *boubou*. You were out of breath and adjusting your neckline. The phone in the sitting room downstairs was not working and, though you had called the NITEL office several times, no one had yet come to repair it. Each time you heard the phone ring, you had to run upstairs to your husband's study, as it was closer than your bedroom, which also had a phone. He had followed you there and was standing by the door. The study had fluorescent lights and gold-colored curtains that were permanently drawn.

The air conditioner trembled to a halt as Biola said, "I won't be able to handle it. I just know I won't."

You laughed. This from your most academic child who had locked herself up in her bedroom to study, unlike her younger sister, Oyinda, who was smart, but lazy. Deji, your only son, needed help. He had to take tutorials during the Easter break to get through his O levels, which he had passed with Bs and Cs.

Next term, Oyinda would be in her fourth year at Cheltenham Ladies' College and Deji in the Lower Sixth at Cheltenham College. This afternoon they were both at Ikoyi Club, a few minutes away by car, meeting up with friends who were in Lagos on vacation, most of whom were students from boarding schools in England. They were either in the air-conditioned rotunda, eating *suya* and drinking Chapmans, or they were outside playing squash and tennis.

Your plan was that Oyinda and Deji would spend a month in Lagos, then you would all fly back to London, where you would join Biola and go on a family holiday to Sardinia before the school year began. Your husband would rent a villa there for a couple of weeks, through one of his clients, an Italian construction company that was building a dam in Sokoto, up North.

"My dear," you said. "You've already got in. Your work is half done."

"But I'll never be able to handle it while I'm there. I'm not that clever, you know."

"How can you not be clever? All you have to do is follow the curriculum."

Biola sighed, as she did whenever you gave her advice about studying. You were not a university graduate. You trained as a nurse at St. Thomas' Hospital in London while your husband was a student at Cambridge. You retired from nursing as soon as you returned to Nigeria and got married in 1961, a year after Nigerian independence.

"It's easy to get in," Biola said. "You learn the right things and write the right things. It's all lies, Mummy. I know I won't be able to handle it while I'm there. I just know I won't."

"Please, speak to your father," you said.

You were tired that day, not just from running upstairs, but there had been power cuts throughout the vacation. You had to supervise your new housegirl, Patience, who burned meals while warming them on the kerosene cooker. You had shed most of your domestic staff now: the cook and the houseboy, who turned out to be thieves. They were stealing rice and beans from your storeroom. You kept the day and night watchmen, the washerman and gardener. You did not have a driver (your previous one upped and left) but your husband did.

You were sure he would be able to ease whatever anxieties Biola had about going to university and perhaps you didn't quite believe what you were hearing from her, either. It was too absurd.

As you handed the phone to him, you remembered Biola had made the same statement earlier in the vacation. "It's all lies," she had said, after you were able to tell her what you had been hiding from her for years. It wasn't that you thought it was an appropriate time, but it was convenient. Biola had left Cheltenham for good and you were both alone in the London house for a while before Oyinda and Deji joined you. Their father was in Lagos, unable to make it to their end-of-term activities, and it was just as well. He would have had to explain for himself why he had married another woman by customary law, a woman who had twins by him, sons who were now four years old.

"I will never, ever speak to him again," Biola had said, almost in a whisper.

"You will," you had said. "He is your father. He cares for you."

"No, he doesn't," Biola had said. "It's all lies."

You couldn't bear to see Biola that withdrawn. You told her he had confessed of his own volition and had begged your forgiveness. He would continue to live with your family and visit his other family.

He had been doing that without your knowledge. He had even bought the twins and their mother a house in Lagos and furnished it. You asked Biola not to say a word to Oyinda and Deji, whom you felt were not yet old enough to understand the arrangement. Biola decided she would not fly back to Lagos. You could have insisted, but it seemed like a fair trade-off and she had worked so hard for her exams. You agreed to let her stay in London. So did her father. Perhaps he was relieved he didn't yet have to face her.

He had little tolerance for defiance at home and Biola could be stubborn. She got into arguments with him whenever he put a curfew on her or stopped her from going to parties. She was against his association with the Italian construction company, which you couldn't understand. How could building a dam be a bad idea? Wasn't everyone fed up with power cuts? Wasn't Biola intelligent enough to know her father's foreign clients paid for the houses in Lagos and London, her school fees, vacations, clothes and pocket money, not to mention the food she let go cold whenever she brought her adolescent grievances to the dining table?

Your husband would ignore Biola as she raised her voice and gesticulated, trying to justify her position, until she wore herself out, which had led you to give her the nickname "Mrs. Lawyer," though your husband thought she might never make it as a lawyer if she didn't learn how to control her emotions.

"Yes?" he said, putting the receiver to his ear. "Yes, my dear, I can hear you. Yes, I'm listening. I said, I'm listening. No, my dear. Slow down. I said, slow down."

He sat on the swivel chair before his desk, facing the wall where the family photo hung. He raised his eyes to the fluorescent light on the ceiling, then frowned at his marble ashtray.

Of course, Biola had since spoken to him. She spoke to him when she called to tell them about her A-level results and again when she ran out of money. He transferred money from his Barclays account to hers. Normally, he would have told her off for spending excessively and ordered her to get on the next flight home. You were certain they had not talked about his other family and you were in some doubt as to whether you wanted them to. It depended on how you were feeling. Sometimes, you wished Biola would confront him, unlike you, who had this response: "There isn't much we can do about it now."

He had seemed so awkward kneeling before you and holding your hand when he confessed. It was uncharacteristically humble of him and you were ashamed for being so oblivious. Most of all, you did not want him to have the power of knowing how much he had hurt you.

Biola must have finished speaking because he said, "I can't allow that."

For a moment, he pulled the receiver away from his ear as if Biola were shouting.

"What is she saying, Frank?" you asked.

He raised his hand and resumed their conversation. "I've told you, I can't allow that. You don't have a choice in the matter. Now, is there anything else you would like to say to me or your mother?"

Biola must have slammed the phone down on him because he replaced the receiver and mumbled, "I don't know what is wrong with the girl."

"What did she say?" you asked.

"She wants to travel."

"Where to?"

"Around Europe, for a year, and she will pay for her trip."

"Since when?"

"Don't mind her. She's not serious."

Summer in England was the rainy season in Nigeria. Your husband had decided to forgo his game of golf at the Club that day because the course would be wet. Later, you both sat on the veranda, which faced your garden of palm trees and tiger lilies. Your fence was covered with bougainvillea and golden trumpets. The veranda was shielded by green netting that kept mosquitoes out, but allowed in a cool breeze and the smell of cut grass.

There was a table-tennis set in a corner of the veranda. You were a table-tennis champ as a girl. In your senior year of secondary school, you took part in matches with other schools. You nearly always won. Your children laughed whenever you bragged about that. You had never played against Biola, who had no interest in sport, but you had defeated Oyinda, who played lawn tennis. Oyinda gave a sorry excuse that table tennis required a different sort of wrist movement. You had also defeated Deji, who was a gifted athlete. You had even defeated your husband round after round, until he gave up trying to equalize.

Your husband slipped a cassette into the stereo in the sitting room: *Ella in Hamburg*. You poured drinks into crystal glasses, a gin and tonic for him and, for yourself, a sherry.

On afternoons like this, he sometimes left home without saying where he was going, but you knew he would be with his other family for a while. You would read paperbacks by Jackie Collins and Harold Robbins. You had a section for them in the bookshelf under the staircase, next to the leather-bound English literature classics. They took you to exotic places, where people's motivations were revealed and you didn't have to speculate as to why they got up to misdeeds. Other times, you knit sweaters in colors like pink, yellow and sky blue, which you gave to your staff. Your cook was always a willing recipient before you got rid of him. He was in his late sixties, but he had several young children. He lived in the boys' quarters in the backyard and his wife and children lived somewhere on the mainland. His wife had just had another baby when you sacked him and your husband couldn't believe that. "These people," he had said. "They never know when to stop."

You took a sip of sherry. "But why would that even cross her mind?"

"Don't mind the girl," your husband said, with a dismissive wave. "She is just spoiled."

"Should we call her back?"

"No. Leave her alone. We can't indulge her. She will get over it."

Ella Fitzgerald was singing "Mood Indigo," part of an Ellington medley. You grew more agitated thinking about Biola's phone call until your sherry began to taste vinegary. Perhaps you should have listened to her instead of handing her over to her father.

The driver brought Oyinda and Deji back from the Club and you snapped at Oyinda, who whined about her tennis coach's body odor.

"A little smell won't kill you," you said.

Deji handed Oyinda a bottle of Coca-Cola from the fridge that he had shaken up, and he laughed when it erupted on Oyinda's tennis whites.

"Both of you," you warned, "don't try me today."

You were particularly tired that evening, of the NITEL boys who had not yet come to fix the phone, and of NEPA. The local office did not restore electricity until nighttime, by which time the smell of kerosene had permeated the house. You switched on the electricity generator and the noise was, as usual, insufferable. Patience's stupidity drained you further. She had left the door of the fridge ajar until it began to leak.

"Look here, my friend," you said. "You do that one more time and you leave this house. You understand me?"

It was just a threat. You needed at least one extra pair of hands around the house because your children were of no use. All they wanted to do was go to the Club during the day and at night, play their cassette tapes or watch videos in the sitting room. Between the electricity generator, their music and the television, you had no peace until they went to bed.

That night, you were sleeping when the phone on your bedside table rang. You answered it and initially didn't recognize the voice. It was Biola, who sounded as if she had developed a cold.

"Mummy?"

No, she was crying. You switched on your bedside lamp. "Biola? What time is it? It's almost eleven. What happened? Why are you calling so late?"

"I've been arrested."

You sat up, your negligée slipping off your shoulder. "Why?"

"I have been arrested, Mummy."

"What for? Where are you calling from?"

"From the station."

"Which station?"

You pictured trains as Biola said she had been arrested at Victoria tube station. A tramp had been following her around and the cops should have arrested him, but instead they arrested her.

The story made no sense. You shook your husband's shoulders. He was asleep, which wasn't unusual. You were the light sleeper in the house. That was why the phone was on your side.

"Frank, wake up. It's Biola again."

It took him a few moments to adjust to the light from his lamp and the information you relayed. You watched as he spoke to Biola. He slipped his hand under his pajama top and scratched his shoulder.

"Yes, my dear. No, that's OK. What happened? I said, what happened?" He frowned. "Why? Of course not. Let me speak to her. Yes, let me speak to her. Please."

"What is it?" you asked.

He shook his head. "Yes, I am her father. Yes, I am a lawyer." He was silent for a while, then he asked to speak to Biola again, this time saying, "Don't worry, my dear. I'm coming for you. No, no. There is nothing to worry about. I will be there as soon as possible. Tomorrow. Yes, tomorrow night latest."

He handed the phone to you and confirmed that Biola was in police custody, but not for the reason she had given. She had assaulted a fellow passenger at Victoria tube station. You held your head as if you were adjusting your mind, rather than your scarf, as he added that the police officer had also said Biola was showing signs of a psychiatric illness. Since she was insisting she had no next of kin in London, the only safe option was to hold her in custody until morning and take her to the nearest hospital that would admit her.

"I will go there tomorrow," he said. "You stay here and look after the others."

He slept that night. It took him a while, but he managed to. You couldn't. You kept thinking of your late sister, Ebun, who at the age of nineteen began to mope around the house. Ebun cut off her hair and was bedridden. The doctors called it brain fatigue, caused by studying, and it wasn't until you were an adult that you learned how Ebun died. Ebun killed herself. How, you still did not know. Suicide was illegal back then and never discussed.

You and your husband had multiple-entry British visas so you could travel to London at short notice. He left on Monday night, via British Airways. He had an account at the Five Star travel agency and his secretary handled his ticket reservations.

You remained in Lagos, as he had directed, and you banned Oyinda and Deji from going to the Club without giving an explanation. They asked why and you answered, "Please, this is not the time."

You did say their father was going to London to bring Biola home and they accepted the news in silence. Perhaps they thought Biola was pregnant, as you had when your sister, Ebun, became bedridden, and you might even have preferred it if Biola was.

You called London several times the next day until your husband answered late at night. He had been to the hospital and had brought Biola back. You asked to speak to Biola and, though you insisted, he said, "Just leave her alone for now. You can speak when she gets home."

"But how is she?"

"She is fine, don't worry."

"Did she tell you what happened?"

"She did. I will tell you when we get home."

Two nights later, the driver took you to the international airport on the mainland to meet Biola and your husband. You found Biola looking skinnier than she had been at twelve. Her jeans were baggy and her eyes unfocused, as if she was on tranquilizers. Her short-back-and-sides haircut, which you had always argued about, was standing on end. She looked like a captive prisoner.

Where had believing your husband ever got you, you thought, as you hugged her. You gave him an accusing look over her shoulder before inspecting her face.

"How are you, my dear?"

Biola managed a smile. "I'm fine, Mummy."

Her skin was dry and her breath smelled of orange juice.

"We'd better get going," your husband said and ushered you through the crowd in the arrivals area.

None of you spoke on your way home and you saw nothing. Not the street hawkers walking between cars and carrying trays of wares on their heads. Nor the market stalls, which were still open and lit up by kerosene lanterns. The driver reached Third Mainland Bridge and you did not even notice the lagoon beneath, though you seemed to be staring at it. It was too dark and the street lights on the bridge had never worked anyway.

You got home and the driver carried Biola's suitcase indoors. Patience took it upstairs and Biola followed with her rucksack. She locked herself up in her bedroom and Oyinda and Deji, who had been waiting for her, remained downstairs looking as if they were guilty of some wrongdoing. They had been watching a video, but they switched off the television now, as if they had lost interest.

That night, you ate lamb chops and roast potatoes for dinner without Biola, and your husband instructed that everyone leave her alone until she was ready to talk. You were irritated by his reticence, not Biola's, and it occurred to you that this was how he had managed to keep his secret from you, by controlling when and how you spoke to each other.

Not until you were in bed did he tell you how he had found Biola at the hospital. She was cursing the nurses and calling other patients "schizoids." She claimed an Indian doctor had given her an injection to turn her mad. He did not want to leave her there.

"The facilities were not the best," he said.

He did not specify what he meant, but you could imagine the starkness of a National Health Service psychiatric hospital. He had thought of taking Biola to a private hospital and had even called around. Then he went back to the NHS hospital the next day and spoke to the same Indian doctor, who told him Biola had a chemical imbalance and would have to take medication to control her condition. He asked for how long and the doctor said, "Probably for the rest of her life."

"What does she mean by that?" you asked.

"I don't know," he said.

He paused as if he was in danger of breaking down and you could easily have asked to read the doctor's notes. Instead you said, "These people. What injection did they give my child? What injection did they give her, for heaven's sake? Now see what they have gone and done."

The weekend passed and Biola did not leave her room, except to go to the bathroom. Patience took her meals upstairs on a tray and brought them down when she was finished, but she was not eating much. She spent too long in the bathroom, which wasn't unusual, and Oyinda and Deji did not bang on the door and shout "Hurry up," as they normally would. Instead they were polite to her, saying, "Hey," whenever they saw her and Biola would reply, "Hey," without returning their lopsided smiles.

On Monday morning you and your husband took her to the teaching hospital on the mainland to see Professor Ajose, the dean of psychiatry. Professor Ajose was one of those. He was married to a white woman and he wore paisley bow ties. He had a bald patch and gray beard. You found him antiquated and his wife snooty. She was a tall blonde who wore her hair in a bun. She had a reputation for being curt.

After Professor Ajose's consultation with Biola, he confirmed that she had been diagnosed with a chemical imbalance. He mentioned the words "depression" and "bipolar" for the first time and advised that Biola continue to take the medication she had been prescribed.

"The important thing is for them to take their medication," he said. "They often fail to take their medication. If she fails to take her medication, we might have to admit her here, so we must continue to monitor her."

Already annoyed by his mention of bipolar and depression, you were infuriated by his use of the words "we" and "they," and the manner in which he talked about Biola as if she was not actually sitting in his office.

You and Biola lagged behind as Professor Ajose gave you a tour of the female psychiatric ward, with narrow beds and dusty windows. Nurses dragged their feet around in the midst of patients who appeared outright mad, the kind who walked the streets naked. One scratched her armpits as you walked past. You could smell urine and antiseptic from the toilet at the far end of the ward.

"Mummy," Biola said, moving closer to you. "I can't stay here."

You patted her back. "You must remember to take your medication, my dear."

Driving from the teaching hospital to Ikoyi, Biola sat between you and your husband in the back of the car. The driver was going fairly slowly. Pedestrians were crossing the median of the highway, commuters were scrambling on buses and children were selling bread and oranges. Most of the children were shoeless and you were confronted with the dilemma that, no matter how much money you had and no matter where you could escape to overseas, you could not save yourself from your own country.

You noticed a woman selling tinned milk. The woman would have an easier time dealing with Biola's problem, you thought. She would take her child to the Celestial Church or to some other superstitious cult for prayers, or to a *babalawo* for exorcism. If she earned enough, she might even take her child to the teaching hospital. You would never consider doing any of that, and soon half of Lagos would hear about Biola's problem, people who were jealous of your family.

"They can't even keep their wards clean," you said.

"Hm," your husband agreed.

"Wasn't Ajose one of those who trained in Russia?" you asked.

"No," he said.

"I thought he was one of those who trained in Russia."

"No, he went to Trinity College."

"Trinity College where?"

"Dublin."

"Isn't his wife Russian?"

"No, she is German."

You shook your head. "I have never liked that woman."

That night, he canceled your trip to Sardinia. Oyinda and Deji again accepted the latest development without a word. Biola didn't care. "I didn't want to go anyway," she said, shrugging.

The week passed and she seemed to be taking her medication. It made her feel like a zombie, she said, but she was sticking to her regimen. She did not want to end up in the teaching hospital.

Another three weeks passed and one morning you woke up to find Biola dressed and alert, which was unusual. She said she was feeling much better. She had just been under a lot of stress from studying. She had changed her mind about going to university. She had been up all night thinking about it. She would go to King's College after all. She wanted to be a lawyer. She would work with her father, but she would only do pro bono work.

Biola followed you to the kitchen as you unlocked the backdoor to let Patience in to sweep and dust. She wanted to eat breakfast on the veranda because she felt grateful to be alive, and the sun was shining and life was absolutely wonderful and she could smell rain.

"Isn't that smell amazing?" she said. "If only I could bottle it. If only I could find the formula, as perfumers do. Actually, who wants to find the right formula for the smell of rain anyway? The only reason people appreciate it so much is because they catch a whiff"—she sniffed—"and then it's gone."

The sky had darkened and, by the time Patience brought her breakfast to the veranda on a tray, the rain was beginning to pour. The tiger lilies in the garden brightened and dripped. You watched Biola make a bulky sandwich out of her sausage and toast, then you went to the kitchen to ask Patience to shut the windows. Not finding Patience there, you were about to do it yourself when you saw someone running into the garden. At first you thought it was the gardener, but he worked fortnightly on Sundays.

It was Biola, raising her hands heavenward. She disappeared for a moment and you assumed she was coming into the house. Instead, she returned to the garden with the watchman, who was wearing his black tunic and white skullcap and carrying prayer beads. She forced him to waltz with her. The watchman was trying to free himself without hurting her.

"That's enough," you called out, as thunder rumbled.

The watchman managed to disengage himself as lightning struck. You went outside to meet Biola on the veranda.

"Are you taking your medication?" you asked.

She was wringing her T-shirt. "Of course I am. What do you mean? Why wouldn't I?"

But later in the afternoon, after the rain had stopped, she interrogated Oyinda's friend who was visiting, a fourteen-year-old who complimented her about the weight she had lost. Biola said it was typical for women to judge each other by their looks.

"I got into King's. You could have asked me about that.

Why don't you ask me about that? Isn't that an achievement? Why is losing weight such an achievement?"

She went on and on, until Oyinda, embarrassed, took her friend by the hand and led her away. Biola went back to her bedroom, just as Deji began to play his cassette on the stereo, a funky song with lyrics that went, "Outside in the rain, let's make love out in the rain, all night." You kept picturing Biola dancing with the watchman.

"Will you turn that thing off?" you asked.

"God," Deji said, "you can't do anything in this house."

You suspected he had a girlfriend at the Club. He was always on the phone to someone in the study while his father was at work. He and Oyinda were enjoying Lagos. Here, they fit in without trying. They rarely bothered to mix with the expatriate children at the Club.

Deji huffed as he switched off the stereo.

What selfish, spoiled children you had, you thought to yourself. England had done that to them, or they had inherited it from their father. Perhaps it was even your fault. He had always said you spoiled them.

You toyed with the idea of calling to tell him what Biola had done, then you decided to wait until he came home, which he did on time as usual.

"I don't think she is taking her medication," you said, in the privacy of your bedroom.

He had taken off his shoes and tie and normally you would give him time to unwind, but you were fed up with talking to him on his terms.

"Don't worry," he said. "I will take care of the matter."

For dinner, you had rice and chicken curry. As you ate, Biola told him about her plans to go to university and to come home to practice law and clean up Nigeria. Even Oyinda and

Deji, who were pleased to see her doing what she normally did at the table, could tell the difference. Biola was never this animated. Her eyes were never this wide, and then there was her absurd conclusion: that Nigeria had so much potential.

"It's just the infrastructure, you know," she said. "The infrastructure that holds us back and, of course, the usual corruption."

Your husband kept nodding as if you were all at an economic summit, but he never once looked at her.

When she was through talking, he said, "I don't think you are ready for university this year."

"Why not?" she asked.

"I just don't believe you are ready for it," he said.

She frowned. "Em, why?"

"In view of your behavior."

"What behavior?"

"Shh," you said, making calming motions with your hand.

"No," Biola said. "I want to know. What behavior?"

"This is not a punishment," you said.

"Can't he speak for himself?" Biola asked.

"Em, may I be excused?" Deji said, standing up. "Because I don't..."

He left without waiting for an answer and Oyinda followed him upstairs.

Your husband finished another mouthful and afterwards said, "I hear you were dancing with the watchman this morning."

"What's that got to do with anything?" Biola asked.

He kept his voice steady. "Were you or were you not dancing with the watchman?"

You shut your eyes. Where did the man think he was? In court?

"I did," Biola said. "I did dance with the watchman. So what?"

He nodded. "I see."

Biola faced you. "So what if I danced with the sodding watchman? What has that got to do with anything? Isn't he a frigging human being?"

"You do not talk like that in my presence," her father said. "I will not tolerate that behavior from you."

Biola slapped the table. "What about you? Let's talk about your behavior for a change."

"Patience?" you called out. "Will you get yourself in here?"

Patience walked in, rubbing her eyes. She had probably been sleeping in the kitchen.

"Wake up," you ordered, "and clear the table."

Biola dragged her chair back. "I hate this family."

Why had you trusted your husband again? Your children had inherited their selfishness and petulance from him. He was still eating, but you left him alone at the dining table. He preferred your cooking, which was why he came home on time. You had fantasized many times before about putting poison in his food. Today, that would have been perfect. Why did he have to say that to Biola? Why couldn't he just wait? This wouldn't be the first time he had withheld information from her.

Later that night you knocked on Biola's bedroom door and Biola didn't answer. You turned the handle and were not surprised to find that the door was locked. You didn't sleep well that night. You kept thinking about your sister, Ebun, and could well imagine the pain that drove her to kill herself.

The next morning, you heard a door creak, which sounded as if one of your children was going to their bathroom. You got up and put on your dressing gown, then you went to see who it was.

You knocked on the door and no one answered. Assuming it was Biola, you turned the handle and opened the door. You found Biola on the floor with her container of pills by her side. She was still conscious.

"Jesus of Nazareth," you whispered.

Oyinda called out, "Mummy, are you OK?"

"It's nothing, my dear," you said, pushing the door shut. "Just call your father."

Oyinda and Deji were in tears when they found out. The driver did not start work until seven in the morning, so their father drove you and Biola to St. Christopher's, a private hospital nearby. The teaching hospital was too far away. Throughout the drive Biola retched.

Patients admitted to St. Christopher's ended up in the teaching hospital because St. Christopher's doctors were not as well trained, but their facilities were the best in Lagos and you knew the owner.

You arranged for Biola to have a single room there. The doctor and nurses called you "madam" and your husband "sir" as Biola, now recovering from her nausea, began to insult you both.

"Illiterate," she said to you. "You have no pride. He treats you like shit." "Hypocrite," she said to her father. "Coward. Bigamist. Bastard."

The door of the room was open and her voice carried down the corridor. Your husband left the room with his hands behind his back. The doctor and the nurse, who had called him "sir," could no longer meet his eyes.

"Go on then," Biola said. "You're used to sneaking off anyway, aren't you? You're the embarrassment, not me." Then to you: "Can't you just leave him? Can't you just kick him out? You're the one that's mad. You're the one that's demented."

You covered her mouth, wondering what to say, but there was no precedence for this. Your sister, Ebun, was quiet and weepy. Ebun never got to this stage.

"Madam," the doctor said, "I don't think this is the right hospital for her."

He sedated Biola. Four nurses had to hold her down. He agreed to keep her for one night because she might end up trying to "harm" herself again.

You left Biola limp and struggling to keep her eyes open. You, too, did the walk of dishonor as patients and hospital staff stared at you.

You found your husband sitting in his Mercedes in the car park, with the front windows down. You had never imagined you could have a pain so immense you would be afraid to cry. You sat in the passenger seat and spoke to each other in hushed voices.

"Why did you leave?"

"She was getting out of hand."

"She didn't know what she was saying."

"She knew. She knew exactly what she was saying."

"I shouldn't have told her."

"That has nothing to do with this."

"She took it very badly."

"That has absolutely nothing to do with this."

"You shouldn't have said that to her last night."

"No. This thing is inherited."

"What thing?"

"We don't have it in my family."

"What do you mean?"

"We don't have it in my family."

You said nothing to him on the way home. It had taken you a while to tell him about Ebun. Madness in the family was enough cause to have second thoughts about marriage in those days, but he had said it was irrelevant to him. After all, he was an educated man, a Cambridge man.

Your anger turned to Biola. How dare she disgrace you by bringing up your private life? Did she do that to punish you? You had trusted her. You had thought she would be mature enough to understand, but oh no, she had to throw a tantrum of that magnitude.

You were no doormat. You had stopped sleeping with your husband once you found out. That was your decision. Once or twice, you thought you would, for yourself alone, but you couldn't. You demanded that he take a bath before he came home after he returned smelling of a musky perfume you would never use. You had heard the other woman was a divorced lawyer, that her ex-husband beat her because she was flirtatious and eventually threw her out. You were not pleased to hear that. What difference did it make? Your husband could marry as many women as he could afford to by customary law and he would not be forced to pay you alimony, so how literate did any woman have to be to stay, especially for the sake of her children?

No, you would not forgive Biola, not for a while. Her father was right in that respect. Her display in the ward was deliberate.

By bedtime, he had changed your vacation plans yet again. He said he would leave for London the following Friday with Oyinda and Deji and would stay there until they went back to school. He would run his practice from there. He had three senior lawyers, who were competent enough. You and Biola could stay in Lagos.

"Why don't we all go back to London?" you suggested.

"No," he said. "She is not in any shape to travel."

"But London is where she will get the right treatment."

"No. She can't travel right now. Besides which, I don't want her harassing her brother and sister."

"So what do you want me to do then? St. Christopher's will not keep her."

"Take her to the teaching hospital. Maybe then she will know she has to take her medication."

You agreed, partly to show Biola what would happen if she didn't take her medication. It wasn't a punishment.

He refused to go back to St. Christopher's the next morning. He said he didn't want to be disgraced. His driver took you there, this time in your Volvo, and he drove himself to work.

Biola was still sedated when you got to St. Christopher's. The driver took you from there to the teaching hospital and Professor Ajose admitted Biola to the female psychiatric ward.

"Where is my friend?" Professor Ajose asked. "He ought to be here."

You said your husband had to go to court. Biola was still too drowsy to care about her surroundings. You asked for the bed by the wall, furthest from the toilet, and made her bed with clean sheets from home. Biola lay down as the patient in the next bed warned her that stray cats were invading the world.

The following Friday, your husband left for London with Oyinda and Deji. You called to give him updates about Biola every day, and took fresh sheets and food provisions to the teaching hospital. You also brought hot meals in Pyrex dishes and left them at the nurses' station. Biola, now aware of where she was, was refusing to see you. She sent messages through the nurses that if you so much as stepped inside the ward, you would live to regret it.

You indulged her. At home the power cuts eased for a while and you spent more time indoors, reading your paperback novels. Patience wanted a couple of weeks off to go to her hometown and you gave her permission to.

One day, while Patience was away, your driver came back from the hospital to say Biola wanted to see you. You immediately called your husband to tell him the good news. You had been hoping for this moment. You told him you would go to the hospital and, once Biola was discharged, you would both come and join the rest of the family in London.

"Ah, no," your husband said. "That can't happen."

"Why not?" you asked. "What is it this time?"

"It's too soon. We can't be sure she won't relapse."

"But she is asking to see me."

"It has only been a day."

"But it's a good sign. Isn't that a good sign?"

"It has only been a day."

He kept insisting that he couldn't be sure and that he was concerned about Oyinda and Deji.

"They, too, have been affected by this. Plus, I have to travel out of town after they go back to school."

"Travel where?"

"I have clients I have to see."

You heard the tone in his voice and thought about his history of hiding information. You were suspicious. Even if his senior staff were efficient, he had never left them for more than three weeks at a stretch before.

"Frank," you asked, intuitively, "are you bringing that woman to our house over there?"

"It hasn't been easy for me, running my practice from here," he said.

"Frank, I'm asking you. Are you bringing that woman and

her boys to our house after my children have gone back to school?"

You slammed the phone down on him when he didn't answer, not before calling him a hypocrite, a coward and a bigamist. Afterwards, you called the Five Star travel agency and discovered that his secretary had booked flights for the woman and her sons, from Lagos to London, and from London to Sardinia and back.

You visited Biola in the ward the next morning and she still appeared sleepy, but she was more lucid now. The patient in the next bed kept grinning at you. The rest looked exhausted and sad. You had brought Biola some *jollof* rice and fried plantains. She managed a few mouthfuls and gave her neighbor her leftovers.

"I'm sorry, Mummy," she said. "It's been terrible for me. You don't know how much. I can't believe I'm in a place like this. I can't even use the toilet. I will take my medication from now on. I will do anything if you just take me home."

She spoke as if her illness was her fault and you said, "It's not a punishment, my dear."

"When is Daddy coming home?"

"Soon."

"Aren't Oyinda and Deji in school?"

"They will be."

"When?"

"Soon."

Biola shut her eyes. "Maybe Daddy will come home then. I'm sure he won't believe how long I have lasted here."

"I'm sure," you said.

But he did not return to Lagos, even after she was discharged from the hospital and Oyinda and Deji started school. They were back to being the little English girl and boy again, sounding self-conscious and answering you in English when you spoke to them in Yoruba. The rainy season came to an end. It was the beginning of autumn in England, and the dry season in Nigeria. You spent more time indoors, even as the power cuts resumed.

Biola was taking her medication and it left her lethargic. She turned what little attention she had to the English literature classics on the bookshelf under the stairs: Austen and Brontë. She joked that Dickens would make her crazier.

You went to the NITEL office, and this time offered a bribe. Within a week the NITEL boys came to the house and fixed the phone in the sitting room. You asked if the phone would remain fixed.

"Yes, madam," they said, ducking and smiling. "It will work from now on."

After they left, you called Oyinda and Deji in school and Biola spoke to them. She actually laughed, which she hadn't in a while. She didn't spend long, though, and then she asked if she could call her father next.

"If you want," you said.

"How come you don't call him?"

"Ah, well," you said.

"But how come he doesn't call?" she asked. "And why isn't he home now they're back in school?"

"I don't know," you said.

"You don't ask what he is doing there?"

"I don't."

"You should ask him, Mummy. You should. Why don't you? Why don't you call him and ask what he is doing there?"

There were times she became anxious, her eyes widening and her tone becoming urgent and it seemed as if her symptoms were on the verge of returning.

"Ask him yourself," you said.

She called and the phone rang, but no one picked it up. After a while, she sighed, her medication subduing her.

"It's all right," she said. "I should have known better."

Her father was still away when she relapsed a month later. She was bloated up from her medication now, but it was no longer working for her. She was the one who packed her suitcase. She was the one who said, "I think I'd better go to the hospital." The driver took you there and she didn't even look back as you left her in the ward.

You came back to an empty house that evening. At the beginning of the summer vacation you had wanted a full house. You had not bargained for the vacation to end this way: two in boarding school and one in a psychiatric ward. Their father was probably back in Lagos and living with his other family. You went from room to room shutting doors. It made the house seem less deserted. There had been another power cut. On the veranda, you picked up a table-tennis bat, smashed the ball over the net and watched it ricochet until it stopped.

LAST TRIP

This time, he wants her to deliver a hundred and twenty-seven balloons of heroin to London. He counts them on her table to make sure there is no question about the number. The balloons are multicolored, a little smaller than her thumb. She is capable of swallowing every one of them, but she bargains for extra pay, a thousand US dollars more.

"I'll do it for five," she says.

She speaks in broken Yoruba because she has to be careful about eavesdroppers. The room she rents for her trips has thin walls. It contains the wooden table, a couple of collapsible iron chairs, and a new mattress that smells vaguely like urine because she sweats more than usual on the nights before she travels. Her son, Dara, is asleep on the mattress, face up. He rubs the eczema patches around his eyes and wheezes. A miniature oscillating fan blows dust over him. She has considered leaving her windows open to give him some relief. The heat indoors is unbearable, but the air in this part of Lagos has a sour taste. For now, she is more worried about sounds that escape her room. Even on afternoons like this, with the horns and engines of the traffic on nearby streets, she can hear her neighbors talking. She guarantees they are listening. They know she has a man in her room.

"Since when five?" he asks.

He goes by the name of Kazeem. He has a lisp that is amusing, potentially. In the past, he has hired killers to dispose of difficult couriers, couriers who have double-crossed him.

After thirteen years of loyalty to their organization, she is not worried about the consequences of betrayal. She is scared of him the way people are of little dogs that jump and bite. His eyes are a sickly shade of pink and the sun seems to have roasted him, the fat in his body melting to oil. His skin is too shiny and clings to his bones. The veins in his arms protrude. He crunches on kola nut and occasionally stops to smack his lips. This habit of his irritates her.

"You can't just demand five like that," he says.

"Why not?" she asks, sitting up. "My life is not worth five?"

She is taller than he is, robust, especially with the brocade *boubous* she favors for international flights. They give her stomach enough space to expand and make her chest look as sturdy as a shelf. Many times before, she has concealed bags strapped around her torso. She eats well to keep her weight up, bleaches her skin with hydroquinone creams to freshen her complexion. In her latest passport photograph she appears much younger than she is, and can pass for her fake age. Her alias is Simbiyat Adisa.

He sucks a piece of kola nut out of his teeth. "I pay you in kind, nothing more."

"No!" she says, waving her hand. "Not in kind!"

She tells him in a whisper, even though he already knows this about her, that she doesn't push drugs.

He shrugs. "So, it's four as usual."

"Five," she repeats, spreading her fingers.

The man sees her as walking storage. He will pay her more only if she swallows more.

"Take it or leave it," he says. "There are many where you came from."

She is one of his best. He will have trouble finding anyone willing to swallow this many balloons. He is testy because last week the drug law agency arrested more of his couriers at Murtala Mohammed Airport. These ones didn't even make it past check-in. They were novices, 200-gram mules. He has had to drop his prices because of seizures like this, and is trying to sell more within Nigeria now, but wealthy Nigerians are not easy to hook: they get high on Mercedes Benzes. He wants to target their children who depend on pocket money, or the masses that would have to give up their meals for one hit.

She has seen addicts like this in her neighborhood. One walks around the marketplace naked and scratches his crotch. Street hawkers pack up and run when he begs for food. Heroin makes people mellow, Kazeem says, but the rumor is that when this addict can't find a little to lace his hemp, he shivers as if he has malaria and vomits on himself. He will steal from his own mother to buy an ounce. What will he do to a stranger?

"Use the boy if you want more money," Kazeem says. "I will pay you well for that. It is not as if he will know what he is carrying, with his mental condition, and no one will bother to check him at the airports. You'll see."

She taps the table. He has never had tact. "This is between me and you," she says. "Never mention my son again."

Kazeem leaves her room muttering about her audacity. Everyone is making life difficult for him of late: his couriers, the drug law agency in Lagos, his shippers in Bangkok, the Turks in London, and Colombians in New York. The entire universe is conspiring to make life difficult for him and deprive him of business.

There was a time when he would brag that their organization was the largest in Africa, that he had established their trade routes from Thailand. He even claimed to have taken over South Africa after apartheid, colonized the whole country with cocaine, he said, and spread heroin use in countries as far off as Russia, New Zealand, South Korea and Saudi Arabia. She used to be in awe when she didn't know a poppy seed from an Asian brown or white. Then she discovered that Kazeem was just a middleman, and not even a high-level one at that.

He reports to bigger men in their organization, and fears them. He is rich in naira terms, but they are wealthy in foreign exchange, these men. Barons they are called. She calls them cheats out of common sense rather than a sense of moral superiority. The balloons she carries are worth over a thousand times more than the amount Kazeem pays her, and packed with a pretty consistent mix. At a time like this, when he needs reliable couriers, if she travels with half a million dollars of heroin in her stomach, is it too much to ask for five thousand?

"Foolish man," she says.

She drinks a bottle of Swan water to settle her stomach, and lies next to Dara. His body is warmer than hers. Every drop of water she's had seems to be leaking out of her pores. Is she menstruating early or falling sick? She pats her neck to monitor her temperature and checks her watch. The minute the hour hand reaches twelve, she gets up and pours palm oil into a plastic bowl; and then she dips each balloon in before putting them into her mouth.

She has to be cautious with the oil: too much might get her stomach juices going again and dissolve the latex. The balloons are bulky to swallow. They block her ears as they go lower, and hurt her chest, so she pauses in between to rest. All things considered, they are easier to get down her throat than the surgical-glove fingers she trained with, and anyway, it is like losing your virginity: eventually one becomes accustomed.

When she first started swallowing, she would gag as if someone was strangling her. Her nose would stream with mucus and her eyes would well up with tears. Kazeem would yell, "You'd better keep it down!" If she threw up, he would remind her of how he'd given her a plane ticket, passport and spending money, handed her a suitcase and driven her to the airport. He sent her to Douala, Accra and then to Amsterdam. She traveled with Indian hemp back then. When Indian hemp became less profitable, he gave her cocaine. Heroin is popular these days. He calls it the big H or H, depending. She swallows the last of the balloons. Her stomach is bloated and hard, as if she's been constipated for weeks.

When Dara gets up, his height overwhelms her, and so does his heavy breathing. Her room is not meant for two. There is not enough space to have a private thought, or smell.

As he dresses, she notes the hairs above his upper lip and in his armpits. He has muscles like a teenager but still has the heart of a child. He sobs whenever she travels, doesn't like staying with his grandmother, and even his grandmother will not keep him this time.

"Take him to his father's," she said, clapping her arthritic hands. "After all, they're both men. Go on. I can't control him anymore. Let his father take responsibility for him—for a change."

In her desperation, she left her mother's house and headed for her ex-husband's to ask if he would look after Dara while she was away.

That one stood in his doorway, in his dirty string vest, and said, "Don't bring that boy anywhere near me! He's not mine!"

She explained that Dara had never been on a plane, and she was nervous about how he might cope.

"I told you," he said, finally acknowledging Dara, "to let the nurses smother him."

She cursed him. His new wife, barely twenty years old, and pregnant again, ran out of the house, and pleaded on her knees, "*Ni suuru.*" Have patience.

Patience she has; she had no home or job when the man threw her out days after Dara was born. She was almost considering prostituting herself when Kazeem came along. She taught Dara how to dress himself, feed himself and helped him to adapt to his handicapped school. She was there when he learned how to weave baskets and kick a football. This month, she has been training with him for his favorite event on sports day, an obstacle race, parent and child. They run through hoops and jump over buckets. He wants to win every time and jeers at the losers. His headmistress is delighted with his academic progress. His report sheet is full of teacher's comments like: "Omodara is an exemplary student" and "Omodara is a credit to our school." She will continue to work for Kazeem to make sure Dara remains a student there. The school is not one of those where teachers beat or neglect their students. They are Christian-based; evangelical. They believe in the healing power of prayer, but their fees are expensive.

It is early evening, and the sky bleeds a light shade of orange. She leaves her room with Dara carrying only a handbag, inside which are their passports and plane tickets. The car that will take them to the airport is parked outside the gates of the tenement —a Peugeot 504 that reeks of lemon air-freshener. The driver informs her that her suitcase is in the boot. She doesn't look too long at his face, in case he is one of those who don't approve of women couriers. She does notice how he stares at Dara.

"BA," she says, startling him.

"British Airways," he confirms.

They drive over potholes, past rubbish piles almost as tall as palm trees. The houses are mostly unpainted. The gutter that runs parallel to the road is thick with slime that resembles boiling tar. Pedestrians cross over it on wooden planks leading to their cement verandas. Street hawkers have already perched kerosene lanterns on their stalls on the roadsides, ready for the night market. Children walk around barefoot. A group of old men have gathered to play a game of *ayo*. One of them, his eyeglasses secured with Sellotape, cries out in triumph. A rooster flaps its wings and scampers.

The driver continues to sneak peeks at Dara in his rearview mirror. He takes Third Mainland Bridge to the airport and drops them off in the parking lot. One good thing about the new government is that they have cleaned up the place. The last government was lax; the airport was teeming with touts, from the parking lot to the departure gates. She would have to forge her way through crowds, and was always worried about being mugged.

Now, the police have erected barriers, and they patrol the airport with guns. They will stop anyone who attempts to cross the barriers without evidence to prove that they are traveling, or accompanying someone who is. The drug agency is also on the lookout, but Kazeem worries more about them than she does. Couriers who get caught look like they are couriers; they appear desperate, for a start. One eyeball from an official and they begin to twitch.

They don't lack guts; they lack imagination. She always ties her headscarf with the aplomb of a Lagos fabric trader, wears conspicuous colors. Her flamboyance helps her to get through passport control and customs. Dara's presence can do her no harm either, since people are too busy gaping at him.

What she fears most are flight delays. An hour is nothing to worry about, two hours and her heartbeat will rise; three, and they will leave the departure gates and find their way back home. She knows couriers who have convulsed and died when balloons burst inside them. That is why she refuses to travel Nigerian Airways. British Airways flights are fairly timely.

Dara keeps playing with the rope that leads to the check-in desk. "Please," she says. "Leave that thing alone, for heaven's sake."

People are looking at him as if he is unearthly. His hand drops immediately. One warning is usually all he needs.

Customs officers ahead are preoccupied with a teenage boy who is traveling business class. They open his suitcase and ruffle his belongings, mostly jeans and T-shirts. The only questionable items they can find are two small ebony carvings.

"Have you got written permission for dis?" one customs officer asks.

"Pardon?" the boy says in an English accent.

"Have you got written permission?"

"Why would I need written permission?"

"You're not allowed to travel with national antiquities."

"But I bought them at Hotel Le Meridien. Daddy?"

The boy waves at a gray-haired man who has been talking to a woman at the first-class check-in desk. The man is definitely his father. The father has a pot belly and the boy is lanky, but they have the same prominent widow's peak.

"What's going on?" the man asks the customs officer.

The boy explains. The customs officer fidgets with the carvings. Perhaps he thought the boy was alone and could get away with hustling him.

"Come on," the boy's father says. "They're just souvenirs."

The customs officer shakes his head. "They're national antiquities, sah."

"I don't believe this," the boy says. "Bookends?"

"He is a student," his father says. "He is going back to school. Now, see how you've scattered his suitcase for no reason, eh? They're common souvenirs for tourists. You can even buy them here at the airport. What is wrong with you people? The work you're supposed to do, you don't do. The one you're not supposed to do, you do, eh?"

"I'm following directives," the customs officer mumbles.

He has to be careful. He doesn't know whom he is addressing. The elite are so well-connected that if this man isn't someone important, he will certainly know someone who is.

The commotion is convenient for her. She checks in without scrutiny. The customs officer, still sore about his dressing down, beckons impatiently. "Step forward," he says, and then lifts his hand and orders, "Step back."

Customs checks are not for drugs, or terrorist weapons, or precious artwork, anyway. They are for bushmeat, stockfish, smoked herring, live snails and all the other foods that people slip into their luggage, knowing that they are prohibited overseas.

Between passport control and the gate, she loses sight of the boy with the bookends. He is probably in a special lounge, not in the row of seats by the gates with faulty air conditioning. There are two Nigerias, after all, two ways to enter and two ways to leave: one for people with a lot of money, and the other for everyone else.

She stops at the airport café to buy Dara a cold Maltina and tells him he deserves one for being good. He laughs; he loves to be praised.

A waitress, in an oversized waistcoat and trousers that are too tight, pours his Maltina into his glass. Dara claps to congratulate himself, and then spits out froth after his first gulp.

"Behave yourself," she says, as she pays the waitress. "You're not a baby anymore."

The waitress says through her nose, "Burt it is nort his fault."

She does not defend herself. First of all, does this waitress imagine she's living overseas because she works in an airport? Why else would she speak with such an odd accent? And who is she to judge? If she cares so much for the handicapped, doesn't she wonder why there are so few of them around, or is there a special country for them, too? Stray animals are more prominent in Nigeria.

"He's making a mess," she says.

Dara knows how to behave in school to impress his teachers. He knows how to frustrate his grandmother so that she will tire of him. He certainly knows how to get the attention of a pretty girl.

"Burt he's nort doing it on purpose," the waitress insists.

"He is an intelligent boy. He knows exactly what he is doing."

Showing off, she thinks, womanizing like his father. Just wait. Wait until he grabs that high backside of yours, then you will know why I discipline him.

Their flight boards twenty minutes late. She stops sweating as soon as the air conditioning on the plane is on full blast. They settle in two window seats by the left wing. Across the aisle, a bald man clears his throat and snorts. She helps Dara to fasten his seat belt and then loosens hers.

If she presses her stomach hard enough, she can feel the balloons. She must not eat or drink, and since the flight attendants are on the lookout for passengers who don't, she will have to switch her tray with Dara's. He can easily eat enough for two. Normally, she hides portions of her meals in her handbag and flushes them down the toilet. For now, she watches Dara as he studies the signs—exit, no smoking—and then the long line of heads in front of them.

The most trying part of being his mother is the guessing; not prompting him to feed and dress himself, not his allergies and ointments and wayward limbs, not even trying to restrain him whenever he gets excited over women. Just as she thinks she has a good sense of what is going on in his mind, it tightens and shuts her out like a knot.

He is fascinated, not frightened, as the plane takes off. The sky is pure indigo. Soon she is able to see the horizon, and the flight attendants walk down the aisles to offer drinks. Tonight, they are serving beef stew or tarragon chicken for dinner. The smell reminds her of baking meat pies. Her mouth waters. The passengers behind her choose the chicken. A flight attendant, blonde with coral lipstick, asks in a chirpy voice, "Chicken or beef?"

She chooses the chicken for herself and the beef for Dara. He plays with his fork. She makes a show of helping him to lift the foil cover of his packed meal. Close up, the beef smells like a burp.

The bald man across the aisle protests, "I specifically requested a meal without salt."

"Give me one moment," the attendant says.

"I specifically requested," the man says, even more loudly, "no salt."

"Just a moment, please," the attendant says in a pleasant voice, as if she is speaking to a willful child.

"For medical reasons," he says and snorts.

The attendant turns to her with a conspiratorial smile and asks, "All right?"

"Oh, yes," she says.

Distractions are perfect for her. Dara is gobbling carrots. The attendant tilts her head as if she is observing a puppy.

"He's got a good appetite, hasn't he?" she says.

"Oh, yes."

You with your skinny self, she thinks. Just don't lean too far over him if you know what is good for you.

The attendant carries on up the aisle. She exchanges Dara's beef for her chicken and whispers, "Well done. When you finish, we'll go to the toilet before you sleep."

He pees on the toilet seat and forgets to wash his hands. She sends him back in and he does as she tells him, but emerges with his head bowed. She ignores his sulky face and follows him down the aisle.

As usual, she bites off corners of the blanket bags before tearing them open. She spreads his blanket over him, and hers over her lap. Dara raises his over his head. She lowers the window shutter, places her pillow against it and closes her eyes.

He begins to snore and she realizes how long it has been since she's had company on a flight. In the days of cocaine, Kazeem would fill a plane with carriers. Sometimes, twenty of them would be on board, smuggling in their luggage, in their clothing, or in their stomachs. Kazeem recruited grandparents, government officials, mothers traveling with their children. In those days, whenever a courier was caught, it caused a scandal. The newspapers would go wild with their reports—*An Epidemic of Drug Mules*, and such. There was the case of the woman who stuffed cocaine in her dead baby and cradled the baby as if it were sleeping, and another case of a society woman who swore she thought she was carrying diamonds. That woman had been smuggling when British Airways was British Caledonian, when British Caledonian was BOAC. Princess So-and-So, famous for cramming a condom of cocaine into her vagina.

These days, Kazeem sends only one courier per flight. He uses just as many men as women, and *oyinbos* from England and America. The *oyinbos* are rarely stopped. He pays them twice as much, and will use children as mules with their parents' consent. There was that eleven-year-old boy who was caught at La Guardia with God knows how many grams of heroin in his stomach. The boy was charged as a juvenile. In England, Kazeem said, the boy would have been handed over to social services and placed with foster parents. "The English are more civilized," he said, "far more advanced than the Americans when it comes to these matters."

He makes assurances like "Confess if you're caught and they'll give you a lighter sentence," or "They have no space in their prisons. They will deport you back home," and oh, oh, his best one is, "They're not looking for people like you after 9/11."

So many of his own couriers have ended up as John or Jane Doe of No Fixed Abode. One was stopped at Heathrow and sent to Holloway Prison for her first offense. She discovered a whole community of Nigerians there. Another was stopped at

JFK. She refused an x-ray, so federal agents chained her to a bed and waited for her bowels to move. She got five years with no probation. Then there was that other man, Lucky or Innocent something or other, who, after spending time in an American prison, was deported, only to spend another nine years in Kirikiri Maximum Security before he was pardoned. He came out swinging his hips like a woman, eventually died of tuberculosis. She has heard of other couriers who were executed by firing squad in Nigeria, publicly beheaded in Saudi Arabia. Granted, they're not flying angels, but given their work hazards, five thousand is not too much to ask for.

She shifts her headscarf to a more comfortable position. After this trip, she can afford to pay her rent. It is paid two years in advance. Her carburetor needs to be replaced, or so her mechanic says. She does not move in circles where last year's *iro* and *buba* are no longer fashionable, but she does like to take care of herself. She will buy herself some lace and a few silk scarves, maybe matching shoes and bags from Liverpool Street market. Of course, she has Dara's school fees to consider first, but in less than twelve hours, she will have earned more money than most Nigerian women spend in a year. She has often wondered what it would be like to be one of those who come to England to work. She sees them at Gatwick Airport, on the Gatwick Express and at Victoria station, walking with the same hurried gaits, and recognizes them by the shapes of their lips and noses. They are all jacketed up like English potatoes and their skin and hair are dried up from the cold. They have more education than she has. Some are even university graduates, but how legitimate can their work be if they are living here illegally?

No, to come and go as she pleases is still the better option for her, even if she ends up spending one night in some cold hotel in North London, with a narrow staircase and worn-out carpet, in a room that doesn't have enough corner space to lay her suitcase down. When she gets there, she will take a dose of laxatives, and hopefully pass the balloons before her contacts arrive. She is humiliated by their expressions whenever they have to wait for her to finish in the bathtub. She herself cannot stand the smell, or sight, as she rinses her feces off. She wonders who would smoke a substance, knowing that it has come out of a stranger's bowels, or sniff it up their noses, or inject it into their blood. She doesn't expect sympathy from the world like the addicts who waste their money getting high. But each trip she makes she plays with death; each trip is her last, until the next. So she, too, is dependent on the drugs she carries. She, too, is living with a habit, after all.

Dara keeps elbowing her; Mr. No Salt across the aisle continues to snort. She has several more hours to go, and wonders what it would be like if the plane were to crash and she never had to work again.

After midnight she falls asleep. She dreams of death by plane crash, car accident; sees herself drowning in Lagos Lagoon, Dara peering over Third Mainland Bridge, and her mother unable to stop him from slipping in because her hands are so crooked from old age they look like a couple of crabs.

When she wakes up it is breakfast time. The lights are on and the attendants are walking down the aisles again. Her eyes are swollen and sore. She shakes Dara's shoulder and he coughs.

"Take it easy," she says, rubbing his back.

The air conditioning is no good for his lungs. She checks his socks are still on. The blonde attendant stops by them with a trolley and offers two trays of food and half a smile. Her lipstick has faded.

"Had a good rest?" she asks, bending over Dara.

Dara reaches up and pulls her hair. She struggles to free herself. He drags her lower. She pries his fingers apart and straightens up with a red face.

"Gosh," she says. "He's got quite a grip there, hasn't he, Mum?"

"Sorry," Mum says. Maybe now you'll leave him alone, she thinks.

The attendant smooths her hair back. As soon as she rolls the food trolley past them, Mum hands her sticky pastry to Dara, and then raises the window shutter. The ground below looks like geometric shapes separated by green bushes. Roads curve through clusters of red-brick homes. From the ground, the red-brick homes are the color of dried dirt, a few of them defaced with graffiti, and their gardens are so tiny, so *chinchini*. She would not like to live in England. She wants to remain here, above the country, suspended.

Dara eats his pastry after hers. The blonde attendant collects their trays and is more careful about keeping her distance. In no time at all the pilot announces they are about to begin their descent.

"Nn," Dara moans when the plane dips.

"Hm," she responds in his language.

Taking off is easier than landing. She clutches her armrest and braces herself. The balloons in her stomach feel as if they are about to drop.

Only Nigerian passengers clap and cheer when the plane lands with a bump, she is certain of this, and they also get up and remove their hand luggage from the overhead compartments before the seat-belt signals are switched off. At Gatwick

Airport there is a rush, as usual, through the corridors towards passport control. She would like to keep up with the rest, but Dara lags behind. He is preoccupied with the clusters of trolleys, and the lit signs saying emergency exit, arrivals and baggage reclaim.

They reach the hall and join the long queue. Her heart beats on her eardrums and she tries to focus on a sign to keep calm: We. Take. Extremely. Seriously. Any. Attempt. To Inti. Midate. Our. Staff. Either. By. Threats. Or Assaults. We take. Extremely seriously. Any attempt. To intimidate. We take extremely seriously. Any attempt to intimidate…

She takes hold of Dara's hand, just in case it strays again. When they stop at the line on the floor that they can't cross over, she mentally pokes fun at the man in the immigration booth so she can speak to him with confidence. The man's head is shaped like a boiled egg. His cheeks are as blotchy as half-ripe pawpaws. His mouth is no bigger than a *kobo* coin.

"Morning," she says, looking at his forehead.

"How long will you be staying?" he asks.

"Too weak…"

"Sorry?"

"Too. Weak."

"Two weeks?"

She nods. This one can't understand her. She herself finds it difficult to decipher what *oyinbos* are saying, especially when their mouths are as small as his, but he enunciates as the flight attendant had.

"What is the purpose of your trip?"

"Holiday."

"Visiting friends or family?"

"Friends."

He stamps their passports after a few generic questions.

She has found that white immigration officers are more lenient than black, and men are more lenient than women.

"Have a nice stay," he says, nodding at Dara.

"Thank you," she says.

Again, she has to remind herself to take even breaths. At Baggage Reclaim, she concentrates on the carousel to avoid making eye contact with those on surveillance. Her clothes don't matter because they can't differentiate between Nigerians. They can only rely on telltale signs like shiftiness and sweating.

She is sweating again, under her arms. People continue to break from the crowd around the carousel to retrieve their luggage. She panics when she doesn't see hers. She will not make this journey again, she tells herself. She should not and cannot. Her nerves will not survive another trip.

"Wait for me," she says to Dara.

She walks around the carousel to stop her legs from trembling, and spots her suitcase with a pink and gray tapestry pattern. She reaches for it, as if it is drifting down a river, and grabs the handle. The suitcase is lighter than she recalls and she loses her balance. She backs into someone, and discovers it is Dara.

"I told you to wait," she says, without raising her voice.

She is not upset. He has been the perfect diversion. Here in England, people glance rather than stare at him, as if they would rather be fake than rude, but he is shivering. Is he nervous or just cold?

"What?" she asks, leading him away from the carousel. "What is it?"

She is using the opportunity to check that there are enough people passing through Nothing to Declare. Two customs officers are on duty. One of them steps forward and her heart beats so loudly it deafens her.

The customs officer stops someone else behind them. She takes steady steps before she is round the corner, and is relieved to see the shop, the one with all the colorful socks. They walk into the crowd on the other side, past people who are waiting for arriving passengers. An elderly woman kneels to embrace a toddler. A row of men display handwritten name cards. Dara raises his fists and cheers. Everyone watches as he runs a victory lap and returns to her.

"*Iwo*," she says, shaking her head. You.

This is the last time she will travel with him, but he has given her so much trouble she has almost forgotten hers. He claps as if he knows she is pleased with him, and she is glad he has no idea why.

News from Home

It is not a good day to tell her. This morning she quarreled with Dr. Darego again. They were upstairs in their bedroom on the second floor; I was on the sofa bed in the basement where I sleep every night. I heard their voices clear as if I pressed my ear to their door. Mrs. Darego called him a selfish man. Dr. Darego said, "Listen, I work very hard." Mrs. Darego said she was overworked. "What are you harassing me for?" Dr. Darego asked. "You wanted help, I got you help. You have your nanny downstairs. Call the girl, tell her to get the kids ready, take the keys to the jeep. All of you, drive to wherever you feel like spending your July Fourth. I'm not going. Finish?"

Mrs. Darego must have been the one who slammed the door.

Perhaps this is why houses like theirs in America are called "dream homes." They are not built with unhappy couples in mind; their walls are too thin.

I fold up the sofa bed and replace the cushions, which are in a pile by the concertina-shaped floor lamp. I untie my black satin scarf to let my braids down, slap lint off my shorts, then listen to a world news broadcast as usual. It is Independence Day here in America. Hopefully, there will be an update on the demonstrators from my hometown.

Forty years it took for our story to reach the front pages of the *Times*: *Nigerian Delta Women in Oil Company Standoff*. The women had occupied Summit Oil's terminal, the report said. They were clapping and singing. If their demands were not met, they would strip naked, and this was a shaming gesture, according to local custom.

I did not know of any such custom in my hometown. I only remembered old-fashioned Catholic women who would consider knee-length shorts like mine a taboo. We Kalabaris were an overdressed people. You had to see our men in traditional attire, with their long tunics, staffs and black bowler hats. Women wore bright silk head ties, lace blouses and layers of colorful plaid wrappers down to their ankles. Why would they bare their bodies for a cause? I thought the newspaper report was a hoax, designed to ridicule Africans and trivialize our protest. I wondered who in my hometown had joined the demonstrators, what had happened to my friend Angelina who was one of them, whether Val had since been found, and if Mama now agreed with Papa when he said that on the arrival of the foreigner, the native must learn to sleep with one eye open.

The broadcast ends without a word about my hometown. In a cowardly way, I'm relieved. I pull the floor lamp to its proper place by the wall, push the sliding doors open to let warm air in. My goose bumps shrink. Outside, the Daregos' small lawn is bordered by flowers I can't name. They are pale compared to hibiscus and bougainvillea, muted like the rest of the house. Indoors, there are beige walls, bronze carvings, ebony masks, mahogany tables, and batiks. African-inspired, I've heard Dr. Darego say about their choice of decor. I've never seen a house in Africa that resembles theirs, so consciously and deliberately

African, so beautifully coordinated. To me it is highly westernized.

"Eve?" Mrs. Darego calls from upstairs.

"Coming," I say.

Fresh air from outside chases me as I hurry to her kitchen. Living in a basement is like living in an underground tomb.

When I was a girl, I was in love with every expatriate I came across in my hometown, Catholic priests especially. I thought they were as pure as God in their whites. I couldn't wait to hop on their laps. I was envious that they seemed partial to boys. My class teacher, Sister, I didn't understand why no man had spoken for her. I would have married her myself. She was as beautiful as the Blessed Mary with her red hair and freckles. She was decent enough to spank with rulers, unlike the tree branches our mothers favored for beatings. She taught us about Mungo Park, the Scottish surgeon who was killed on an expedition trying to find the source of River Niger. He was trapped in swamps, fell ill with fevers, was ambushed by natives who stole his equipment and shot at him with bows and arrows. The textbook said he eventually jumped into the river to save himself, and drowned.

I cried for Mungo. I thought natives were wicked people, too ugly in the book illustrations. I grew up, and missionaries like Sister left town. The only expatriates I came across worked for international oil companies—British, Dutch, Canadian, Italian, and American—like the human resources director of Summit Oil who interviewed me for a nursing position at Summit Oil Clinic. He signed the rejection letter addressed to me. Most nurses I graduated with were selling bottled water, bathing soap, tinned milk for a living. Few people in town could afford to buy such provisions. We were one of them. Papa was an electrician; Mama had a Coca-Cola consignment. Still, I was lucky to come to America to work as a live-in nanny.

Mrs. Darego is wearing a flowery housecoat. Her face looks freshly washed. She has the kind of dark skin I admire, almost indigo. This morning she appears gray under her fluorescent kitchen lights. She narrows her eyes as she speaks.

"I'm sorry, Eve," she says. "It's me and you today. We have to take the children to the barbecue. Their father doesn't want to go, and I don't know what else to do."

She was going to give me a day off and spend her time shopping for groceries and cooking. I was looking forward to doing nothing useful.

"Shall I get them ready?" I ask.

"Yes, please," she says. "I'll pack the cooler and make sandwiches."

I head for the children's room, but she stops me by the fridge.

"Is everything all right?" she asks.

I smile to assure her. She has sensed my mood.

I arrived in America in February of 2002. I saw snow for the first time. To me it looked like granulated sugar, this white sprinkle on trees, streets, buildings and the expressway to the Daregos' house in New Jersey, so pretty I reached out in their yard for a handful and licked it. I loved snow more once I was indoors and warm. Through the sliding door in the basement, I watched the flakes fall. I stepped outside one night to feel them settle on my head and thought the wind was playing a terrible joke on me, the way it cut through my cardigan to my bones. In Nigeria, we had a dry season most of the year, rainy season in summertime, harmattan winds over Christmas and New Year. None compared to the chill of winter. Out there, under the black-blue New Jersey sky, I thought that living in America was exactly what it was like to live in a mortuary.

In my first week, I caught a flu so severe I wished for mere malaria. I sweated from fevers; headaches pounded my temples. Mrs. Darego worried because I had no health insurance. She treated me with lemon drinks and vitamin supplements. I was meant to relieve her, but already I was a burden. I recovered and found I was down to my weight as a teenager. In my spare time, I went for walks to the mall to increase my strength. There, I saw shops for underwear, shops for pets, and thirty types of breakfast cereal. Pancakes with blueberries, raisins, honey, nuts, chocolate chips. Disinfectants and air-fresheners for every germ and odor. Scented toilet paper!

"Where are you from?" Americans often asked. Sometimes they smiled, other times they looked at me with suspicion. I was from Africa, I ended up saying, because I quickly learned they didn't know Nigeria. They asked, "Algeria? Liberia?" I started to say West Africa, to make things easier for them. They said, "Oh, South Africa!" I met people in New Jersey who had never been to New York. I began to understand their sense of the world.

"Hello, Auntie Eve," Alali says as I rub her back.

"I had a bad dream," Daniel groans.

They sound like frogs whenever they get up. Daniel is five and Alali eight. They have their mother's half-moon eyes. I untangle their legs from their Disney bedsheets and notice new lumps on their skin from mosquito bites. Here, there is no risk of malaria.

"Bath time," I say.

When I met them, their expressions were Who-are-you? and What-d'you-want? Their accents were wanna, gonna, shoulda.

"You talk funny," Alali said, once she was comfortable with me living in the basement. "Are you one of those people who call candy sweets and cookies biscuits?"

"Yeah, are you from Africa?" Daniel Junior asked through his missing teeth.

Alali pointed out imaginary locations on the tablecloth. "Now, my mom is from this little village here in Africa. My dad is from this little village here in Africa. Which village are you from?"

"A town," I said. Her parents were from cities. Her father grew up in Port Harcourt in the Niger Delta, and her mother was from Lagos, though she was raised in Tanzania and Cuba—her parents were in the diplomatic service.

"I sawed the picture of Africa," Daniel said. "And the boy had no hair, and his belly was all swelled up, and he lived in a hut, with, um, no windows, and I don't like Africa. Africa women have droopy boobies."

Alali laughed. "Huh?!"

"My dad's name is Daniel," Daniel said, ignoring her. "That's why I'm called Junior." He paused as if contemplating a serious political issue.

"And my mom's name is Pat," Alali said, pushing her chest forward. "She's a doctor, but she hasn't got her papers, so she can't work yet."

I smiled so she wouldn't be envious. Between them they would reveal all their family secrets.

Daniel shook his head. "My mom really wants her papers, because my dad is controlling."

"Come on," Mrs. Darego says. "Out of the tub, both of you, or someone is going to get smacked today." She claps her hands as she leaves the bathroom. She never hits her children. She shouts at them, especially if they are reluctant to get out of the tub. "I'm not playing," she warns from the corridor.

She is recovering from her call the night before. On a day like this, she has little patience for nonsense.

"You heard your mother," I say. "You want trouble?"

Alali plants a big foam ball on Daniel Junior's head.

"I'm telling," he whines.

"So?" Alali retorts.

Daniel crosses his arms and turns his back on her. His bottom cheeks are clenched. In school they think he has Attention Deficit Disorder. He won't listen; they want to medicate him. His mother says the teacher who suggested this must be on drugs herself. Cheap ones. Alali continues to gather foam with her bloated hands.

In my hometown we had rainbow-colored water. It tasted of the oil that leaked into our well. Bathing water we fetched from a creek. This smelled of dead crayfish. Our rivers were also dead. When rain fell, it rusted rooftops, shriveled plants. People who drank rainwater swore that it burned permanent holes in their stomachs. Our roads had potholes as big as cauldrons because of the rain. Only in the villages on the outskirts of town did we have one smooth road. The road ran straight from a flow station to Summit Oil's terminal. The villages had perpetual daylight once the gas flaring started. The flare was where cassava farms used to be. Summit Oil bulldozed those farms and ran pipelines through them. The land was now sinking. The gas flare was as tall as a giant orange torch in the sky, as loud as a hundred incinerators. It sprayed soot over coconut trees. From the center of town we could smell burning mixed with petrol. People complained that their throats were as dry as if they swallowed swamp mahogany bark. Elders feared the gas flare was like hellfire. Children wanted to play. Sometimes they played near the flare. Their mothers cuffed their ears if ever they caught them. We'd all heard the story of one little rascal nicknamed Boy-Boy. Boy-Boy wore glasses that belonged to his dead grandfather. He was always with his homemade catapult trying to kill birds. He burned in a gas-flare fire. His family held a funeral for him. They had nothing but his ashes to bury. They buried them in a whitewashed wooden casket.

I help the children out of the tub after the bathwater runs out. Their bodies are warm and slippery. I throw towels over their heads to make them laugh.

"Oh, Auntie Eve," Alali says, hugging me. "I'm so glad you're staying. If you left, I would just die."

She smells of raspberry bath wash. She hugs me too tight.

"My dear, don't curse yourself," I say into her ear.

She knows her mother is angry with her father again.

During the months I was out of work, I stopped at Summit Oil Clinic to see my friend Angelina. She too was a nurse, and she got her job because her aunt was the midwife there. I'd pass the line of patients sitting on benches in the admissions ward. There were the usual malaria cases and children with stomachs bloated from *kwashiorkor*. There were also patients with strange growths, chronic respiratory illnesses, terminal diarrhea, weeping sores, inexplicable bleeding. We had too many miscarriages in our town, stillbirths, babies dying in utero, women dying in labor. People blamed the gas flare. They came to the clinic and sat for hours. The nurses turned them away. There were not enough beds, so patients slept on raffia mats on the floor, even women in labor. New nurses were quick to develop lazy walks. If a patient called out for help, they snapped, "What?!"

One old man who was a regular, he came by canoe from a hamlet on the other side of our main creek. He lived in a bamboo hut near mangroves. In his youth he was a member of the Ekine Society, those masqueraders who paid tribute to Ekineba. Folklore said Ekineba was this beautiful Kalabari woman who was kidnapped by water spirits, and she returned to the land to teach the masquerade dance. People said this man was over a hundred years old, and his body was refusing to die. Some claimed his soul was possessed. He would sit on the admissions bench cursing and prophesying disasters. The land was our mother, he said, and we would suffer for allowing foreigners to violate her. One afternoon, I went to the clinic, and he was there again, naked from the waist up. His chest hairs were white, and his skin clung to his ribs.

"Nurse," he said, to Angie, "I'm choking here, can't you see? There is something terrible in the air. Our seasons are not as they were. Our ancestors are spiting us." He held his hands towards us. "Deliver me."

Angie whispered that we should get as far away from him as possible.

He stood up. "You turn your backs on me? Oil is a curse on the land, you hear? You will suffer for your complacency. Your fathers will cut off their penises to feed their sons. Disease will consume your mothers. Daughters will suckle their young with blood. Nurses! Prostitutes in white!" He spat with such force he staggered.

Angie and I rushed to his aid. We sat him on the bench.

"He's senile," Angie said with a smile. "Honestly, Eve, we all pray that he will die."

The man's bones were as strong as iron.

"For goodness' sake, be quiet," Mrs. Darego says for the second time during our drive. Daniel and Alali are asking if we are there yet.

"We'll be there soon," I say. "Alali, don't put your hand out of the window."

It is cool enough for us to drive with the windows down and the sunroof open. The jeep is as big as a hut, with three rows of leather seats and a DVD player. I've heard people on television complain that vehicles like these use up too much fuel. I wonder why they are built so large, considering Americans have such small families; why they are so sturdy when the streets I see are flat and wide. The critics on television say that people buy them for status. They have no idea what status is. Nigerians, given a chance, would drive jeeps as huge as mansions for show. But at least we have plenty of children; at least we have appalling roads.

Unfortunately, no one asks my opinion. Instead, I end up arguing with television pundits, after I get tired of the soap operas and their never-ending dilemmas; the talk shows with cheating lovers, cross-dressers and women who are miserable because they can't stick to diets; reality shows; infomercials. Twenty-four hours of programs to entice me into one studio-produced existence or another. It is a struggle not to click on the television in the basement and be transported into a Hollywood movie. Fuel consumption is not the only indulgence in America, and at least the supply of fuel is limited.

The barbecue we're going to is for a community of Nigerians who live in New Jersey, mostly doctors and their families. Mrs. Darego is in a yellow sundress. She wishes her stomach were flatter. She had both children by C-section. Today, they are in their usual coordinated Old Navy and Gap clothes. We stop at a traffic light. This part of New Jersey is all mountains and expressways. She taps the steering wheel.

"Eve," she says, "you forgot to give me your passport again."

"Sorry." But I didn't forget.

Her nails are clipped for work. She is not wearing her wedding band.

"No, no," she says, "don't worry. I just need to send off your renewal by tomorrow, understand? Immigration is tough these days. Me, myself, when I came, I made the mistake of applying on my husband's visa. Seven years, and I'm yet to see a green card. Everything is delayed since September 11."

She has just started a pediatric residency program and needs me to be at home with her children. She is hoping to have my visa extended. I can't tell her I am looking for a green-card sponsor now. I am ready to work as a nurse. What will she say to that after flying me over to America?

"I'll give it to you today," I say. Here in the land of free speech, I've learned to keep my mouth shut.

"You too talk, Eve," Mama used to warn me. "You no see your friend Angelina how she quiet so? If Val marry you, make you no carry dat mouth go 'im house, oh!"

My nickname at home was Tower of Babel because my legs grew long before my torso. I was never mouthy; I just wasn't fluent in silence like most women I knew. I envied them, the way they expressed their opinions and emotions clearly, without opening their mouths. Elderly women especially, they terrified me with their shrugs and side glances. I thought they were dishonest. Why couldn't they just say exactly what they were thinking? I felt compelled to explain myself with words. I couldn't trust people to understand me otherwise.

I never told Mama the source of my vexation, though, which was Val. He was my boyfriend from secondary school, tall and fine, except for his pointy ears, and brilliant. The whole town celebrated when Val was accepted at the University of Port Harcourt. He never returned to town after his graduation. He stayed in Port Harcourt and got a job with Summit Oil as a public relations clerk. He moved into his uncle's servants' quarters to save on rent money, kept telling me about the man's Spanish-style villa, the man's Benz, the man's golf-club membership, yacht and trips to Europe. What was my concern? Was the man willing to hire me as his private nurse? I attended nursing school in Port Harcourt or PH, as people called it, or Garden City. Val was my shadow there. We rocked to the days of jazz funk. We disvirgined each other. I cried when I couldn't find a job and had to return to our boring town. All we had was a bungalow ambitiously called the Grand Hotel, one main road called Mission Way, a marketplace, Summit Oil Clinic, and one of the oldest Catholic churches in our country. Val never asked me to visit him after I left Port Harcourt, much less talk of marriage. We argued whenever he bothered to come to town to see me. Yes, I provoked him. Sometimes I wondered why he chose me and not Angelina. They were friends from church. Angelina was the sort of person who smiled at everyone, and everyone loved her for her dimples. She would have made him a perfect wife: the quiet, graceful sort of woman who was praised for the peace she brought into a man's home. The sort of woman my mouth would not allow me to be.

The barbecue is in a park. People have set up picnics in separate territories the way folk in America socialize within their communities. We find our group under a tree.

Nigerians don't appreciate the sun beating down on them. Next to us is an African-American family all wearing the same yellow T-shirts saying, "Knight Family Reunion." There is also a Hispanic family, and their music sounds like the music we call highlife at home. I seesaw my shoulders to the rhythm of salsa and observe our small gathering. We are homogenized in our T-shirts, baseball caps and sneakers. What gives us away as Nigerians is the way we barbecue our hotdogs and hamburgers. Women are manning the grill. Nigerian men have their limits to being Americanized. Some have not quite mastered their wannas, gonnas, shouldas. Everyone laughs loudly and talks as if they haven't been out in years. They are lonely people, I think.

In the Daregos' house, friends rarely drop by. When they do, they telephone first. Dr. Darego once said that the fewer guests he has, the better anyway: Nigerians gossip too much and wish bad on others. He complains about Americans the same way, saying how rude they are, how arrogant and prejudiced. I've heard him call the Indian and Filipino doctors he works with a bunch of ass-kissers. My father would have said to him, "Young man! Check your own stinky armpits before you walk into a room full of people and begin to complain about foul odors!"

Dr. Darego works all week and moonlights in his spare time to pay for his dream home. He is too tired for his family. He has no intention of returning to Nigeria. The place is a jungle, he says. But does he like America, the land and people? He loves his children, and they are American. He loves his dream home in America, but America the place is nothing more than a giant mall and workplace to him.

Will living here be different for me? Sometimes a shop assistant follows me in a store, and I want to turn and scream, "If not for the havoc your people have wreaked in my country, would I be here taking shit from you?!" Then, on a day like this, I think of the guerrilla politicos in my country, petroleum hawkers, who treat the land and people of the Niger Delta like waste matter. I look around the park, see trees I can't name, clear skies, smell the clean air in New Jersey that is supposedly polluted, and think, "Well, Gawd bless America."

Alali is teaching Daniel Junior the pledge. "I pledge allegiance," she says, with her hand over her heart. "To the flag. Of the United States of America. And to the republic for which it stands. One nation under God, indivisible—"

"I'm bored," Daniel says and runs off.

He has two boys his age to play with. Alali watches her new friend who looks like a giant Bratz doll. Such a pout on this new friend, and she seems to know all the hip-hop dances. She dips, rolls her head and pumps her skinny arms. Her jeans are riding low, her navel is exposed, and her fingernails are sparkly blue. I know Alali will demand a bottle of that as soon as we get home: "Aw, I wanna have nail polish!" Her mother will certainly say no. Mrs. Darego believes girls should not be little women.

There was a girl who lived on my street; her name was Amen. Amen was Teacher's daughter. She was sixteen and in secondary school. She bought Coca-Cola from Mama and looked like a bottle of it: small, shapely, slim and dark. Amen liked to style her friends' hair. She wanted to be a hairdresser. Her father was against that. He asked me to encourage her to apply to nursing school. Amen said, "But look at you, Eve. Since you graduated, you have no job."

I used to watch her whenever she passed our house. She wore jeans and funky fake imported T-shirts: Calvin Klein, Fruit of the Loom. She giggled and showed off her pretty dark gums. Towards the end of her school year, I noticed how Amen started walking on her own. She relaxed her hair and started wearing it in a tight ponytail. She shaved her eyebrows and painted her nails bright pink.

"Something is going on with Amen," Mama said after she'd sold her a bottle of Coca-Cola. "She's just growing up," I kept saying. I thought Mama was being critical like other women in town. "No," she insisted. "Something is going on with Amen, I tell you. She is looking too advanced." We argued over this. I told Mama she should leave the girl alone. Did she expect her to be sweet sixteen forever?

Then one day I passed Amen on our street. She turned her face away from me and started to cross over to the other side. "Amen, you can't greet somebody?" I asked, jokingly. Perhaps she was expecting another lecture from me about nursing school. She eyed me. "You yourself, can't you greet somebody?" I stood there with my mouth open as Amen strutted off.

Mama was the one who told me. Amen ran away from home and her father thought that she'd been kidnapped or murdered. He rushed to the police headquarters in Port Harcourt to file a missing person's report. There, he learned that Amen was one of the girls arrested by the Naval Police off Bonny Island, where the Liquefied Natural Gas project was based. Amen was now a resident of Better Life Brothel in Port Harcourt. Amen's father came back to town without her.

Teacher was a skinny man and he stood with his hands behind his back. His shoes had holes, and yet people called him a dignified scholar because he spoke big English. Whenever someone asked, "Teacher, where is Amen?" he answered, "Amen? Amen expired. Most unfortunate. Ah, yes, it was unanticipated. A great loss to our family. A tragedy of calamitous proportions."

Amen should have gone to nursing school. She ended up hanging around the port, edging local customers, looking like smoked fish. Prostitutes with college educations had better chances of finding expatriate customers who would keep them.

Mrs. Darego has her sunshades on. I can tell her eyes are wandering.

"You're upset about something," I say.

"Me?" she says. "I'm just thinking. Why?"

"You're not mixing much."

She raises her brows. "Me? I came because of the children. They need to play. I want them to meet other Nigerians. In this country it's so easy to forget your identity."

I've been to birthday parties with both children at places like McDonald's, KidZone and Chuck E. Cheese's, places with contraptions to distract them. They have soccer practices, ballet lessons, and karate lessons after school. Their mother says they have no time to play.

I dust sand from my sandals. "Everyone is so excited to be here."

She shrugs. "These people, they are my husband's friends, not mine. Most of them I would never have met in Nigeria."

She is someone I would never have met in Nigeria, a diplomat's daughter. Back home, for the amount she's paying me, she would have a housegirl for each child, a cook, a washerman for her laundry, a driver to take her to work. Here, she worries about who will look after her children while she's in a hospital taking care of other people's children.

Mrs. Darego is a "butter-eater." I know this because she eyes her husband when he crunches on chicken bones. He grinds them to the marrow, flexes his jaws, spits the pulp on his plate. She watches him as if she would like to punch him in the mouth. Dr. Darego won't clear the table, load the dishwasher, cook, or bathe his children. One day she joked that he should add these initials to his medical qualifications: B.U.S.H.M.A.N.

"Do you have picnics for October 1st?" I ask.

"It's too cold in the fall," she says.

October 1st is our country's Independence Day. It is hard

to imagine America as a former British colony. That is, a country like mine, broken down and forever recovering from military coups.

She takes off her sunshades. "Eve, I want to tell you something personal. Please, and I don't want you to tell anyone else."

Everyone found out what happened between Val and me; that Val had a woman in the city, a woman who was pregnant by him, a woman who was older than him. At first he claimed it was a vicious rumor spread by those who resented his success. I forced him to confess, slapped his head as if he were my son. "Tell me the truth! Tell me the truth!" Then I cursed him and cursed the woman. I stopped short of cursing their child. Val lowered his head until I finished shouting. He was probably thinking, someone please get this lunatic away from me.

I could not leave home for a while after we broke up. Whenever I did, people stopped me to give advice. "Go there and fight her, Eve." "Sit on his doorstep and refuse to leave." Cook him a good meal, one old woman said. There were people who blamed me for breaking up with Val. He was intelligent, so his head had to have been turned by this other woman. And I, to let a man like him go, a man with a job in an oil company, something had to be wrong with me.

When I heard about the interview for the nanny job, I saw it as a way to escape our scandal. I went to the man who was hiring. He was Dr. Darego's grand-uncle, the head of their family who lived in our town, but he had no money, and no one really respected him. He sat in his cement compound, on a varnished cane chair, cooled his face with a raffia fan. Behind him was his bungalow with a rusty corrugated-iron roof. The man was almost blind. He kept calling me Helen. "Are you spoken for, Helen?" "Do you have a clean reputation, Helen?" He said he chose me because I didn't look like someone who would run wild in America and chase after men. I told him I was very grateful for his commendation. Some of my colleagues said it was below my qualifications to apply for such a job, a mere housegirl. I knew they were jealous. Angie hugged me, and then she burst out crying in the clinic. She said she could never leave her mother.

Angie was her mother's only child. The rest died as babies. Her father was killed in a motor accident on Mission Way. Her mother was always in church saying novenas. People said she was paying for the sins of her fathers.

I couldn't imagine such a burdensome love between mother and daughter. I was Mama's last born, her only daughter. Mama said, "Go. You're unhappy living here anyway. Everyone knows how Val disgraced you, and they won't employ you at Summit Oil Clinic. Nanny is not what we sent you to school to study, but it's not as if you're going to Heaven and you can't come back."

There was a time I thought going to America was as fantastic as going to Heaven. When I was a child and I used to sing that song, "Come and see American wonder. Come and see American wonder." When I fell in love with Michael Jackson. I was twelve and walking around town saying I was going to be Mrs. Michael Jackson, and Mama would tell people, "Leave her alone. The Jackson family is coming to ask for her hand soon." I had my white church glove, I had a poster of Michael with his glittery glove. I wrote to Neverland. The post office clerks used to laugh at me. I thought they were all mistaken. But accepting the job was a question of common sense. Dr. Darego offered me ten times the salary I would earn working as a nurse. Nothing else mattered, not missing my family, or standing in line at the American embassy in Lagos, being ordered to step forward, step back, answer only when I was spoken to. Certainly not being held up by a gap-toothed Nigeria airport official who was looking for a bribe: "Where you get dis? Dis passport is fake!" Least of all being inspected and questioned at Immigration and Customs at Newark Airport. "How long are you staying?" "May I check your baggage, ma'am?"

"I'm moving into hospital accommodation," Mrs. Darego says. "Yes. I've been thinking about it for a while. My commute is long. I'm in the hospital most of the time. Would you mind being alone in the house with the children and their father?"

I say I'm not sure. Her voice is insistent.

"It will only be for the next six months. I have to. I mean, you're not going to be with us forever. I supported my husband when he was in residency. I stayed with the children, but now I'm Dr. Darego, too. He has to learn how to support me, see?"

I saw.

"Do you think you can manage?"

"I'll try."

She taps my shoulder. "What you've done for my family, I cannot tell you. The children are so fond of you. It puts my mind at ease when I'm at work."

Please, I want to say. Don't sweet-talk me today.

One evening, I took a shower after the children went to bed. Mrs. Darego was on call and Dr. Darego was out. I was sitting on the sofa in the basement with nothing but a towel wrapped around my body. I was rubbing Vaseline on my elbows and knees. The kitchen door opened, and I heard footsteps on the stairs to the basement. I stood up and held my towel tight. It was Dr. Darego. He had shoulders like a football player, and his head was shaved. At first I was angry he didn't seem embarrassed. Bastard, I thought, in fluent silence, and my expression must have given me away. He walked down the stairs without saying a word, searched behind the sofa bed and found a magazine. He rolled the magazine up like a baton and walked back up the stairs. As if I wasn't there. He lost favor with me after that, even though he never did it again.

"You yourself," Mrs. Darego says. "You seem quiet today."

"My mind is at home."

"The demonstrations?"

"Yes."

"Have you heard from your people?"

"No."

She pats my back. "Don't worry. At least women are involved this time. The world is focused on their cause. No one can harm them with this much media attention."

"I hope not."

"Definitely not," she says. "And it is good that women are involved this time. Women, we are always the first affected and the last heard."

Who knew the women's union would start with Madam Queen? Madam Queen, the drunk who talked too much. I used to pass her house on my way home from school. She was one of those we called half-castes. Madam Queen's mother was Kalabari and Italian. Madam Queen herself, her father was German. She was the color of beach sand and over six feet tall. She couldn't find shoes to fit, so she wore men's sneakers. Divorced and no children, and she drank like a man. People said that had to come from her foreign blood. I was always a little scared of her. She had bluish eyes, black hair down her back. In the afternoons, she sat on her veranda with her wrapper pulled up to her knees. Her varicose veins were thick. She couldn't bear the heat. Sometimes a few women gathered in her compound like disciples.

Madam Queen told folklore, and I found such stories boring, so I never really stopped to listen. The first time I did, I was coming back from school and heard her booming voice: "Hurrah! Congratulations! We celebrate when someone we know gets a job at Summit Oil Clinic. We hope they will bring us into the fold. We forget about what the company is doing to our land. Kalabari people, we are not like that. We come together. We don't allow foreigners to rule us by dividing us, or we are no better than those who sold their own for bounty when the Niger Delta was the Slave Coast…"

I thought she had to be drunk to talk like that. I stayed to hear more.

"The oil companies," she said, "they drill our fathers' farms and they don't give we, their children, jobs. We eat okra, cassava, grown in other parts of the country. We use their yam, plantain and palm oil to cook our *onunu*. There are no fish in our rivers, no bushrats left in our forest. We don't use natural gas in our homes and yet we have gas flares in our backyards. We can't find kerosene to buy and we have pipelines running through our land. Some of us don't have electricity. Some of us don't even have candles to burn. Are you listening, women?

"Young men are kidnapping expatriate employees and demanding ransoms. They are locked up. We call them thugs. Young girls are turning to prostitution to service expatriate employees. They are locked up, too. We shun them. We say they bring AIDS. Meanwhile, the oil companies spill oil on our land, leak oil into our rivers. They won't clean up their mess. All they do is pay small fines, if they pay at all. Our community leaders write petition letters to their directors and they don't give us the courtesy of replying. When they do, they call us liars. We protest because they continue to breach regulations and they call security forces to handle us. Women, listen to me. I'm telling you this, as we speak we are dying. We are dying of our air, we are dying of our water. We are dying from oil. We are not benefiting from it. Must we continue to stand by in silence and wait for men to fight our battles?"

I went home feeling like I'd fallen under her spell. Superstitious people said Madam Queen had such a sweet mouth that she could hypnotize her listeners. At home I saw Mama and Papa sitting under the framed poster of Jesus. Jesus was nailed to a wooden cross and his eyes were raised heavenward. Around the frame Mama had stuck photos of my brothers, Solomon, Benjamin and Ezekiel, to protect them because they'd left home. Papa was in his cane chair, taking a pinch from his snuffbox. Mama was sitting on the chair next to his. She wore her hair in a neat plait. She thought untidy hair was a sign of inner turmoil.

"I listened to Madam Queen today," I said.

Mama frowned. "Queen?"

"Yes," I said. "She is speaking against the oil companies."

"That old drunk?" Mama said.

Papa raised his pinch of snuff. "Yes, indeed, Queen does that. She speaks the truth about the foreigners on our land.

She has their blood and she detests them. She is fearless, that woman." He sniffed and sneezed. "Just like a man."

Mama pouted. "That's why she can't keep a man. Please, Eve, don't listen to Madam Queen again. She is trying to get people killed. Remember what happened to the Ogoni people?"

Papa and his pronouncements. My brothers laughed at him behind his back. He was short, with a nervous twitch from the Civil War where he narrowly escaped a detonating landmine, but no one dared challenge him.

Mama, whose idea of a major fight with Papa was to make his *onunu* extra lumpy, so that he might ask, "Ah? My wife, your *onunu* is not smooth today. What have I done to deserve this?"

They actually argued that day. Papa gave his usual proverb about natives sleeping with one eye open. Mama said she would rather trust a foreigner than an Igbo, knowing full well Papa's mother was Igbo.

"My good customer Mr. Obrigado," she said. "He's never done any wrong to me. He's perfectly charming."

She didn't know his real name. He was a journalist with the biggest nose I'd ever seen on a white man. Sometimes he said "obrigado."

"Foreigners," Papa muttered. "They can't keep their hands off our women."

"Obrigado doesn't stray," Mama said.

"He strays to our town center," Papa said. "He's lucky no one hijacks him. He should speak to the Americans at Summit Oil and find out why they keep away from us."

"Obrigado comes here to take photographs," Mama said.

"What for?" Papa asked. "How would he like it if a group of us went to his country to take photographs?"

"Obrigado thinks it's unfair that our government attacks us," Mama said. "He thinks our government should do more to protect our land."

"Obrigado should clear off our land!" Papa shouted. "Is he deaf and blind?! Isn't it the oil companies who arm our government? Now, every useless man in uniform has the gall to attack us! I must not see that foolish fellow in your shop again!"

Yes, I heard about the Ogoni people, how they protested against Shell. Security forces came and shot at them, burned down their homes, beat up women and children. Ken Saro-Wiwa and others who led the movement were tried by a secret military tribunal and hanged in Port Harcourt. I was in nursing school when General Sani Abacha detained oil and gas union officials after the strikes. In Port Harcourt people queued for days to fill their car tanks. Students from Val's university marched to the governor's house and threw petrol bombs through his windows. Kill-and-Go police came and opened fire on them. Eight were struck, five were killed. One had a bullet through his forehead. The governor shut down the university and our nursing school for public safety. Val and I returned to town. No kerosene to buy, was all we heard. Women from the gas-flare village tapped a burst pipeline one morning. There was an explosion. The women, all seventy-three of them, perished. The villagers refused to accept the mass grave Summit Oil offered. They blocked access to the flow station in protest. Summit Oil called in soldiers. The soldiers threw tear gas at the protesters, butted their heads with rifles, kicked a pregnant woman in her belly until she miscarried, beat up one old man until he was comatose. The government said the reports were grossly exaggerated, the dead people were illegal scavengers and lawless rioters, ordered a dusk-to-dawn curfew. I'd never demonstrated in my life. Why would I?

"We should go home soon," Mrs. Darego says.

It is getting cloudy. The sun has disappeared and there is a cool breeze. I call out to the children, "Alali! Daniel! Time to go!"

"Aw, man," Alali says and stamps her foot.

"I don't wanna go," Daniel whines.

They never want to. The word "go" sounds as terrible as "die" to them.

"Not now," I say. "Soon."

A white man and his son are flying their multicolored kite. The son laughs and twirls.

We arrive home early in the evening. Alali and Junior have to stop their Harry Potter DVD, and as we drive into the garage, they complain that they are bored.

"I work all night," their mother says, yanking her car key out. "I go to a... a picnic on my day off because of you. You can't even say thank you, and now you're bored because you can't see the end of Harry Potter? Get out of my car. Get. Out."

Her voice is too low to trust that she won't smack them. I make them apologize. They scamper. Their pupils are dilated from a DVD overdose.

Dr. Darego opens the door. "Hey," he says. "What's going on here?"

Alali jumps on him. "Daddy! We went to a park! You should have come!"

"Hi, Dad," Daniel says and hugs his knees.

Mrs. Darego and I walk past carrying the empty cooler

and tray. She is still not speaking to her husband. Me, I avoid looking at him; I don't want trouble. We reach her kitchen and she says, "Eve, please don't forget your passport."

We hear Dr. Darego laughing with the children. Sometimes I believe every child needs two mothers: one who gives birth, and another who can easily forgive fickleness.

The sliding doors in the basement are shut. I search my suitcase for my passport and find Angie's letter first. I've read it many times before.

> Dearest Eve,
>
> I hope this finds you in good spirits. If so, splendid. We miss you terribly here. Your parents send their greetings. My mother sends her greetings. We are all fine, but unfortunately I don't have good news for you. You won't believe it, Val was sacked from his job shortly after you left. That woman he thought was carrying his baby was well-known for target-ing men at Summit Oil and feeding them the same story about being pregnant. She was going with Val's direct boss, a married man. The man found out about Val and wrote him such a bad appraisal that Summit Oil sacked Val. He came back to town.
>
> He was bitter, Eve. He talked about revenge. He said Summit Oil's terminal is like Hollywood. They have a clinic, cafeteria, video games, watch television from overseas. He said that not one person on the senior staff in Summit Oil head-quarters is from the Niger Delta and from day one

he was treated as an outsider. Now, he's missing.
The police have charged him as an accessory in a
kidnap case involving an expatriate employee.
They arrested him and no one knows where he is.
We are all waiting for news. I hope you've forgiven
him. He made a mistake and he's paid a huge price.

I go to meetings at Madam Queen's house
regularly now. I've even recruited my mother
because of what happened to Val. Madam Queen
says we will get him released. She may drink but
the woman is a force. She says we should not be
afraid. She is rallying as many of us as she can to
join other women of the Delta to demonstrate at
Summit Oil's terminal. We will block their airstrip,
jetty, helicopter pad and storage depot. We will
demand that they give us electricity, clean water,
better roads, schools, clinics, jobs. Pregnant women,
too, and mothers with babies on their backs. She
said Summit Oil may send the security forces to
stop us, but we will not be stopped. We will carry
nothing but palm leaves in our hands and respond
to their threats with songs.

Eve, you can't come back. There is nothing
here for you. You must take your nursing exams
while you're there. I hear they need nurses over
there in America. You can always come home to
visit. A nurse here told me of her friend called
Charity. Call Charity. Her number is...

Charity lived in the Mississippi Delta. I called her the day
I received Angie's letter. "Who sent you to me?" she demanded.

She was angry that I had her telephone number. Then she said parts of the Mississippi Delta were as bad as the Niger Delta, but there was a strong possibility of finding work there and getting a sponsor. She advised that I kept my plans secret from Mrs. Darego meanwhile. "Who knows? You know how women can be. She might frustrate your career to further hers. Study in private, take the exams. Once you find work, take off without giving her notice."

I said I couldn't do that.

"Why not?" she asked. "Did she feel sorry for you when her husband brought you here to work illegally? Are they paying you minimum wage? Are they declaring your wages in their taxes? Do you realize you can have them jailed for breaking federal laws and sue them?"

I told her that wasn't my intention, to ruin the Daregos' lives, only to find a legitimate way of staying in America and earn enough to continue sending money home.

She said, "Ah, well, you will soon learn how things work over here. We Africans, we only get attention when we need help, when we have no hope, and oh yes, most especially when we are naked."

"Eve?" Mrs. Darego calls from upstairs.

"One moment," I say, reaching for my passport.

"Come here! Please! Now!"

I drop my passport. She is never rude or impatient with me. I find her standing by the computer desk in the family room, under the mud-cloth painting of two gazelles. She hands me a photograph printed from the internet.

"Aren't these the demonstrators from your hometown?"

The photograph is clear, although greenish. I recognize Madam Queen, Angelina's mother, Angelina with her big dimples, and—"Mama!" I shout. Her beautiful, troublesome face. What is she doing there?

"Your mother is one of them?" Mrs. Darego asks.

I nod. Amen's mother is there, Val's mother and his older sister, Sokari, who counseled me. Never lose hope in men, she said.

Mrs. Darego hugs me. "They've brought Summit Oil's operations to a standstill! Can you imagine? Can you? The company is negotiating with them. See?"

The women are dressed in traditional attire: lace blouses, plaid wrappers and head ties. They are waving palm leaves. Mrs. Darego laughs. Her body feels warm. Why am I afraid? I think. We hold each other for a while, and then I pull back.

"I have something to tell you, but you may not want to hear it."

"Eve," she says. "What can be worse than me abandoning my children to you?"

GREEN

This is going to be really boring. I forgot my book in the car. We are in the immigration office in New Orleans. The television is on CNN not Disney. A news woman is talking about the elections again. I don't vote. I'm only nine.

We sit in plastic purple chairs joined together, Mom and me. Dad stands in line for one of the booths. The booth curtains are purple too. They are open like a puppet show is about to begin, but real people sit behind the glass windows, stamping and checking. I hope my parents get their green cards. I really hope we can drive back to Mississippi in time for my soccer game.

Booth A is for information and questions. Booth B is for applications. Booth C is for replacement cards. D is for forms and E is for adjudications. I know these words because I read, especially when I'm bored. What I don't understand is why do they explain the rules in different languages here?

No Smoking is *No Fumar.*

No Drinking is *Khong Duoc Uong.*

No Eating is *No Comer* and *Khong Duoc An.*

I ask Mom, "What language is that?"

"Spanish," she says. She is not wearing her glasses so she can't see far. She is holding the yellow envelope for their passports.

I should have guessed Spanish. I take lessons in our after-school program. Mr. Gonzalez won't let us leave until we get our words right. He is always telling us to shut our mouths or else. Then you should see him at Mass on Thursdays, eating the body of Christ and drinking the blood of Christ.

There are people here who look like Mr. Gonzalez. Indian-looking people too, like my friend Areeba who left our school because Catholic religion was confusing her. There are people who look Chinese to me, but whenever I say this, Mom says, "They're not all Chinese!" Sometimes she gets on my last nerve. I'm just a kid. There is one family who looks African like us, but Mom says they must be Haitian because a man next to them keeps speaking French to their son.

A pretty woman comes out of a wooden door. "Mr. Murphy?" she says. "Enrique Morales?" The third name she says sounds like Hung Who Win?

Mr. Murphy is the French-speaking man. "*À bientôt*," he says, when he gets up. No one in the Haitian family answers him. Maybe they are too tired to be polite.

I tell Mom, "Bet that's where the green cards are hidden. Behind that wooden door."

"Like lost treasure," she says.

"Why green?" I ask.

"I don't know."

"Maybe because green is for go?"

"Maybe."

"Remember when you ran a red light, Mom?"

"When did I ever run a red light?"

She did. She ran one and said it was too late to stop. I was small and I yelled, "Oo, that's begainst the law."

"Can I please go and get my book from the car?" I ask. "Please?"

"No," she says. "Absolutely not. What if they go and call us?"

Green is for vegetables. I will never eat mine. Green is for Northeast soccer field, especially when it rains. Green is for envy. My best friend Celeste is trying to make a move on my man, just because their names both start with C. His name is Chance. I told Mom my true feelings when she forced me to share. She said if two women are fighting over a man they've already lost. "What if your best friend makes a move on your man?" I asked. "*Kai*," she said and bit her finger. "I blame that Britney Spears."

Dad hands over their passports to an old woman with orangey lipstick in the booth. When he comes back, he sits next to me.

"How long will it take?" I ask.

"You never know," he says.

"What if it takes all day?"

"We'll wait."

"Aw, man."

"'Aw man,' what?"

"Nothing."

Last year, when Grandpa died, Dad couldn't go for the funeral in Africa. Mom said this was because they were out of status, waiting for their green cards. If Dad went to Africa, he wouldn't be able to come back to America. Dad cried. Mom said people didn't know the sacrifices we had to make. Then on the day of Grandpa's funeral, a white pigeon landed on our roof. She said that it was Grandpa coming to tell Dad his spirit was at peace, which made me scared, so I sneaked into their bed again, in the middle of the night, even though I really didn't believe that pigeon on the roof was my Grandpa.

"How I wish we can get back to Mississippi before six," I say.

"What's on at six?" Dad asks. "Some Disney rubbish?"

"Never mind," I say.

If I tell him, he'll think I'm selfish. I want to get back to

Mississippi in time for soccer. Already he is watching the elections on CNN.

Green is for my parents' passports. Green white green is the color of the flag of their country in Africa, Nigeria.

The pretty woman comes out of the door again. What she says sounds like Oloboga? Ologoboga?

"That's you," I say, pulling Dad's jacket. "Come on. Come on."

"Ah-ah, what's wrong with you?" he asks.

"Calm down," Mom says.

Sometimes my parents act like I'm bothering them all the time. I walk behind them. I don't even want to be in the same footsteps as them. The pretty woman says, "Hey sweetie."

"Stop sulking," Mom says.

"Are we getting your thumbprint today, sweetie?" the pretty woman asks me.

"No, she's the American in the family," Mom says and smiles.

On the other side of the door, I don't see any green cards, only a room with a table and a copier. The pretty woman does Dad's thumbprint, then Mom's, and then she writes our address in Mississippi to send their green cards. Mom won't stop thanking her.

"You have no idea. We waited so long. When will they come?"

The woman leads us to the door saying, "By regular post. Yes, you can travel as you like. Yes, yes, you're officially permanent residents."

I don't think she cares.

"Can we go now?" I ask, after she shuts the door.

The Haitian family is still sitting out there. The lines for the booths are longer. An Indian boy spreads his arms like plane wings and makes engine sounds with his lips. Brr! Brr!

We walk to the elevators.

"Mardi Gras parade," Dad says.

"Is there one this afternoon?" Mom asks.

"Shall we?" he says. "To celebrate?"

"Do you want to stay for a Mardi Gras parade?" Mom asks me.

Dad is dancing. Limbo. The yellow envelope with their passports is under his armpit. It's so embarrassing.

"Em," I say. "No."

Last year we came for Mardi Gras in New Orleans. The weather was sunny. We watched the Oshun Parade on Canal Street. I was trying to catch the beads people were throwing from the floats. I preferred the golds. My neck was weighed down. Mom kept yelling in my ear, "Oshun is African. People here don't know. She is the Yoruba goddess of love." Her breath smelled of the beignets we ate for breakfast. Dad was saying, "Don't just reach out like that. That's why you keep missing them. See, there is a technique to catching the beads." "What technique?" Mom asked, and Dad stepped in front to show us and a huge black bead smacked him in the face. Then we had to eat lunch. I said I wanted Chinese. They said they wanted Thai. Mom said it was all the same. "Chinese is not Thai!" I said, and Mom asked, "How come you know the difference when it comes to food?" We ate King Cake on our way back to Mississippi. It was creamy and glorious. I got the pink plastic baby Jesus inside and Dad said, "That's great," and Mom asked, "What if she choked on it?"

"It's too wet for Mardi Gras," I say.

Mom says, "The American has spoken. Back to Mississippi for us."

Green is for Mardi Gras beads. Green is for sugar sprinkles on King Cake and St. Patrick's Day in my school. Green is for green onions in Pad Thai. I had to pick them out last year.

There is a big lake in New Orleans called Pontchartrain with little bungalows on sticks. Whenever we drive over it, on a roller-coaster-type of bridge, I know we'll soon be in Mississippi. The car is warm. Dad is going on about the elections again. Gay marriages won't make a blind bit of difference, blah, blah. Mom is yawning. I know exactly what she will say very soon. She will call out the names of creeks and rivers we pass: Pearl, Wolf, Little Black, Bouie, Hobolochitto, Tallahala, Chunky. Then she will say, "It's terrible. Names are all we ever see of Native Americans."

My parents are predictable. Whenever I say this they laugh, but they are. My mom is for woman power. Everything in the world is her right. Even shopping is her right. In Mississippi, she argues in the mall whenever they ask her to show her ID. "That's discrimination," she'll say. "That is dis-cri-mi-nation." In JCPenney too. At home, she acts like she's the boss of me and Dad. "Eat up. What's this doing here? Can't you flush?" My dad says that's because she is a lecturer. He is a doctor. He gets mad with the President, and still he wants the President to win the elections, to teach the people who are against the President a lesson, because they are not getting it together, especially with Health. Every day, when he comes home from work, he yells at the television because of the elections. Whenever the President comes on, Mom says, "Ugh, turn him off. That man can't string two words together." Yet she tells me it's not right to be rude about people who can't speak English.

Last election, we voted in school. All my friends voted for

the President—before he became President—because the other guy killed babies. "Who said he kills babies?" Mom asked when I told her. "Your teacher? Your friend? What kind of parent says such a horrible thing to their kid? Well, they must have heard it from somewhere. Well, I think grown-ups should keep their political opinions to themselves." I told her I voted for the President. She said, "What? Why?" "Everyone else did," I said. She said, "Listen, I brought you up to stand your ground. To stick up for what you believe in." I said, "Oh, please." First of all, it was her ground not mine. Number B, I believe in fitting in.

"What's it like being African?" my friend Celeste asked when we used to be friends. "I don't know," I told her. I was protecting my parents. I didn't want Celeste to know the secret about Africans. Bones in meat are very important to them. They suck the bones, and it's so frustrating I could cry. My mom is the worst, especially when she eats okra stew. Afterwards she chews the bones to a mush and my dad laughs and asks, "What was that before your teeth got to it? Oxtail? Chicken wings? Red snapper? Crab?" I'm like, get some manners.

Being African was being frustrated again when my teacher showed pictures of clothes from all over the world. When she showed the pictures of Africans, that lame Daniel Dawson asked, "Why are they wearing those funny hats?" and everyone in class laughed.

Green is for the color I like most—yellow. Green is for a color I can't stand—blue. Green is a mixture of blue and yellow. Green is for confusion.

Dad is still talking about the elections. "Where are the weapons of mass destruction?" he asks.

Mom points out of the window and says, "Pearl River."

"You guys," I say. "I have a soccer game tonight."

They start yelling.

"For goodness' sake!"

"Again?"

"I don't remember that being in my calendar…"

"Why didn't you tell us before?"

"Soccer is meant for the summer. Only the British play in the spring…"

"Only Americans call football soccer."

My parents are so predictable.

"These people are crazy," Dad says. "The weather is not conducive."

Mom says, "What people? Don't put prejudice in my daughter's heart."

"I didn't mention any race," Dad says.

I'm like, what in the world right now? "You guys," I say. "If you're going to live in this country you might as well get used to soccer. It's part of life. I'm American. How do you expect me to feel?"

"You know," Dad says, "she's right."

I can't believe he fell for that.

"What time's the game anyway?" Mom asks.

"Six."

"Shit."

"Don't cuss, Mom."

"Sorry, baby, but I hated sports in Africa and I hate them here."

We've passed Chunky River. I've finished my book. I think we'll make it in time for my game. Mom asks, "Are you still mad with us?"

"A little," I say.

"Sorry. Today has been a bit…"

"I know. Are you happy about your green cards?"

"You have no idea."

"America will soon be number one in the world for soccer," Dad says. "You wait and see. Look at the way they organize themselves. From the grass-roots level. Everyone involved."

"Girls too," Mom says, and raises her thumb at me.

I'm not into all that. I know what girls like Celeste can do.

"Even if they don't have any talent," Dad says, rubbing his chin, "they have the money to import talent. Did you hear of that fourteen-year-old? Highest paid in the soccer leagues. Freddy Adu. His family came from Ghana. Immigration will save America."

"Because of soccer?" Mom asks.

Green is for the Comets' color. I hope we beat the Comets tonight. I really hope we beat them.

We made it to the game. Mom and Dad stayed, maybe because of guilt.

You should see me. My color is red. My number is 00. I'm ready to blast those Comets to kingdom come. I'm dribbling down the field. The lights are like stars. The grass is wet. I have to be careful because Mississippi mud can make you slip and slide. Everyone is cheering, "Come on! Get on it! Get on it!"

I kick that sucker. It zooms like a jet, lands in the corner of the goal post, neat as my bedroom when I get two dollars for cleaning up. Girls in my team are slapping my back: "Way to go! Good one!" My parents are cheering with other parents. This is it. Me, scoring. My mom looking like she loves soccer. My dad looking like he really loves the President. Three of us, looking like we really belong. It's better than finding the baby in King Cake, and my team hasn't even won yet.

YAHOO YAHOO

I once asked Popsi, "Why do people break laws?" We were in his bedroom that day. He had been an officer in the Nigerian police for most of his life and he was about to get ready for work. He was wearing what he called mufti: an ankara tunic and trousers. His uniform was laid out on his bed, starched and pressed. I was sitting by his beret and he was standing over his shoes, which I'd just polished.

"Um…" he began.

Popsi always took a while to answer the simplest of questions. I thought that was because he was a serious thinker, but Momsi said it was because he drank too much. He was a regular at the local palm-wine parlor, where he went to relax and perhaps get away from her. He was standing with his back towards me. His Y-fronts had a hole in the waistband, through which I could see the scar where a vaccination needle had snapped in his yansh when he was about my age.

"Because people are immoral by nature," he said, dropping his trousers.

Popsi spoke several Nigerian languages and acted as an interpreter for criminals who couldn't speak English, but he never simplified words when he spoke to me. I knew better than to ask him to explain himself and I went straight to Momsi, who was sewing in the sitting room. She worked there because she liked to have the television on to watch her talk-show hosts, like Funmi and Adesuwa, and her DVDs with Nollywood actors like Aki and Pawpaw, even though she couldn't hear a word of what was being said because of the noise her sewing machine made.

"What is immoral?" I asked her.

She sewed all Popsi's mufti and was wearing an up-and-down that matched his. Sometimes they went "and co." like that, to show their togetherness. Her head was bent and she pedaled fast as she eased a white net through her machine needle. One of her customers had ordered a wedding train and the wedding was the next day.

"You're bad," she mumbled. "Very, very bad..."

"Sorry," I said, retreating, in case she was about to backhand me. I also knew better than to interrupt her while she was working, especially towards a tight deadline. Momsi was so short the top of my head could touch her shoulders, but her reach was like an American basketball player's. She stopped pedaling.

"Sorry for what?" she asked.

I took a step forward. She was resting.

"Are people bad by nature?" I asked.

"Who told you dat?"

She spoke fluent pidgin, but at home she settled for a diluted version whenever she spoke to me. She could have been a primary-school teacher. She'd dropped out of training college to marry Popsi. She might have had to because she was pregnant, but she would never admit that. "I wasn't an illiterate when he met me," was all she ever said about their wedding.

I repeated the answer he had given me and she eyed the faded gold-brocade curtain that separated my parents' bedroom from the sitting room, and made a sound I can only describe as a "hm."

"Will you," she said, patting her machine, "CLEAR OUT OF HERE BEFORE I CHANGE MY MIND ABOUT YOU?!"

I ran out of the front door before her voice went into turbocharge. My head was too big for my body; so were my hands and feet. I was shoeless and almost broke my toe as I jumped down the stairs of our block. Our flat was on the first floor and I could hear her when I reached the ground level.

"See this *pikin*, oh! How many times have I told you not to disturb me, eh? I'm sitting here working myself to death! And you, Mr. Esprit de Corps, what have you been telling your son this time?"

Popsi was the only policeman in Lagos who was too proud to take a bribe, she said, and that was the cause of her suffering. She went on about how difficult he was to work with and how he thought he was superior to everyone else on the force. That was why no one would promote him. I could imagine her, bags under her eyes and cheeks trembling.

I escaped a serious thrashing that day, but I still remember the dream I had for the first time that night. In my dream, Momsi is sewing the wedding train. She is in our sitting room. There is quiet, for once, and the room smells of burned beans. The walls are brown from the soot of her kerosene stove. The wedding train keeps getting longer. It reaches out of our front door, slides down the staircase, crosses the compound of the barracks and passes through the side gates, creeps into Mammy Market, where police wives sell provisions, circles Falomo roundabout (Church of the Assumption Way) and rises over Lagos Lagoon, like the bridge. It reaches Victoria Island, edges through the traffic on the streets and ends up in Bar Beach, dips into the sea and rides over the Atlantic. I walk on it, trying to keep my balance, knowing I could fall at any moment and drown—I can't swim—but nothing like that happens until I reach the shore of a foreign land, where I wake up. The ending is always the same.

Sometimes, the easiest answer to give is a story. At least, that is how the prophets handle moral issues in the holy books. I am now old enough to know there is no point asking my parents about right or wrong, but when I was thirteen, I probably wouldn't have. We were still living in the police barracks; I was still stuck in that stunted body of mine while I was beginning to discover that my mind didn't have to be.

I was heavily into Genevieve Nnaji, the only Nollywood actress worth my while. She was the face of Lux. There were billboards of her everywhere in Lagos. At night, I fantasized about lambasting her. I was no innocent, but I was facing my studies. My hard work had got me through my Junior School Certificate exams a year earlier than I was supposed to sit them. It was my biggest accomplishment so far. English was my strong subject. I thought I might end up as a newspaper columnist, like Reuben Abati, and work for the *Guardian* or *This Day*.

I was in my fourth year of secondary school. My school was one of those in Lagos, state run and free ed, which meant zero education for people whose parents couldn't afford to buy books. I was not one of them. There were not enough desks or chairs, especially on the odd occasion when everyone bothered to show up to classes. Our classrooms had no doors and our windows no panes. The buildings were not painted. They looked like a series of piled-up cement blocks. But I'd had an excellent attendance record all year, even though my class teacher, Mr. Kolawole, was the worst in school. He was also my English teacher. He may have been in his mid-twenties, but he was already balding and what was left of his hair was in tight, greasy Jheri curls, so we called him Koilywoily.

I was one of his favorite students. He saw potential in me. I could have wept when he told me that. What that meant was that he could whip me whenever he felt like it, in the teachers' mess, on my yansh, and I had to say, "Thank you for disciplining me, sir," afterwards. He had this expression on his face, post-caning. I could never come up with the right word to describe it, but it was the same expression on our president's face when he held a press conference about the pollution problems in the Niger Delta and told the people there to go to hell.

I would ask myself, Why? Why?

Why couldn't I have just a mother that whacked me, or a teacher that whacked me? Why both? The worst part was that I couldn't even complain to Popsi about either one, no matter how severe the beatings, because he would ask, "What did you go and do?"

Koilywoily was perverted. I was convinced he was because of the way he squared his shoulders when he walked, and because of his grimy collars and skinny yansh. He drove a red, fairly used Daewoo and parked it by the teachers' mess so other teachers who couldn't afford cars would be jealous. The teachers' mess was so small that I couldn't imagine what would happen if all our teachers were present for once. Where would they sit? How would they mark papers? There was barely enough room for Koilywoily to cane me. On the morning I sneaked out of school, I was scared he was going to corner me in there again.

"Idowu Salami," he said in his nasal voice.

"Yes, sir," I answered.

He was taking the class register. Like every other Idowu, people called me ID.

"A salami is?" he asked.

"An Italian sausage, sir."

"Speak up!"

"An Italian sau…"

I had to go through the same routine with him, whenever the spirit caught him, and if I didn't give him the correct answer, he would cane me.

Koilywoily knew whom he could pick on. He knew I would not lie in wait for him somewhere outside the school premises and jack him up. There were boys in our school who would do that. Big boys with beards, who could tear him to pieces, like a roasted ram. They were area boys. They came to school for fun, with implements, to break into the office or teachers' mess. One was recently expelled for hoarding a spanner in his shorts. How anyone could even walk straight with a spanner in his shorts, I didn't know. But he did, and he would have unscrewed the tires of our principal's van and sold them, had he not been caught.

Girls, too. There were girls in school who would deck Koilywoily if he dared to touch them with a cane. They would slap his face so hard he would lose all sense of hearing, or sleep with him if he was interested. That was going on as well. It wasn't prevalent, but one or two were prepared to offer themselves in order to pass tests.

I had to piss after Koilywoily took the register that morning, very badly, so I ran all the way to an area behind a half-finished building. Boys who couldn't brave the toilets pissed there. Girls had no choice, but I'd caught one or two lifting their skirts. There was graffiti on the walls: *Hip-hop Rules*; *Bandele Woz Here*; *Man Must Shit*. I was unzipping my shorts when I saw Augustine sneaking in through a section of the chicken-wire fence that had been cut open by truants like him.

The bobo was strange. He was absent most days but, whenever he did show up, his uniform was starched and pressed, as if learning had become a festive occasion for him. His neatness reminded me of Popsi's and I was curious to know where he spent his time when he wasn't around. It was the final term of the year, exam term. Everyone had to buck up and study hard.

"Tss," he hissed.

It was hard to shrug off my junior-boy mentality. A year ago, I would have had to answer, "Yes, Senior Augustine."

"Yes," I said.

"I don't wanna bother you or anything," he said.

I had forgotten about his American accent. His eyebrows joined over the bridge of his nose, which was as narrow as an *oyinbo*'s. I noticed that only because I had inherited Popsi's nostrils, which were as wide as River Niger.

Augustine was in his final year and failing all his Senior Certificate subjects except for English. He scored as high as ninety percent on his English tests—or so he said. He had a reputation for being a liar who was no good at lying. So, if he said "Good morning," you could guarantee that it was nighttime and the world was coming to an end. He was a fabulizer. His mouth was sweet to listen to, though, and his ears were as thick as land snails. His classmates called him Yankee because he spoke with an American accent and everyone knew he could not have traveled an inch beyond the borders of Lagos, let alone overseas.

"Is it true you gorranainenglish?" he asked.

"What?"

He covered his lips with his forefinger as he spoke, as if to make sure his lies remained hidden. I remembered a gist about him: how he'd told his ex-girlfriend that he had connections at Virgin Nigeria and the Nicon Noga Hilton. He had promised to take her for a romantic getaway, for Valentine's Day. The nearest the girl got to the Hilton was when she discovered that his father had applied for a job there as a cook, and the closest connection he had to the airline was that he was a virgin. She told her friends.

"Did you get an A in the English JSC exam?"

"Yes. Yes, I did."

I raised my hand like one of those effico classmates of mine who couldn't wait to give correct answers.

"So your vocabulary is good, huh?"

His front teeth were chipped and looked like a W.

"Well…"

Only when I was fantasizing about having sex with chicks. In which case, my vocabulary just flowed: lambaste, discombobulate. What did he want? He was wasting my time. My math teacher was on sick leave again and he had set us exercises. I didn't plan to do them until I got home, but I needed to get back to first period. I had people to play cards with, gist to catch up on.

We were in a secluded area. There was an almond tree where students plucked fruit at break-time. A laborer was walking by with a bowl on his head. He was wearing shorts alone and his skin was covered in cement dust. "Do be quick," I wanted to say.

"I've got a proposal for you," he said. "Would you like to earn some dollars?"

"How?"

"You'll have to learn how to get on the internet. Have you ever heard of the internet?"

He pronounced the word "inner net" and was rubbing his hands together now. Who did he think I was? Some backward bobo?

"Of course."

"Have you ever used a computer?"

"Nope."

I'd never even touched one. Our school didn't have a computer, even though we had a subject on our syllabus called "Intro to Tech." The last class we'd had was on word processors and facsimiles.

"You can earn dollars working with computers," he said. "Would you like to?"

He reached into his pocket and pulled out two twenties. I hadn't swallowed since I'd owned up to getting an A in English, and now I had too much saliva in my mouth.

"Yesch," I said.

Then I remembered I had English with Koilywoily that afternoon. I didn't have to think twice. I asked him to wait, hurried back to class and told Dolamu, who sat next to me, that I'd vomited on the wall and now I had severe shivers.

"Since when?" he asked.

We called him Dolamumu, because he was one—a complete *mumu*. He was repeating his fourth year again. He couldn't spell. He transposed letters.

"Please," I said. "Just tell Koilywoily I'm sick."

I left the classroom hunched over. Only one teacher stopped me in the corridor, our biology teacher. She had taught us about the reproductive organs and this term we were on the digestive system.

"Salami, what's wrong with you?" she asked.

"I'm experiencing vomiting and diarrhea, ma."

"Eh? Go home! Don't spread it!"

She hurried away from me. She'd also taught us about hygiene. The woman was pregnant again. She had been pregnant ever since I'd known her, and she was skinny to top it all.

Had Augustine not shown me those dollars, I would have dismissed him as a jiver. I would have gone back to class to say yes, the gist about him being a liar at least was true. But he showed me the lalas, and here was the problem: my parents had never told me, "Don't do such-and-such when someone tells you to come and make money on the internet." I was sure they hadn't heard of the internet. To me, it was an abyss. They had warned me many times before to stay in school, though, and I was smart enough to realize that what Augustine had called me to do wasn't as clean as he appeared. On the other hand, he had shown me hard currency and, by the way my eyes bulged when I saw it, he might as well have unzipped his shorts and rolled out his jomo all the way to the ground.

We busted school that morning. We sneaked out through the chicken-wire fence and tried to blend in with the rest of the Obalende crowd, even though we were in uniform and carrying schoolbags. A few other truants like us loitered around the shacks displaying leather slippers, DVDs, broken televisions and secondhand suitcases. At the top of the street was an upside-down wheelbarrow next to a pyramid of mangoes. We bought meat pies from the corner shop; their sausage rolls were too flat. I finished off my meat pie before we reached St. Gregory's School.

As we approached Keffi, there were fewer hawkers around. They were selling manicure sets, glasses for drinking and for seeing. A sign on a wall read *We thank d Lord*, and another, *Prayer moves mountains*.

I asked Augustine why he had approached me.

"I've seen you around," he said, "heard about your skills. I need a partner. I'll explain later."

The bobo was somehow amusing, especially the way he covered his mouth.

"By the way," he said, "what are those beads on your wrist? Native insurance?"

"No."

They were. I was the youngest in the family and there was such an age difference between Brother, Sister and me that I wasn't allowed to call them by their names. The twins, who were born before me, had died when they were babies. They convulsed, which may have been as a result of cerebral malaria, but Momsi believed that someone put a hex on them. Someone who was jealous of her sewing business, she said. I used to wonder; had I been that jealous of her success, I would have tried to ruin her business rather than try to kill her children, but I had to wear the beads she bought for my protection and I hated them because they looked bush, extremely local. We were in the new millennium after all. Anyone cool was wearing those colorful plastic bands saying *peace* or *love* or *stay strong*. They were cheap and plenty, plenty in the bend-down boutiques on the streets.

Augustine took me to an internet café in Keffi. Outside the café, a group of Hausa traders were hawking padlocks and medicine. One had a cauldron with ashes and raw goat meat on skewers, ready to roast into *suya*. The building was residential, like most on the street, but they had been converted into shops and beauty salons, and there was a *bukateria* next door, where workers from businesses nearby came to eat.

Popsi often talked of a time when there were commercial hubs in Lagos. I couldn't imagine that, a hub. Now, there were hubs everywhere. That was the reason for the increase in crimes, he said. But this was the only Lagos I knew.

Augustine bought a phone card from a woman who was sitting under a yellow umbrella on the street corner. He had a cell phone, which he pulled out of his pocket. I wanted a cell phone like that, one that I could whip out like a gun. I listened as he talked.

"Hullo, *oga*? It's me. Yes. It's me, Augustine. What is the format? I said, what is the format today, sir? OK, OK, Monday then. I'm recruiting. I said, I'm recruiting right now, sir. Yes, this one has brains in his head."

I pretended to be interested in a hawker who was roasting plantains across the street. Her plantains were haphazard on her grill and she waved the fumes away with a piece of cardboard. My stomach growled. I was still hungry.

"Sorry," Augustine said. "That was my *oga* I was talking to."

On the gate of the café was a painted sign saying *No 419ers. No internet Scammers AKA Yahoo Yahoo Boys.*

The front door was shut. The protective iron-grille door was open. The sign had been screaming at us but, as soon as we were inside, I could tell it was for someone else's benefit. I had not been in an internet café before. The place looked like a classroom in a private school, with wooden desks arranged side by side, but I knew that every single bobo I saw sitting before a computer was a Yahoo Yahoo. They could pass for office clerks, some of them, with their shirts and ties. Others wore sports clothes with logos like Nike and Adidas. One bobo was in school uniform, like us. There was even a chick. She had a gold-colored hair weave and a Red Sox cap.

Augustine paid for internet time and led me to a table by a window, also with protective iron grilles. I pulled a chair from an empty desk and sat next to him as he pressed buttons. I was nervous. The café was like an examination hall. Actually, more like a typing examination. No one was talking and all I could hear was the tap-tap-tapping of their keyboards. Augustine spoke quietly enough to remain below the sound. He moved an oval object on a black pad on the table. "This is what is called a mouse…" The screen came to life. "This is what is called logging on…"The screen blacked out, returned in dazzling colors and patterns, then settled into a page. "This is what is called the internet…"

He pushed the mouse around, prodded buttons and got into his Yahoo account, and then into his inbox. He had twenty-seven messages. He clicked on the first one, which was blank but for two words in capital letters: *SOD OFF*.

"This is what is called retrieving email," he said. He typed *YOU TOO*. "This is what is called sending email…"

I was sure I would never learn. The process was too complex. He repeated it and then guided me through my first try. I could barely press the keys for fear of causing an explosion. As for the mouse, I mastered that pretty quickly. I was nervous about the clicking part, though. Did I have to click with my forefinger or little finger? Augustine meanwhile talked in that voice, as if I were a *mumu*: "This. Is. What. Is. Called. Logging off."

The internet was anachronistic. That was exactly the word for it. Outside, there were stagnant gutters, because the drainage system was permanently blocked. Indoors, I was tapping into the future, as people did in science documentaries when voice-overs with echoes announced: "Tap into an undiscovered territory and discover the unknown" and nonsense like that.

The business was like gambling, he said. Every reply we received would increase our chances of winning until we hit a jackpot. He showed me a sample letter in circulation that he had plagiarized. All I had to do was learn how to extract email addresses and send it out.

From the desk of Alhaji Ahmed
Public Relations Office
Foreign Remittance Dept.
Bank of Nigeria

Dear friend,
I am the manager of Bills and Exchange at the
Foreign Remittance Department of Bank of Nigeria.

In my department, we discovered an abandoned sum of $25.5 million in an account that
belongs to one of our foreign customers who died
along with his entire family in a plane crash.

Since we got information about his death, we
have been expecting his next of kin to claim his
money, because we cannot release it unless somebody applies for it according to our banking guidelines and laws. Unfortunately, we learned that all
his supposed next of kin have died, leaving nobody.

It is therefore this discovery that has led I and
other officials in my department to decide to make
this business proposal to you and release the money
to you as the next of kin and subsequently disburse
the money to you. We don't want this money to go
into the bank treasury as an unclaimed bill.

The banking law and guidelines here
stipulate that if such money remains unclaimed
after six years, it will be considered unclaimed. Our
request for a foreigner as next of kin in this
business is occasioned by the fact that the customer
was a foreigner and a Nigerian cannot stand as
next of kin to a foreigner.

SEFI ATTA

We agree that 30% of the money will be for you as a foreign partner, in respect to the provision of a foreign account, 10% will be set aside for expenses incurred during the business, and 60% will be for my colleagues and I.

Therefore, we will visit your country for disbursement according to the percentage indicated, to enable the immediate transfer of this fund to you. You must apply first to the bank as next of kin of the deceased, indicating your bank name, bank account number, your private telephone and fax number for easy and effective communication.

Upon receipt of your reply, I will send you by fax or email the text of the application. Kindly contact me as soon as you receive this letter.

Yours faithfully,
Alhaji A. A. Ahmed
Bills and Exchange Manager

We were online for an hour. When we finished, I was sweating and my heart was racing. I might as well have been at PE. Augustine resumed his normal speaking voice as we stepped outside.

"You want to know why I approached you?"

"Yes," I said, shaking out my arms and legs.

"I didn't want anyone to see us together at school. The timing was right. You must not act as if we know each other. Understand? It's important. If someone asks you, 'Do you know Augustine?' deny me. Deny me on the spot. Straight-away. From now on, we meet here. If this works out well, I will get you a phone. We will communicate like that…"

I hopped over a gutter full of green slime and he followed and stumbled as he landed, because his hands were in his pockets.

"The internet is your link to *mugus* overseas," he said, recovering his balance. *Mugus*, *magas*, *mumus*, they were all the same. Dullards.

"All you need to learn is how to handle a computer and tell a story, and *mugus* will send you money. Do you know how to tell a story?"

"Yes."

We looked left and right before we crossed the street. On the other side was a yellow sign saying *Loan Without Collateral*. A man ran towards me and I almost collided with him.

"Are you s-stupid?" he asked.

I didn't answer. We got to the other side. I was hot and had to confess.

"My popsi is a policeman."

Augustine frowned. "What?"

"My popsi is a policeman."

He spat on the ground. "Ehen, so? It doesn't mean."

Of course it meant. Of course it did. I was angry with Popsi. No one believed he was law-abiding. What was the use?

"He's not corrupt," I said.

Augustine hissed. "Nigerian police. They are all corrupt and poverty-stricken."

"What about your popsi?" I asked.

I smirked, so he would know I'd heard about his connection to the Hilton.

"My father?"

"Yes," I said. "Your father. What does he do?"

"My father is a chef."

A houseboy. A lackey, as Popsi would say. A rich person

could call his name or ring a bell and he would come running: "Yes madam, no madam. Yes sir, no sir. Yes *oga*, no *oga*."

"He is retired now," Augustine said. "We used to live on Lekki Peninsula, you know. He worked for an American family, the Savages. Mr. Savage was with Summit Oil. Their headquarters is on Lekki Peninsula…"

Lekki Peninsula indeed. He was back to his American accent.

As he launched into a long explanation about how he had grown up eating the Savages' food, like spaghetti and meatballs and burgers and fries, and played table tennis with their kids, Chip and Peanut (their father's name was Dick), I deliberately yawned. They called table tennis ping-pong. Their nanny, a Calabar woman, borrowed their books about Tom Sawyer and Huckleberry Finn and taught him how to read and write. When the Savages returned to America, they left his father their VHS player and a library of videos.

"You should see Pacino in *The Godfather*," he said. "Nicholson in *The Postman Always Rings Twice*."

"Me, I'm into Jet Li."

The latest DVDs were available in the police barracks, bootleg copies from overseas.

Augustine was just jiving and his family had since relocated to Ajegunle. "I'm telling you," he said, "they don't call that area Jungle City for nothing."

He wanted to travel to America. He had a cousin who lived there and had got married to get a green card. He planned to apply for a visa by pretending to be dying. He would get a fake doctor's report saying he had a hole in his heart and needed an operation. His sponsors were an NGO dedicated to saving Nigerian children with chronic medical ailments. That was the only reason he came to school. If the United States

Consulate so much as suspected he was a Yahoo Yahoo, his application wouldn't stand a chance.

The United States Consulate's website had a section warning visa applicants about Yahoo Yahoos, apparently. On their visa requirements page, they asked for general forms, special forms for men aged sixteen to forty-five, and proof of sufficient funds. Applicants had to make appointments for their visa interviews and pay a non-refundable fee.

"They're the original Yahoo Yahoos," he said. "They collect the fees and turn down everybody, even rich Nigerians, let alone a poor man's son like me."

I had grown up believing Momsi was a cash madam. With the money she earned from her business, she'd bought our Panasonic television and Sanyo fan. Her sewing machine was a Singer. Society women would come from Ikoyi with copies of *Hello!* magazine and ask her to copy Princess Diana's outfits. They drove through our gates in their old Peugeots and wore ordinary ankara up-and-downs like hers, so she couldn't guess how rich they were (and end up jacking up her prices), but she could tell from their watches and gold rings, and their need for clothes: always fast, fast and now, now.

"You," one said, pointing at me, when she met me playing in the compound. "Go and call your mother. Do quick, I beg." She spoke pidgin in that pretend down-to-earth manner and she couldn't even be bothered to walk up our stairs. Customers who did wrinkled their noses when they entered our flat. One of them told Momsi outright, "I hope you're not going to return my clothes smelling of beans. I have no money to waste on dry-cleaning."

They had massive yanshes most of them, huge hips, big bobbies that no brassiere could contain, and no gratitude for Momsi, who would adjust Princess Diana's outfits to suit their bodies.

As for me, I'd begun to peruse their photographs of Princess Diana. She wasn't a bad chick: that smile, those eyes. I mistook my crush on her for wishing she was my mother and took that out on her sons, William and Harry.

"Look at them," I would say to Momsi. "Spoiled. She's always hugging them and taking them out."

Momsi would say that was how *oyinbo* women raised their children. They didn't teach them any discipline.

I was her personal assistant at home, helping to measure cloth, fetching buttons and zips. I knew too much about fashion and foreign celebrities I would never have heard about but for *Hello!* magazine. Brother and Sister teased me about behaving like a middle-aged woman. Brother in particular was concerned that I was too effeminate, but things were much more complex than that with me.

One day, for instance, I lost patience with that William for burying his face in his mother's belly because a paparazzo wanted a snapshot of him. "It's not his fault," I said. "He has no home training. He thinks he can do anything he wants."

"He can," Momsi said. "His father has money. He is not a poor man's *pikin*, like you."

I had never considered Popsi poor. Nothing had prepared me for that. Not our block of flats with laundry hanging on balconies and wooden boards nailed across windows. Not our compound with chickens running around and sewage leaking from the septic tank. Our walls were filthier than they were in my dream, and from my bedroom I could hear our neighbors shouting and babies crying. It was a miracle to have electricity and running water for a whole month. On the other side of the lagoon were mansions on Victoria Island, with electricity generators and swimming pools. I still had never thought we were poor until she said we were. I disliked William and Harry even more.

Momsi made money when Princess Di was alive, though, and I remember the day she died. Momsi cried out, "Heh, what am I going to do?" I too walked around the flat saying, "Heh, what am I going to do?" until Popsi kicked me in the yansh and asked, "Was she a relation of yours?"

Momsi explained she was worried about her customers, and they did stop coming as frequently. Her outbursts became more unpredictable—or rather, more *sporadic*. One day she might say, "Hm, if only Popsi was less upstanding." The next, she might say that anyone who could stitch two pieces of cloth together was now known as a dress designer. Foreign fashions went out for society women—or perhaps they were just too fat to wear what was fashionable overseas. The latest trend was the up-and-down. They copied styles from photos in local magazines like *Lifestyles* and *Heritage*. Every seamstress in Lagos could replicate those photos. The competition became too much. We were eating beans and *garri* every day, and beans made me spoil the air. Popsi was not only a drinker, but a smoker, and he gave up his Gitanes cigarettes to save a little on the side.

"I can't miss school," I said to Augustine, "unless I am sick. Malaria, chest colds…"

"Don't worry about that," he said. "I will take care of your attendance record."

"How?"

He waved. "I have people on my payroll."

We passed a woman under a Coca-Cola umbrella. Was he fabulizing again?

"Like who?"

He laughed. "I say I have people on my payroll. Look, I fake my school reports at the end of the year. I even buy WAEC papers. Forty dollars is all you need. What? What?"

I was shaking my head. West African Examination Council papers. That wasn't a surprise. They were available on the black market. The only reason students in our school didn't buy them was because they had no money.

"WAEC," I said. "They will catch you."

They recalled papers every year and students had to re-sit exams.

He nodded. "You have to be a real *mugu* to be that obvious. A big one. But it is not by force. If you don't want to do it, then don't. All I'm saying is that you can talk about WAEC from morning till night, but who is selling the papers? I'm not the one selling the papers. I just buy them. And let me tell you another thing: even if you pass your WAEC exams and end up going to university, you will never get a job that pays as much as I make on a daily basis, so what are you wasting your time in school for?"

The sun was beating my head. Above us was a banner saying *Royal Finishing School. How to be a lady, gentleman. Dining etiquette.*

"It's not every day you have to come," he said. "We can alternate. Me, three days a week. You, two, once I teach you what to do."

I was thinking about Popsi again. He had only ever shared one fraud case with me, a case involving two grandmothers. They were first cousins. One needed money for her seventieth-birthday celebration and the other for her youngest daughter's engagement ceremony. A man had arranged to meet them at a hotel. The man claimed he had a link to diamonds smuggled from Sierra Leone. He asked for an initial investment to grant access to them.

These women delivered their entire savings to the man. In the middle of the transaction, the hotel door burst open and policemen charged in. They ordered the women to disappear or else. The women ran to reception shouting that they had been waylaid. They refused to say by whom. Come to find out that their link to the diamonds had disappeared. Come to find out that the police had never raided the hotel.

It was a classic Section 419 crime, Popsi said, and the men were neither found nor apprehended, but 419 was local. Yahoo Yahoos operated in cyberspace.

Popsi also said that not everyone who lived on Victoria Island was rich, but the word "poor," to him, was for people of Maroko. I was not yet born when the place was leveled and the land sold off as part of Lekki Peninsula. He was one of the policemen who were dispatched to drive the people out. The police were merely following orders, he said, but, as usual, the majority of them got carried away. The word "poor," to me, referred to people like those who lived in fishing villages like Sokoro under Third Mainland Bridge. Their communities were propped up on sticks. They swam past their own shit to reach their wooden huts. Perhaps they didn't even consider themselves poor.

"I'm not sure," I said to Augustine.

He raised his hands. "You're not sure? You're not sure? What else is there to be sure about? Look, it's because you have not been near the other side, to see how they live. In this place, we may all be in the same, em, em, vicinity, but there are

SEFI ATTA

invisible barriers between us. It is a class system. A class system, you hear me? You know what a class system means? I don't think you do."

Now, I was walking behind him, listening to his sweet talk, as if he were one of those child-molesting street prophets Momsi had warned me about. We were heading away from school. Had school been less dry, I would not have bothered. I would have said, "It done do," and returned there. But I'd never met anyone who behaved like Augustine before. He was a performer. I could tell he was putting on a show for his own enjoyment as much as mine, as if all he needed was an audience of one, and that was enough for him.

He had to talk. He needed to and that made me pity him a little. I might have been the only one in the world who had time to listen. My legs were cramping. I kept up with him, though, as we passed rusty gates, piles of sticks, rotten banana plants, phone-card hawkers sitting under umbrellas and a wall with a sign saying *No urinary*.

He found a sandy patch by the gate of a block of Public Works Department flats. Pedestrians and hawkers were walking past. We were obstructing their path. He didn't seem to notice or care. He picked up a stick near a street gutter and drew a lopsided circle in the sand. Then he drew a line across to divide it in two and poked dots all over the place.

"These are the haves," he said. "These are the have-nots. This is you and me. Consider yourself part of the masses. Now, of the haves, there are two types: the nouveau riche…"

The word "nouveau" put me off. It was like a French lesson.

"They are taking over Lagos. They are the ones who have made stupid money recently. First-generation money. That is the difference between them and the elite. The only difference.

Now, the elite are a dying breed. They have money going generations back, only three at most, but they can't stand to see the nouveau riche around them. They think they own Lagos and they are no better than the nouveau riche. They both made their money the same way. Mostly by *wuruwuru*: stealing from the government, from a bank, from somewhere. A generation later, they are looking down on others. You see? Don't let anyone fool you. They are no better than you. In every rich family, the first person to make money was a poor man's *pikin* like you. Come."

His mouth was too sweet. I was mesmerized. Or had he jujued me? What was the use of my beads? We continued up Awolowo Road in the wrong direction. The road had changed from residential to commercial in the olden days—the early eighties, to be precise. At one end was the Command Officers' Mess, at the other was the French Consulate where people queued up to apply for visas, and somewhere in the middle was the shopping center.

Oil, he said. That was the ultimate source of wealth, but there were others: the new-generation banks and the wireless-phone companies. The elite were just jealous of other people who were discovering these outlets. They were the cause of the class barriers that existed. Their trick was to intimidate the rest of us by mimicking *oyinbos*, whom they claimed they didn't look up to. They would swear they were superior to *oyinbos*, even, but the evidence of their colonial mentality was there.

"They can't stop traveling overseas to shop," he said. "Their clothes, their homes, their mannerisms. They are influenced. Look at their clubs. You can't join, but *oyinbos* can join. What does that tell you?"

His father had friends who had worked as chefs in most clubs nearby—Ikoyi Club, Golf Club, Polo Club, Yacht Club, and the Motor Boat Club. As soon as the nouveau riche joined these clubs, the elite checked out. They couldn't handle the competition, not even from foreigners as dark as they were. They stopped going to Ikoyi Club in the nineties when Indians took over the place.

"They are snobbish and yet they have no class. Overseas, they would call them bourgeois. Here, they are elite, but only in a useless place like Lagos can they be. Don't let them keep you down psychologically. That is what they want, to preserve the order and keep themselves on top."

Bourgeois. More French. We walked for almost half an hour and got to the Motor Boat Club. It was still a safe haven for the elite, he said, because the nouveau riche wouldn't know what to do with a boat.

The clubhouse stood there white and firm, like some establishment that was never ever going to budge. How many times had I passed the place and seen the car park packed with jeeps? I loved jeeps. Sometimes when I was stuck in traffic, I imagined myself driving the biggest jeep on the road and banging other vehicles out of my way. The boats were tucked away in sheds.

"On the weekends," Augustine said, "they go to the beach to get away: Tarkwa Bay, Ibeshe, Ilasha. They eat lobsters in there, you know, as big as chickens."

They also dressed better than *oyinbos*, he said, who sometimes wore torn T-shirts, even though they owned beach homes.

"But why?" I asked.

"That is what is called reverse snobbery," he explained. "Stepping up by dressing down. But the elite will never go that far to prove they have class. They are too insecure and vain." A silver Benz poked its nose out of the exit gate. The driver lowered his window.

"*Oga*, sir," he hailed the gateman.

The gateman bowed in response. The driver raised his window. No tip. He was wearing sunshades and a light-blue T-shirt, one of those with the logo of a man charging on a horse. He was definitely an elite. That horse T-shirt was their uniform and the Benz was their official car.

Why call the gateman "*oga*," then? Was that also reverse snobbery? And why did they have to pretend anyway?

I remembered a couple of girls who came to the barracks to get dresses made in the time of Princess Diana. Their car had a flat tire in the compound and, as they waited for their driver to fix it, one said to the other, "Bloody hell, this place is a dump." Then she added, "I mean Lagos in general," when she caught me staring. When I wouldn't stop eyeing her, she turned her back on me and whispered to her friend, "What's that one looking at?"

I was looking at the woman in the passenger seat of the Benz, now. She, too, was wearing sunshades. Hers were so large they covered half her face. Her bare feet were on the dashboard. I was sure she was cool in the air conditioning. You couldn't get close to a woman like her. The nearest you could get to her was by sewing her clothes or cooking for her.

"They always look clean," I murmured.

Augustine nodded. "Yes, but their shit still stinks, which is what I've been trying to tell you."

The road was clear. The bobo in the Benz didn't even look at us as he drove off.

In a way, I thought I was privileged, at least within the police barracks. I had a room of my own. Everyone else I knew had to double up, if not triple and quadruple up. We even had a spare bedroom, into which Momsi sometimes moved because of Popsi's snoring. At night, he sounded like the broken-down engine of a *kabukabu*.

Our block was one of two in the barracks that were painted. It was the color of curry, with a red roof and green shutters—perhaps because we were right across the road from Sterling Bank and the bank customers might complain about the view. The other blocks in the barracks were cement gray. Their roofs and mosquito netting were rusty. Their balconies were cluttered with pans, boxes and tires. We had only laundry hanging on ours.

"Do you want to go back to school?" Augustine asked.

"No."

For what?

"You want to come to Victoria Island?"

Why not? If my teachers noticed my absence, they would just assume I was becoming one of the bad boys in school, one of the slackers, NFAs—students with no future ambition—and that wouldn't be a surprise.

We hopped on a *danfo* bus. I was so close to Augustine I could smell the starch on his uniform. Popsi had once told me criminals picked their victims. They could smell the vulnerability in people. I asked if a criminal would be able to smell mine. I didn't know what "vulnerability" meant at the time, but I had been the target of bullies in primary school. One classmate just used to headbutt me; another, a girl, used to trip me up. Popsi had tried in vain to teach me how to fight back. I had inherited Momsi's stature, he said, but not her character.

Augustine was the insecure one from the beginning: his father's occupation, his virginity at the age of seventeen, eighteen, or however old he was, and his reputation for being a liar. But I allowed him to carry on thinking he was in charge and initiating me, and impressing me, because of the money. Long before he came along, I'd wanted more of that in my life. I had my reasons—our school, for one. Why else would I have ended up in such a useless school, unless Popsi didn't have enough money? I was smart enough to get into a private school.

On our way to Victoria Island, I couldn't imagine living anywhere else in Lagos or having to move to a place like Jungle City. I knew this section of Awolowo Road so well, from the Boat Club to the federal fire station—which was abandoned, but for an old red Mercedes truck—to Bacchus nightclub, Jazz Hole and the YMCA with flats that I suspected were not occupied by any youths. To escape the traffic, I sometimes took the back roads, which could be just as jammed, but once in a while I might bump into the artists who hung out at the Bogobiri guesthouse or the born-again Christians of Mountain of Fire and Miracles, arriving for their spiritual clinics and revivals. They revived until after midnight, apparently, and kept people in the neighborhood up with their clapping. At Falomo, of course, there was the Church of the Assumption and Mammy Market. If I wasn't in the mood to go home, I could head up Kingsway Road, past Golden Gate Restaurant and the national petroleum building, which had closed down since a suspicious fire, to Fantasyland. This was my area in Lagos, my hood.

On Awolowo Road I'd seen a Honda driver run over an *okada*. Luckily, the *okada* didn't have a passenger, but he fell off his motorcycle and lay there wailing. There wasn't a drop of blood in sight, but within minutes his fellow *okadas* began to arrive like rats. They rode around the Honda, shouted insults and threatened to beat up the driver. Passersby gathered around to watch, including me. The driver had locked his doors and was staying put until the road was clear and he could speed off. The *okadas* got off their motorcycles and began to bang on his windows.

Okadas were serious about instant street justice, but none of them helped their fellow *okada*, who now was curled up on the road and still wailing. They would have beaten the shit out of that Honda driver, had he not escaped by reversing down the pedestrian part of the road. He knocked down all the hawkers' stands and they scampered.

I'd seen worse. One day, a man fell out of a *danfo*. He was wearing a white skullcap. He just fell off, picked himself up, ran after the *danfo* and hopped back in with his skullcap stained with blood. Another day, I passed a man with a cheek as big as a pawpaw. He had a malignant growth. Two men behind him carried a poster stating this. One of them called out through a loudspeaker, "Support this man! Give in the name of Jesus!"

I thought of Momsi as our *danfo* bus passed over the bridge to Victoria Island. She was a major obstacle. My juju beads were never able to protect me from her. My legs did, when they eventually grew and I became too tall for her to reach, but before that, I used to run, or "miss," as Brother would say. I would miss to the kitchen, miss to my bedroom, or miss outside to the compound and sit on the cement surface of the septic tank until she cooled down. I knew exactly what she was capable of. I had seen how she dealt with Brother when he was at CMS Grammar School and associating with a group of boys she suspected were Indian-hemp smokers.

I remembered how these boys loitered around the gates of our barracks, with their red eyes and school shirts unbuttoned almost to their navels, when they were supposed to be studying for their matriculation exams. They were "doing guy" as she would say. She had this friend, Auntie Florence, who had a provisions store in Mammy Market. Brother used to call her

"Babylon." She was like a satellite dish in orbit and she disturbed me. She was bulky all over, yet from her nose to her chin she was gorgeous. She had these lips, these teeth, and the cleanest mouth I'd ever seen, which was always filled with Bazooka Joe gum. Whenever I saw her and smelled that Bazooka Joe, I had an overwhelming urge to kiss her, just slip my tongue into her mouth and lick her teeth for a moment, but I couldn't stand the sight of her. Her neck was so plump her gold chain had disappeared within the folds of her flesh. She wore so much makeup she resembled a clown. Momsi thought the makeup made her skin fresh. "You look fresh, Florence," she would say, and Auntie Florence would answer, "It's my Posner."

She perspired because of her Posner. I was also drawn to her toes. I couldn't help looking at them, even though they were unsightly. They stuck out of her sandal straps and her nails were thick and painted a shiny pink.

Whenever Brother missed school, she would be at home with Momsi, both of them waiting for him like two detectives.

"He-eh, you've been playing with your education and deceiving this woman who carried you in her womb for nine months?" Auntie Florence would ask him, stamping her foot and waving her arms.

"My children are crazy," Momsi would say. "Crazy children I have. They become teenagers and their heads turn."

Auntie Florence's children had all attended good schools and they had graduated from Lagos State University. They were decent and well-behaved of course.

Through her, Momsi got to hear that Brother was going to Bar Beach with the boys, to smoke what he claimed were Popsi's Gitanes cigarettes, and to Shrine to see Fela perform at Sunday Jump, instead of attending his exam-preparation lessons. The boys were Shrine boys, and Popsi didn't care to hear Fela's name mentioned, after Fela released that record *Zombie* mocking policemen. In fact, the police hated Fela so much at the time that Popsi could have arrested the boys for no reason and thrown them in jail, and no one would have queried or reprimanded him. But it was Momsi who locked Brother up in our toilet and made him swear he would never go to Shrine again. It was Momsi who took off her slippers and chased the boys from the barracks gates when next they came around. She flung one of the slippers and it spun like a boomerang and bounced off one of them. I witnessed that. The bobo's eyes were shut tight when the slipper struck him, *ko*! Then he caught sight of her advancing and he looked as if he might piss on himself.

"Nonsense," she said, as they ran. "You think I'm playing? You haven't heard of me yet. You don't know who I am."

Brother, who was teaching me how to act like a real man, was howling away in the toilet and Popsi was begging for his release. She didn't let him out for a whole day. From then on, Brother began to face his studies squarely. Then Sister started to adjust her pinafores. At first, I didn't know what that meant exactly, but that was how Momsi put it when I asked what Sister had done wrong. She said, "Hm. Your sister is adjusting her pinafores."

Sister was at New Era, prettyish and sort of plump. What she was doing was sneaking into the sitting room when Momsi wasn't there and shortening her school uniforms, stealing Popsi's shaving blades and using them to scrape her eyebrows. As far as Momsi was concerned, that could lead to a pregnancy. In fact, in her mind, the pregnancy had already occurred, because she took Sister to General Hospital for a test. They got there and the doctor asked Sister when last she had seen her period. Sister said she was menstruating right then and there. Momsi told him, "Don't listen to her. She's miscarrying."

I don't know what the doctor did, but Sister was sobbing when they came back home, quivering like a wet chicken. Her hands could barely hold Popsi's blade straight (one of those she had stolen) as she let down the hems of her uniforms. Momsi was threatening that next time she wouldn't spare her from the speculum. Popsi said to her, "Come on, remember what happened to you," and she started going on about how she wasn't an illiterate when he met her, and he kept insisting that that wasn't the point he was trying to make.

I was not looking forward to growing older. Maturity seemed to cause friction in our family, with Momsi in particular. She couldn't stand adolescents, and Brother and Sister warned me that she would show me pepper when I got into secondary school. "She is too wicked for words," Sister said. Brother said, "I swear, that woman is a demon." A beast of no gender was the description he later used, and it was confusing because Popsi was the policeman. He was meant to be the inhuman zombie, not her, but he was not at home as much as she was. Never present. He was either at work or at the palm-wine parlor.

To be honest, I secretly pitied Momsi: first of all, for losing the twins; secondly, for always sewing in that sitting room; and thirdly, Popsi's salary was never paid on time. Brother and Sister eventually graduated from university and completed their national-service years. They got jobs and sent money home once in a while. Brother at first worked as a cash and teller's clerk in a bank up North, until God called him to train as a Pentecostal pastor. He married a deaconess in his church and she was yet to give birth. Sister got a PR job in the capital with a non-governmental office dedicated to the empowerment of rural women. Their patron was an American actress. She visited the capital and met with the president. That made headline news, so Sister was promoted. Then Brother was posted to Ghana, to minister to at-risk youths, and Sister got pregnant by one of her wealthy sponsors who was in the House of Reps.

She had promised us she wouldn't Monica Lewinsky herself. He was a married man, but she agreed to marry him anyway, by native law and custom. Popsi was against a polygamous union. He thought Sister was selling herself short and would be mistreated as a junior wife. Brother thought it was probably best for her child, so long as Sister could squeeze in a church blessing. Momsi was busy trying to find the right shade of white polyester for the wedding gown. "At last," she said, "one rich person in the family."

There was a time she could easily slap my head. Now, I was getting too tall for her to reach. She used to inspect my schoolbooks. She could no longer follow the subjects I was studying. All she did in the evenings was sew. She was making a replica of a wedding gown for Sister, Vera Wank or something. Sister had sent her a picture of the gown, ripped out of a bridal magazine, with her latest measurements. Momsi thought she could adjust the design to hide Sister's pregnancy and leave enough space to accommodate her belly.

One day she and Popsi actually fought over that dress. I came back from school and there was netting all over the sitting room floor. She was crouched over and laying it down as if it were a sleeping baby. She was humming away.

Her hair was threaded and she had not dyed it in a while, so it was partly gray and partly jet black.

"What is this?" I asked, after greeting her.

I tiptoed on the narrow space leading to my bedroom door. Sweeping the floor was my worst chore at home, closely followed by ironing. The broom picked up dust I didn't notice, loose threads and sheared cloth. I was used to seeing them and I automatically looked out for stray pins. The corners of the room were blocked with cardboard boxes. Clutter just accumulated in our flat and piled up each time I cleared it up.

"Tulle," she murmured.

I had long stopped helping her in her sewing business, but I knew that whenever she used a highfaluting name to describe a fabric, the fabric was of a lesser quality. The same way she had called the polyester cloth she was using to make Sister's wedding dress "duchess satin." The same way she described herself as "petite" and not "short." Her tulle was as coarse as a mosquito net. The roll of white polyester was leaning against the wall by the poster of Jesus.

I carried my books into my bedroom, as she continued to hum. Momsi couldn't sing or hum in tune and she did both in high trembling tones. I recognized the song: "I Believe I Can Fly." She sounded miserable. The netting across my doorway reminded me of my dream. The smell of our neighbor's okra stew had drifted through my window and seeped into my mattress.

Popsi came back while I was doing my homework. I got up to greet him and, as I expected, he took one look at the netting and asked, "What is this?"

Momsi was at her table now, sewing pieces of the white polyester together. She had a pin in her mouth.

"I beg," Popsi said to me. "Gather up this rubbish from my floor."

"Just leave it," Momsi said, removing the pin. "I will take care of it. I spent a whole hour pinning it together."

Popsi unbuttoned his uniform. Unlike me, he didn't tiptoe. He trod on her net and I was sure he would leave footprints, but he didn't.

"If you like you can spend twenty-four hours pinning it together," he said. "I've told you my position. There will be no wedding until that man sends his family here to ask for my daughter's hand in marriage."

"See," Momsi said. "My whole body is paining me. I don't want trouble. Let it not be said that I am a difficult woman. All I have ever asked is that you do what is best for this family, but what else can one do when someone keeps throwing his salary away in a palm-wine parlor?"

I couldn't believe she would dare to accuse him, even in that underhanded way. She couldn't even call him by his name, out of respect. What was she saying? At least she had the grace to eye the floor. Popsi was not one of those violent policemen who beat their wives so badly the entire barracks came out to beg. A month ago, one crazy one beat his wife as she tried to leap off the balcony. She was halfway across and the man was beating the parts of her body he had access to. He stopped only to fetch his gun from their bedroom and that was when Popsi and a group of men seized the opportunity to rescue her.

He narrowed his eyes at Momsi and spoke with such dignity. "I am warning you. Do not cross my path today. Do you hear me? You have been forewarned."

No reference to what she was trying to insinuate. As I backed into the poster of Jesus, I wondered if he secretly was a big boozer. Why else would he always let her get away with insulting him? Momsi adjusted her wrapper. She had bags under her eyes from years of sewing under poor lighting and not sleeping well because of his snoring. Her bones—clavicle or cervical—were sticking out. She slapped her arms.

"I used to be fat when you married me," she said. "Eh? Fat and yellow. Now, see all my body, shriveled and black."

"D-did I ask you to g-go all over the place under the h-hot sun s-searching for fabrics?" he asked, faking a stammer to show how serious he was.

She patted her chest. "Why not? Why can't I search for fabrics? Is it not for my daughter's sake?"

"Which daughter?" he said and hissed: "The one you almost drove out of this place?"

She nodded. "Yes. I was shopping for my daughter."

He returned to his room. "Suddenly she is your daughter. Suddenly, because she is marrying a senator, she is your daughter."

"He is not a senator!" Momsi said. "He is in the House of Reps!"

A cockerel crowed outside. A neighbor was clanging pots. It done do, I thought.

"No one has come to me to ask for her hand," Popsi was saying. "No one. And until then, she is my daughter. My daughter. You hear me? I didn't give her away to anyone, certainly not a man who has not had the c-common decency to send his people to my house."

"His people are in Gandu Biyu," she said. "You expect them to travel all the way here?"

"Yes," he said. "Yes, because he cannot come and face me, after what he has done. Under normal circumstances he would not be able to face me anyway, as my prospective son-in-law, so what is it you want to say, woman? What is it you want to say?"

Her voice trembled. "You're too proud. Too proud. The girl is pregnant. It's not as if she is pure, and even your own son said so. He said it was best. It was best for them to marry. He said it."

"He would," Popsi said. "If he doesn't, will his church s-send him as a representative to meet Benny Hinn? Will his church send him on a s-spiritual retreat to Jamaica?"

She was sobbing. "Heh, what is my own with Benny Hinn, oh? What is my own with spiritual retreat?"

I had never even heard Momsi cry. I thought she was completely heartless. Popsi then accused Brother's church of thievery. He said Benny Hinn was a 419er. He also accused Sister's NGO. He said they got funding from dubious government officials and spent the bulk of their money on SUVs.

Augustine and I got to Victoria Island and we were able to talk freely as we walked. He told me he was part of the community at the internet café—the daytime Yahoos. Some worked overnight. The chick with the Red Sox cap was one of them. She targeted foreign dating sites. *Mugus* fell in love with her fake photographs and sent her money. Once in a while she was on eBay. Most of the guys were using the lottery format. They sent emails asking *mugus* to wire funds in order to claim non-existent prizes.

He said the lottery format was overused. He would start me off with begging letters. I was to keep them as simple as possible. I could write as an orphan, or an elderly man. Pretending to be a woman helped; so did having a terminal disease. The most effective format was that I needed money to complete my education, or my child's. That would guarantee me a sympathetic response, but I might also get replies telling me to fuck off or go to hell. One woman from South Africa wrote him a whole page telling him off for ruining Nigeria's reputation. "We despise Nigerians over here," her email ended. He was tempted to write back and abuse her forefathers, Boers, or whatever they were, but he didn't. That would be a waste of internet time. He also warned me about scam baiters.

They were pranksters, who wrote back pretending to be fooled. If I was not careful, I could end up exposed on their websites. The English were notorious for that. Targeting them had become a huge risk.

The real masters in the business, the real P-I-M-Ps, were the *ogas*, the Yahoo millionaires. Those guys did not play around. To trap a *mugu*, they would print fake certificates and letterhead paper, rent a government office and furnish it if necessary. They would put on any charade. Any. Augustine had worked for one who didn't pay his commission. He tried several times to reach him by phone, only to hear his number was no longer in service. He went to his house, found him there and the man claimed he had been in Côte d'Ivoire. Augustine asked when he was likely to pay his commission. The man said the money was in a domiciliary account and the balance had to be wired to a local account.

What excuse didn't he give Augustine after that? Augustine's account number was missing a digit. The wire was awaiting one security clearance or another. He had had no electricity for weeks. Armed robbers attacked him. He managed to jump out of a window and escape. His leg got sprained. In fact, he had been sick with malaria.

"He thought I was a *mugu*," Augustine said.

Mugus were not only fools, he said, but they were also the victims of their own vices. Those who sent money in response to our begging letters were somehow relieving their guilt about how extravagant their lives were, or they were prejudiced about Africans and believed we were all desperately in need. Those who sent money to claim lottery proceeds were plain greedy, and anyone who responded to transfer-of-funds letters had to be corrupt as hell.

"You can be anyone you wanna be," said Augustine. "Anyone on the internet. These *mugus* are ignorant about us, man. Ignorant. They don't know jack about Africa. They think we're still swinging on trees. You've gotta realize the level of ignorance you're dealing with here."

His new *oga* went by different aliases. Solomon Goodhead was one and Alhaji Ahmed was another. He would give me money to buy food to eat at the *bukateria*, next door to the café. They had *edikang ikong* and pounded yam on their menu, rice and stew with plantains and assorted meats.

It occurred to me that there was nothing more precious in the world than satisfaction. That it was possible to end up committing a crime just because you were contaminated by a little discontent. You could convince yourself that you were satisfied, then someone could come along and say, "But I can offer you more," and then you could begin to think, My life is not worth much after all. In fact, you could tell yourself, My life was completely worthless from the start.

That was exactly how I felt as I listened to him, and I blamed everyone we came into contact with. The bobos in their Benzes, for one. I would never be them, picking up chicks and taking them to private clubs. Beggars, for another—one in particular who sat cross-legged on the street with his hand extended. They were too humble, far more than they needed to be.

Augustine had this new girlfriend whom he called his "shorty." Her name was Glory. She was older than him and worked as a receptionist at a hotel on Victoria Island. The hotel was four star and French-owned. The hotel management didn't encourage people like us to walk in. Security guards hovered around the gates, ready to pounce on us, but Augustine seemed to know them. He raised his fist and called them "chief" or "*oga*." They nodded in response. He asked one of them to get Glory. We couldn't walk into the lobby so we stood on the cement ramp outside between the casino and banquet hall. A curved ixora hedge bordered the ramp. A popular police-band song was playing: "Guantanamera." Momsi knew all the words: "*Wancharamera. Maria, wancharamera .Wancharameeera…*" Moments later, when Glory came out walking in time to the music, my mouth fell open. This was the chick he was calling his "shorty"? She was practically a palm tree. Her legs could have reached my shoulders, and she wore high heels. She was in a black skirt and waistcoat. Her hair, which had to be fake, was halfway down her back.

Augustine had said she had recently been attacked. An area boy had tried to grab her handbag outside a Chicken George, but she refused to let go. The area boy pushed her into a gutter and ran off. Passersby pulled her out and said how lucky she was that he hadn't stabbed her. Glory just sat on the side of the street and howled. She was putting serious pressure on Augustine to leave Nigeria, now. She could help him get a visa, she said, through her expatriate connections. He didn't have to pretend he was dying, but she needed him to buy her a plane ticket.

"How now," she said, coming to a stop.

The breeze was strong enough to lift her hair weave and we had to raise our voices. Cars and taxis crawled up and down the ramp.

I strained my neck. Close up, she had pimples on her forehead and her lips were lined black. She was most unattractive. Augustine introduced me as his cousin and she bent to hug me, as if we were friends.

"Oh, he's so cute! How old is he?"

Her perfume was strong, yet I could smell her hair weave, which had a similar odor to sour milk. Chicks usually responded to me as if I were one of them. Glory wasn't my type, but if she was not careful I would rummage through her belongings, I thought. Augustine said I was twelve.

"What's your name?" she asked, rubbing my head.

"Idowu," I said.

She looked at Augustine. "But he's Yoruba. How can he be your relative when he is not from our side?"

Augustine's people were from Warri. They had English names. His parents were called Eunice and Enoch. He mumbled an explanation about me being related by marriage as we walked away from the ramp. People who talked about tribes amused me. Who the hell cared where our forefathers were from?

The hotel was full of prostitutes, packed with them, and they were dressed in western attire. They could easily pass for proper elite. What gave them away were the crooked-legged walks they acquired from parading up and down the diplomatic district. Glory called them "*va bene*," not "*ashawo*," as everyone else called them. So many of them ended up in Rome, she said. She did not dislike them as much as the other staff did. If the *oyinbos* at the hotel were not screwing someone out of their money, what were they looking for in a place like Lagos?

"That's why I love you," Augustine said. "You're egalitarian in your thinking. Very enlightened."

"Ega what?" she said and smacked his shoulder.

She was too old. We found a bench by the car-hire service, near a mosque, beauty shop and magazine store. Kuramo Waters was before us. Behind us was a red-brick bazaar where Hausa traders sold arts and crafts. Above us was what looked like an air conditioner's yansh trapped in an iron cage. It blew hot air over my head and dripped water occasionally.

"But you know I love you," Augustine insisted, stroking her arms as she sat there pouting.

"Then buy me a ticket," she said.

He said he was saving up and it would take time, then he began to compare her to beauty pageant queens as she denied his praises.

"You're my Miss Nigeria," he said.

"At all," she said.

"My Most Beautiful Girl in Nigeria."

"At all."

"My Face of Africa…"

She gripped his hand like a wrestler. "Face of Africa? Please, don't remind me of that. You know they are holding the next contest here?"

"Eh?" he said.

"Yes," she said. "The preliminaries will be held here and I am not allowed to participate because I've passed the age limit. Can you imagine? And if you see the monster they chose last year, you will run. One girl with a square jaw, like this, and a shaved head. Face of what? Who wants to be that? It is the ugly girls they want. The ones with flat noses. They look like lesbians."

She pronounced the word "lexbian."

He reached for her hair weave. "It doesn't matter. You would win if you were allowed to enter. Who is finer than you?"

The Face of Africa girls were not bad at all. What they had in common was that they were not rich. The last Nigerian who won was offered a modeling contract for a hundred thousand dollars. She went to live in New York. The rest had to return to their hovels or wherever they came from. The winner had never held a passport before. She was taller than Glory and her body was tight. Any girl who could manage a haircut that low had to be beautiful. This one didn't have a dent in her head, but a chick that tall was beyond me. If I wanted to have sex with her, where would I begin?

Glory's phone rang. "'Scuse me," she said, flipping it open with her fake nails. "'Lo? Yes? No. No. I'm otherwise occupied. I said I'm otherwise occupied. Yes. Later."

She returned the phone to her pocket as Augustine watched her.

"Who were you speaking to?" he asked.

"My sister," she mumbled.

"Are you sure?" he asked.

"Look," she said, raising her hand. "Don't come here and accuse me of all sorts. I've told you before, this body is not for sale. I don't give it up easily. I'm not a *va bene*. I may not have money, but I am coming from somewhere. My father was a famous footballer in this country. If not for his leg injury..."

"OK! OK!" he said.

She herself was like a footballer. She was all thighs. Her calves were as thick as her thighs and so were her ankles; there was no in or out. A simple "Are you sure?" and now she wanted to give her life history. All that talk was like his bragging about sex anyway. If her father was that famous, she wouldn't have to say he was.

Augustine was a *mugu*, big time, or too much in love to care. He had probably paid for her nails and her phone. How they would qualify for visa interviews, I didn't know, but rather than sit there as he continued to toast her, I excused myself and decided to explore. There was enough vegetation to hide behind: traveler's palms, mango trees, frangipani and *kinikan kinikan*.

The arts and crafts bazaar was open. *Oyinbos* were shopping there for souvenirs like ebony busts, bronze masks and malachite ashtrays. No self-respecting elite would buy any of that. From what I'd observed, they preferred to surround themselves with objects that reminded them of Europe.

I saw a woman with an *oyinbo* man who looked old enough to be her grandfather. Her T-shirt was tight and short, and her bobbies stuck out. He had a hooked nose and his hair was wet with sweat. So was his shirt. He carried a brown briefcase that seemed to weigh him down.

"Is good the eh, eh, art effects?" he asked.

"Yes, of curse," she said. "They have a lot of artifacts here. Any artifact you want, you can boy."

Nigerians. Why did we always change our accents whenever we spoke to foreigners?

"Is eh, eh, hex pensive?" he asked.

An illiterate would have been more articulate.

"Oh, my gourd, no," she said, patting her chest. "They are not expensive at all if you convert to naira. They won't cost you much."

From his appearance, he didn't seem to be worth much, wherever he was coming from, but that was the trouble with the naira. Anyone could come to Nigeria and become rich, once they converted their currency to ours.

The Hausa traders called him. "*Oyinbo!*"

He refused to acknowledge them, as if he was too scared to without her protection. They came out of the bazaar and beckoned at him, "*Oyinbo! Oyinbo! Oyinbo!*"

"Heave," he cried out as their calls grew louder.

He clutched his briefcase to his chest. Eve? That was her name? He was most likely French, then. I'd heard they had problems with their H's.

"*Oyinbo! Oyinbo! Oyinbo!*" the traders kept shouting.

"Heave," he cried out again.

She hurried over to rescue him. He was now using his briefcase as a shield against the Hausa traders as she shooed them away.

Heave indeed.

The new wing of the hotel was to my left. Other women walked in and out and I tried to guess which ones were the prostitutes. It was hard to tell. They all moved with such pride. I counted about three suspects who were accompanying *oyinbo* men and then got bored of watching.

The hotel had a swimming pool. Guests in the new wing would have to have direct access to the swimming pool—to avoid walking through the reception of the main wing scantily dressed. Nigerians despised unnecessary nakedness. *Oyinbos* enjoyed swimming. I could find my way to the swimming pool through the new wing.

I was right about the alternative route. The outdoor corridor from the new wing led there, past a bougainvillea courtyard and fountain. I smelled the chlorine long before I reached the pool, and I was also right about *oyinbos*. The place was full of them, chock-a-block with them. There was only one Nigerian in the shallow end and he was performing stretching exercises. Then he crouched and did breaststroke movements with his arms while walking underwater.

Nigerians couldn't swim—Lagosians, who lived on the mainland. Island people from fishing villages could. They swam better than the fish they caught. Perhaps that was how they caught the fish. People from the Delta could swim, too. As for people from Lagos, *Eko* people, despite the water that surrounded us, we were useless swimmers. Even the elite didn't appreciate getting wet, I'd heard, for all their attempts to be like *oyinbos*. The women especially, with their expensive hair weaves and extensions. The smallest drop of water could revert their looks to African.

Oyinbo people were a mystery, though. Why all that lying in the sun? Were they trying to be as dark as us or what? They lived in their little communities, sometimes with their own special schools for their children—American International, the French School, or the British School—and I'd heard that they restricted Nigerians. There were also Chinese, Lebanese and Indians around. They were not exactly *oyinbo*, but white South Africans were.

Popsi once told me a story about an *oyinbo* bobo who was constantly being stopped at Awolowo Road checkpoint back in the eighties. He called him an English chap. This chap would be on his way back from Lagos Motor Boat Club. The policemen at the checkpoint would bank on him being drunk, even though his driver was always at the wheel. They would stop his car for speeding and demand a Christmas gift. All year round. The English chap would laugh and tell them he'd had one too many and hand them a few naira notes. This continued until the policemen got greedy one night and arrested him for not having his particulars in order. Popsi was on duty at the station when they brought him in. "I'm pissed as a fart," the chap said, raising his hands in surrender. His face was red. Popsi set him free because there were no grounds for his arrest and the chap was so grateful he taught Popsi a song before he left: "Four and twenty virgins came down from Inverness."

At the swimming pool, a blonde woman was lying face up with her bikini straps loose. I observed her to see if her bobbies would flop out. The Nigerian man who was pretending to swim came out of the pool looking a little gray and the chlorine fumes began to sting my eyes. I got tired of waiting.

When I returned, Glory was ready to leave. She hugged me again.

"You're so cute," she said, with regret.

"Thanks," I said.

"You must come and see me again. I'll give you a non-alcoholic cocktail."

I noticed those pimples on her forehead again and her black lipstick. Did she emit an odor? That had to be her secret. She was also attracting the attention of a few Hausa traders in the bazaar, one with tribal marks on his cheeks. He polished a beaded necklace with a rag as he watched her.

"What about mine?" Augustine asked, stepping forward.

"Be patient," she said, wriggling her fingers.

I almost vomited. Her hands looked like crabs. He hugged her and the top of his head barely reached her neck. He wouldn't leave until she'd walked back up the ramp. Her hair weave was like a horse's tail and her heels were shredded.

"Come," he said, turning towards me. "Are you trying to chase my girlfriend or what?"

"Me?" I asked, smacking my chest.

Of all questions!

He pushed me. "Is it because she said you were cute? Is that it? Oh boy, do you know how old she is? Do you think she is your rank? Are you mad? Who told you she likes you? Look, take time, oh! Relax yourself well, well! You'd better have been expecting a non-alcoholic cocktail from her. If you were expecting more than that, you must be very stupid."

Their roles were reversed. He was meant to be the deceitful one, not her. What was going on? It was like an invasion of extraterrestrial creatures, when they took over your mind and controlled your inner thoughts.

"You're crazy," he said. "Because I brought you here to see her? Where would you have been allowed to enter a hotel like this without me? Your head is not correct. You think you can take my girlfriend from me?"

"She's not my type," I said.

"What?" he asked, squinting.

"She's not my type, *jo*. Anyway, I have a girlfriend."

"You?"

"Yes."

"You're lying! What is her name?"

"Fausa."

He smiled. "Is she fine? Is she fine?"

"Very."

"But Glory is fine, too, eh?"

I nodded. We couldn't help our attractions. I couldn't explain mine to Auntie Florence. Glory's father was a famous footballer, he said. The bobo had suffered an injury early in his career and, instead of retiring, he carried on playing until he was eventually crippled. Now, she had to fend for the family. You had to praise her for that.

Fausa was a girl in my class. I fell in love with her the year before, even though I'd heard a rumor that she had slept with a teacher. To be honest, I couldn't hold that against her. She was too fine. I just had to forgive, and she wasn't one of those who laughed at me behind my back because of my height. She used deodorant and smelled sweet. I didn't even blame the teacher in question. I wouldn't have minded a chance to discombobulate her for one night.

Actually, "exquisite" was the correct word for her. She was that perfect—in the mornings when she came to class and her face was a little dry from scrubbing, and in the afternoons when her face was less dry and had a glow. I noticed all that about her. She didn't smile much and she was strict. Yes. You couldn't crack a joke about her. I'd tried. I asked her, "So Fausa, my dear, when is our honeymoon?"

Any other girl in my class would have said, "Ee-yack! You? God forbid. See your head like coconut. Get away from me, short man devil," and all that.

Fausa just gave me a dignified stare, so I watched her more closely. She came to school on time, listened in class, didn't get into arguments and didn't associate with louts. She hardly even spoke to the likes of me. The girl was too proud.

Her parents were illiterate. They couldn't even understand simple "come" and "go." I'd seen them before at our school gates, dressed up in green lace. They might have been off to an *owambe* party. They waved at me and I'd never met them before. At least they were cheerful people. I asked, "Are you looking for Fausa?" I was trying to impress them. They immediately lowered their arms and didn't budge until I'd addressed them in Yoruba.

It was obvious that Fausa grew up speaking only Yoruba. Her voice was unusually soft. You had to listen carefully to hear what she was saying, and perhaps that was why I began to love her even more.

It had to be hard to come from a family of illiterates. Illiterates were the butt end of our insults and jokes in school. If someone took a little while to answer a question, they were illiterate. If someone got a question wrong, they were illiterate. Dolamumu was a bloody illiterate and I almost (almost) racked with one bobo because he called me a stupid one. "Me? Me?" I said, smacking my chest. I didn't mind the stupid part. And some senior even got suspended because he said another senior's father was an illiterate from the village, and there was Fausa, with not one, but two parents like that.

The first time I toasted her she'd scored the highest in an English test. I passed by her desk and said, "Congrats."

"Thanks," she said. "So what did you get?"

Her eyes were white as blank paper. My heartbeat increased because I remembered the dirty thoughts I'd had about her.

"Ninety-five," I said.

She got ninety-nine percent. She was an effico.

Soon we were alone in class. We could hear our classmates chatting and laughing in the corridor and schoolyard. It was my chance. "Aren't you going for break?" I asked.

"I don't want to," she said.

"Why not?"

She shrugged. "I can't let anyone come and insult me."

She had twisted braids. Were they fake? I could never tell with braids, and some girls had those fat ones that looked like the ropes cattle herders used. I remembered the gist about her sleeping with a teacher. Who would spread such a rumor about her?

"Don't mind them," I said. "They're just jealous."

There were two camps: one was a minority of classmates she no longer spoke to (they said she did it), while the other camp said of course she wouldn't do it. She wasn't always in the top five, but she was taking extra lessons from her neighbor, a Mr. Mensah.

"It's Molara who started it, you know," she said.

"Opolo?"

Frog. That was Molara's nickname. Her eyes bulged. I mimicked her and Fausa laughed. They used to be best friends.

"You're funny," she said.

"Really?"

"You look like a hyena."

"When have you ever seen a hyena?"

"In a cartoon."

"Which cartoon?"

"*The Lion King.*"

I smiled. "Was the hyena cool?"

"Not really."

She, too, smiled. Oh, the girl was so delectable and incorrigible. I was sitting on the edge of her desk. It poked my yansh and I had to change positions.

Fausa, unfortunately, had a body that old men appreciated: sturdy in front and behind. Only she could make the brown skirts and beige blouses with butterfly collars that girls had to wear look sexy. She was taller than most of our class, including me, and older. She probably mistook me for an innocent bobo. I genuinely wanted to encourage her to go outside. The rainy season was round the corner. There were not many dry days left to spend in the schoolyard at break-time. Exams were also round the corner, which meant that we would soon begin to study in class during break.

Girls were so sensitive. How could she let someone like Opolo upset her? I made frog noises, but she didn't laugh this time.

"Come," I said. "Let's go and yab the hell out of her."

"No."

"I will yab her for you then. Free of charge."

She shook her head. "No. I leave it to God. God will judge her."

Those eyes again, as white as heaven. God? But why? With all the worries He had in the world, was it Opolo that God would be concerned with? But Fausa seemed so sure of herself. She sat there and insisted she was going nowhere.

"What if He forgets?" I asked before I left.

"He won't," she said. "He never does. He only forgives."

Fausa was a Muslim, so was Popsi. Momsi was born into a Muslim family, but her mother was a Christian and raised her as one. She raised us as Christians with both a Muslim and a traditional twist, which meant that we were scared of divine punishments and juju.

As for Opolo, she was sucking the pulp out of an orange and spitting out seeds when I got to the schoolyard.

"Opolo!" I called out. "Stop spreading cholera around!"

"Eh?" she said and spread her crooked fingers. "Your head is not correct!"

I laughed. Opolo was unfortunate. All she wanted was to be popular. There was no need to bother with the likes of her.

The next break-time I stayed in class, as Fausa did, while our classmates were going out. She turned around after the usual shuffling of feet and squeaking of desks, to see who else was around.

"Aren't you going outside?" she asked.

"No," I said.

She had cornrows and her head was perfectly round. I'd never thought the rumor about her was a big deal. I'd never even judged her—OK, I did, but I didn't mind bad girls. I asked her about her lessons and she told me about Mr. Mensah.

"He was a teacher in Ghana. He can teach you how to study."

"I don't need lessons."

"You don't know Mr. Mensah. He can work wonders. He is fantastic—"

"I don't need lessons. I'm too sharp for them."

She hissed. "It's not your fault."

She lifted a packet of plantain crisps out of her schoolbag. Her crunching was annoying at first, then the noise got ridiculous.

"What do you want to be?" I asked.

"A lawyer," she said.

Typical. She ought to be a judge, a chief one. Chief Justice of the Federation.

"Your jaws are strong, oh," I said.

She smiled. "You're not well."

I hoped she wasn't a bad girl. I was concerned about the rumors, as a parent would be. I wanted her pure, pure.

I convinced Popsi that I needed to go to Mr. Mensah's Junior Certificate lessons so I could be with her. What a butterscotch she was. What a botanical bouquet and Brussels sprout. Because of her, I couldn't concentrate. Her father was a mechanic. He vulcanized. Her mother was a Mama Put by trade. Her *jollof* rice was excellent.

Mr. Mensah also tutored students who attended private schools. They were taking O levels, SATs and the Baccalaureate. He came to Nigeria during a difficult time in Ghana, when food and soap were scarce. He stayed during the "Ghana Must Go" campaign, when illegal Ghanaians were driven out. He never went back, even after the situation in Ghana improved and Ghanaians became better off than Nigerians, and Nigerians who could afford to began to escape to Ghana for Easter and Christmas.

Ghanaians had good personal hygiene; I discovered that with Mr. Mensah. He always smelled of soap and he was fair to me, even though I couldn't help imitating his accent, the way he said "all of the abeve."

I almost got thrown out of his class, with Fausa, for causing trouble and I was afraid of what her mother would do to me if she found out. Not that the woman was strict, but she treated Fausa like an egg. I would hear her calling out after lessons: "Fausa, come and eat! Fausa, come and sweep!" She praised Fausa for doing her chores and laughed whenever she saw me. Mothers were usually nice when they spotted a short guy like me hovering around their daughters. Not because they trusted me, but they just didn't believe their daughters would ever be interested in me.

Fausa loved me because I was short. She was proper. She had class, but we eventually broke up because I was getting in the way of her studies with my silly pranks.

"You're lazy," she said. "Too lazy and you're disgracing your parents who suffered for you. Stop disgracing your parents who suffered for you."

How I begged her, "Please, please, please," and I held on to her ankles. I tried to explain that I was a genius and needed no extra tutorials until she finally fell on top of me and kicked me.

Mr. Mensah wanted to quench me, in the meantime. He made me work until I almost died in his lessons. He also taught me study techniques like using mnemonics. Mine were so filthy I couldn't share them with anyone, but they helped me to get through my Junior Certificate exams.

Would God judge Augustine, I wondered, outside the hotel gates, as he bought a newspaper from a vendor who was tooting a bicycle horn. The headline story was about the police inspector general. The man was in the newspapers nearly every day. He had stolen millions from the police pension fund, and Popsi had a few years to go before his retirement. He was furious about that.

Augustine rolled the newspaper into a baton as we walked past a street construction site. The laborers were stepping on cobblestones. They were shirtless and their torsos were covered in sand. I couldn't wait for the rainy season to begin.

It was too hot. During the rainy season, the streets on Victoria Island sometimes flooded like rivers, but at least we had some respite, in the form of a breeze. Victoria Island was another commercial hub, crammed with billboards advertising products I didn't want, like bleaching creams, or products I couldn't afford, like Kia cars. I didn't mind the Maggi woman with her plate of *jollof* rice, but I couldn't stand the Ribena boy. I imagined knocking him off his bike.

We walked to Bar Beach. I remembered Brother saying that Bar Beach was a happening joint in his day. He and his friends would go there to chill. Perhaps he meant to smoke Indian hemp. He didn't mention that, but he did say there was once a public beach there with thatched tents and chairs that you could rent.

Now, there was a dirty marketplace where street hawkers had set up provisions stalls. They occupied the thatched tents— they and the drug peddlers. There were also crooked-looking wheel contraptions that if your child sat on, he or she would surely fall off. The beach had receded and resembled a cliff. Every so often, a wave leaped out of the sea and landed on the street that ran parallel to the beach, and washed up so much sand that cars could only drive on one side.

That was the case today and Augustine thought it was a spectacle worth seeing. The street had been reduced to a one-way. He and I walked on the less sandy side, by the government guesthouses for out-of-state officials. Cars, lorries and *danfo* buses waited in line for their turn to pass. A few of them had braved the sandy section, only to find themselves stuck and their wheels spinning, as helpers from the beach, probably the drug peddlers, offered their services.

We watched a group of them lift a Peugeot. They were shouting, "*Oya, oya, oya!*" The owner was at the wheel, stepping on his accelerator. His Peugeot was wobbling. One of the helpers banged his bonnet and said, "It done do! It done do!"

"That car is going nowhere," Augustine said.

It needed to be towed. The bobos were wasting the driver's time. I was frustrated just watching them. The street would be cleared within a day, and by the end of the week another enthusiastic wave would leap over the beach and land flat on the street, spilling its guts. What was the use?

When I was much younger, a dead whale was beached right there. Lagos State didn't know how to handle the situation. The whale was all over the newspapers. Momsi went to see it. People were hacking away at its meat. They hacked until they unearthed the rotten fish in the whale's belly. The smell reached Falomo. The police were dispatched to control the crowd. Popsi was one of them. He said that every year the beach receded and eventually the whole island would become smaller until it disappeared. Banks, finance houses and mobile-phone centers had taken over most of the residential streets and those who couldn't bear the traffic were packing up and moving further into the mainland.

My school sandals were beginning to fill up with wet sand.

"Let me shake them out," I said to Augustine.

We walked to the pavement in front of a state governor's lodge and I kneeled down, removed them and began to bang them on the pavement. I was super hot now, sweating in my uniform, and had to ask him more questions. He was standing over me, his Nike trainers inches away. They were fairly clean, yet he ran on the spot to get rid of the sand that was stuck in his soles.

"So what do you want me to do?" I asked, without looking up.

I banged my sandal so hard it bounced out of my hand and somersaulted.

"You catch," he said. "I follow up."

He explained. I would forward my email responses to him and he would send them to his *oga*. I retrieved my sandal, which was lying on its back, and began to bang my other sandal's head against the pavement. There was no way of checking that he wasn't cheating me.

"What about the *mugus*?" I asked.

I gave my sandal a concussion before I let go of its neck and stood up.

Augustine stopped running on the spot. *Mugus* came from Ireland or from towns in England like Wigan, and in America from states like Wisconsin, Wyoming and Idaho, he said. Anywhere there was a high concentration of dullards.

"I feel bad for them," I said.

"Why?" he asked.

I shrugged. He wouldn't care anyway, but before I knew it, we were arguing and he was lifting his newspaper to stress his points.

"What are you feeling bad for? If you're feeling so bad, maybe you should go back to playing cards or whatever you do during your free periods at school. Let me tell you, you should be feeling bad for yourself, as a black man. Ever since slavery, these *oyinbos* have been taking advantage of you..."

He raised his newspaper so high I thought he was about to strike me. Slavery? But I wasn't yet born and neither was he.

"And they're still taking advantage of you," he said. "Economic imperialism. Have you heard of that?"

I imagined a white man as a Nigerian traditional ruler, wearing an *agbada* and a conical crown. His chiefs were white as well. They wore coral beads around their necks, and their servants were all Nigerian.

"No," I said.

"*How Europe Underdeveloped Africa* by Walter Rodney, with a... with a postscript by A. M. Babu. Have you ever read that book?"

"No."

"*Stupid White Men* by Michael... Michael Moore?"

His cousin worked in a bookshop at Falomo Shopping Center. He borrowed books and returned them, as if the bookshop were a library, he said. No one bought the books he read, or missed them. They stayed on the shelves for years, while the Christian books by Creflo Dollar, Bishop T.D. Jakes, Joel Osteen and Joyce Meyer were gone in a matter of days.

I knew the bookshop. I used to go there after Fausa broke up with me. The rainy season was in full force, and I was so heartbroken I was beginning to suspect that certain clouds in Lagos were following me. It was like a conspiracy. The minute I stepped out of our block, the lightning would locate me, then the thunder would laugh, "Ha ha, found him," then the clouds would pelt me. Some days, I wouldn't retreat. I would walk through the rain, refusing to run. I would end up at the bookshop. The place always smelled clean, unlike the barracks that stank of overflowing septic tanks. I would pick up exercise books and sniff them when no one was looking. They were the closest I could get to freshly cut grass. I would pick up pencils and erasers. School supplies, that was my section. I never bothered with any books.

The books and newspapers Augustine read had influenced his views. He talked about Halliburton, Nigeria, and the bribery allegations. I was not interested. He told me about the G8, Paris Club and that U2 bobo, Bono. I told him I was not the one who borrowed money from the International Monetary Fund or whoever, so no goddamn individual or club in the universe could forgive me for debts I hadn't incurred.

His views reminded me of Brother's, during his Shrine days, when he would come back from Sunday Jump and start singing Fela songs like "Why Black Man Dey Suffer..." Brother was conscious in that way.

"You just sit there," Augustine said. "You don't know your history. You don't know what's going on in the world or how it affects you. You haven't even heard of the International Monetary Fund or globalization."

I imagined the world as a white man's head gobbling me up. Opening up its wide mouth and just gulping me down with one big globalization.

"Oh boy, do you read the papers at all?" he asked.

"Yes," I said.

Scandalous headlines only, in the *Sun* especially. If I saw one that said "Bombshell" or something like that, I was immediately drawn in. The juicier they were the better. A mob had recently burned a man in Idi-Araba to death over some commotion near a mosque. I wasn't sure of the details.

"You don't," he said. "I have not seen you buy one and yet you say you want to be a journalist."

My voice rose. "I listen! I remember! I make observations!"

Koilywoily had told me that. What he had actually written in my report was that I was highly articulate and had an eye for detail. I had never thought of myself as being articulate and I believed my eyes were just good for figuring out the size and shapes of bobbies, but after he wrote that, I supposed he was right.

"Observations my ass," Augustine said. "How can you write if you don't read? Do you think Reuben Abati got where he is by not reading?"

He took the little I had told him, twisted it, and used it against me. I would never again confide in him, I swore, and I would pay him back. All those stories about Chip and Peanut, how he played ping-pong with them at home and tennis at Ikoyi Club. He was probably fetching their balls.

"Eh, what about the Savages?" I asked. "Weren't you running errands for them?"

He shouted, "Peanut and Chip? Yes, they treated me like their houseboy. So what? So what if they did? You think I enjoyed it? Was it my fault my popsi was their cook? Was it my fault they were sending him up and down? Yes, we were living in their boys' quarters, and if you saw the way they were enjoying life in the main house, you would know what I mean about economic imperialism."

He was squeezing the newspaper so tightly it crumpled in the middle. The headline said *IG Probed*.

"Don't feel bad for *mugus*," he said. "These *oyinbos* are stealing from us right, left and center and they are prejudiced. Yes. They never want to acknowledge any good in Africa, never want to see any progress, and if they are so advanced, how come we Yahoo Yahoos are the ones controlling the World Wide Web? Answer me that."

I honestly couldn't. He tapped his temple to imply I was crazy.

"You have to read the papers. You have to. You can't just sit here and be ignorant, especially if you want to make it as a journalist. Look, this same Summit Oil Mr. Savage worked for, do you know what they are doing in the Niger Delta?"

I sort of found out from another headline, when our president told the people there to go to hell. The petroleum companies were destroying the environment.

I faked a yawn as he began to tell me about his cousin, Magnus. Magnus grew cassava and maize on his grandmother's farm to pay for his matriculation exams and got into Port

Harcourt University to study mass communication. After he graduated, his uncle gave him a camera. That was how he began to take photographs and eventually became a photojournalist. Now, he had a gig with the Associated Press and covered the Delta region. The AP paid him in hard currency, but the bobos who flew in from wherever with their better equipment were paid much more, even though they had less experience. Magnus said the minute they landed in Lagos, they would leave the international airport and head for the nearest refuse dump, the higher the better, to take photos. If they had assignments in the villages, they looked for the nearest pot-bellied child. Their photographs would end up in this or that *Times* and everyone would congratulate them and hand them awards. *Oyinbos* didn't give a shit about the true picture of Africa, panoramic or close up. If they needed credibility, they found Africans to do their dirty work for them, and there was always one spineless, short-sighted buffoon of an African who was willing to sell his soul for a little money and foreign acknowledgement.

Magnus sounded like he had a bad mouth, but Popsi was also against the press. The press were always picking on the police, he said. They never wanted to acknowledge the problems that police families faced. The foreign presses were worse. Always the bad stories about Nigeria they reported. Never the good.

"Do you know all the *wayo wayo* America is doing in the Middle East because of this same oil?" Augustine asked.

I knew less about that. In that long email from the South African woman, she'd mentioned that Yahoo Yahoos were as unpopular as Americans were, worldwide.

"Don't get me wrong," he said. "I don't support what Osama bin Laden did. In fact, I completely condemn it as a supporter of non-violent protest. I do, and I don't understand why these Muslims always have to go around destroying buildings because they are outraged. That is why I choose to fight my battles on the internet. There is free speech there. Total freedom, and no one can come and burn down the internet because they are offended. But do you know why bin Laden chose to attack the Twin Towers?"

I had no clue.

"Because it was a symbol."

A symbol of American economic imperialism, he said. One moment he was trashing the place and next, he was planning to escape there. How could he dislike Americans and still sort of worship them?

The day the Twin Towers went down, Popsi wouldn't talk about them. Momsi said, "But what bin Laden has done is wicked." Popsi said, "Please don't mention his name around here." He didn't even want to hear the word "bin." Shortly after, he banned the word "bush." He was even sadder after the explosion in Ikeja Cantonment that shook Lagos. People were going there to commiserate and calling it our own Ground Zero. It was a disgraceful display, he said, and Nigerians were desensitized to human tragedy.

The sun was too hot; I was exhausted. This was like an economics lesson. Economics and current affairs. I felt sick.

"Listen," I said. "I just want a mobile."

"A mobile?" Augustine said.

"Yes," I said. "A cell phone. That's all I want."

"Why didn't you ask before?" he said. "I can give you a phone if you want. Ah-ah? If it is a phone you wanted all this time, you should have said. I can easily give you one. Here."

He pulled out a phone from his trouser pocket and handed it to me.

"You're talking about feeling bad for *mugus*. *Mugus*? They don't care about the reality of your situation. You're not deceiving them. You're just telling them exactly what they want to hear."

We stood there like a couple of pallbearers, burying our grudges. The man with the Peugeot was standing on the street. His helpers had dispersed. Waves were crashing onto the beach. The sea was greenish blue.

"It's as if we have been here before," I said.

"It's a trick of the mind," Augustine said. "That is what is called a *déjà* view."

He was an ITK, an I-too-know, and he *was* a liar. He fabulized more than me. He insisted we cross over to Bar Beach. We got there and he said he wanted to buy Trebor mints. He bought the Trebor mints from a hawker and somehow made a detour to a prostitute's shack. He said he was looking for Schweppes bitter lemon. The prostitute was sitting there with her bronze hair standing on end. She was wearing just a bra and denim shorts. She was not like the sophisticated ones that came to the hotel. She looked pregnant and her bobbies appeared cross-eyed. I had x-ray vision for bobbies. I could tell what shape they were, how big their nipples were.

"You wan fock?" she asked.

"*Ashawo!*" Augustine said.

She spread her fingers at us. "Nothing good will come to you!"

Ever, ever, she said. *Lai, lai.* We ran. That was funny, but it gave me anxieties, marital ones. One had to be careful these days. I couldn't imagine a time when sex was safe. It was like the commercial hubs. All the sex I'd ever had was in my head and how would I ever get any experience then? Worse, what if my jomo was too small and I got married to a woman who laughed at the size of it, or spread rumors that I was a virgin, as Augustine's ex-girlfriend had?

"I beg," he said. "I done tire. Let's go and get some grubbies."

The phone was a Nokia. I could have French-kissed it. It was chunkier than his, and plastic. His was metallic. He loaded my phone card and handed it back to me during our meal at Tantalizers. He had a plate of *jollof* rice and chicken. I had *jollof* rice as well, but with beef. I preferred beef.

"This place is for the masses," he said, munching on his chicken leg. "The food is sweet, but I can treat you to a better meal. A meal with class."

His lips were glossy with oil. Glory's hotel, he said. He would take me to the restaurant there and she could arrange the best plate of steak for us, a steak *au pauvre*. The way he was wolfing down his chicken, one would think he was satisfied with Tantalizers. The place had air conditioning, marble floors and leather booths. For dessert, they had Golden Scoop ice cream and fruit cake.

Tantalizers was a happening joint, as far as I was concerned. People were striding in and waddling out like pregnant women. They looked like office workers. The owner of the chain was an entrepreneur. I wished I could get into a legitimate business like that. I was gobbling my beef. The rice was peppery. My nose was running. I wiped my nostrils with the back of my hand and fiddled with the buttons on my phone. The power on and off was the most important. I would have to remember to keep my phone turned off at home.

"Leave that phone alone for one second," Augustine said, pointing with an oily finger. "You want to spoil it?"

"I'm just checking."

He sucked his finger. "I beg, don't disgrace me here. Are you a bush boy or what? How can you be acting as if you've never seen a phone before?"

Popsi had a cell phone. He used it for work. Momsi wouldn't know how to use one. Modern contraptions confused her, but she needed one for her business. Her rich clients had up to two, three or even four phones. I promised myself I would buy her one, the best phone ever, whenever Augustine paid my commission.

Augustine wiped his lips with a paper napkin, which turned orange and translucent.

"What about my commission?" I asked.

He frowned. "What about it?"

"How will you pay me?"

He flexed his fingers. "Why?"

"I don't know. I'm just thinking of where to put it."

He pulled his phone out of his pocket and began to press buttons. "Your commission, your commission," he muttered. "You haven't even started to do the work yet."

My phone rang. I yanked it out of my pocket. My eyes widened as I searched for the right button. I expected to hear Momsi's voice when I raised it to my ear.

"Hullo," Augustine said.

I hissed and returned the phone to my pocket. He placed his by his plate, which was clean, but for a chicken bone, crushed at both ends.

"That phone you have is the cheapest of the line," he said. "The cheapest, let me tell you. Every market woman in Lagos owns one. You know what they call it? Free water. You know why? No one will steal it. That is why I gave it to you."

Poverty was no excuse for foolishness. I, too, was poor. Yes, I was. I embraced that label now. Why not? Was I responsible for falling into a statistical bracket? I had already accepted that I had limited possibilities. Even if I had dreamed up an idea like Tantalizers, who would give me capital?

Nigerians were too enterprising. That was our problem, not that we were immoral by nature, but there was too much pressure to succeed—or to be on top. A Nigerian couldn't just be satisfied working for someone else's business. We had to own our own: fast-food chain, maternity clinic, law firm, primary school, even.

A common undergraduate degree was not enough. We had to have a master's degree and then a Ph.D. For writers, it was the Nobel, like Soyinka, or the Booker, like that Ben Okri bobo that Koilywoily was always going on about, the one who wrote *The Famished Road*. It didn't matter that the majority of Nigerians had not read his novel and could not even afford to buy books, even if they could bloody read. He won, and that was all Koilywoily cared about.

Nigerians. We couldn't just work for one of the new banks and wireless-phone companies and be grateful. We had to be the MD, COO or CEO. Traditional titles, too: *otunba*, *balogun*, *bashorun* or *erelu*, instead of ordinary chief. Even in church: deacon or deaconess or pastor and not just an ordinary member of the congregation. President, instead of governor or senator.

Now, look where we were today: it was every man for himself.

In Keffi, where the café was, people were employing themselves any which way, selling hand towels, phone cards, socks, fresh grapes, Aquadana and Boost. In Obalende, seamstresses and tailors were designing clothes. Mama Puts were cooking away on street corners. At Mammy Market, you could get your hair cut, your nails done, photocopies made, buy frozen food or medicine. All down Awolowo Road, there were eye clinics, car rentals, art galleries and consultancies. Nigerians provided consultancy services like no man's business, and we were always in training. Training for what, I didn't know, but unfortunately our presidents came one after the other and messed up our lives. So there I was, and there was the internet. It would always be there for me and it was infinite. I had begun to see it as not cyberspace, but outer space. The patterns that emerged when I logged on were now planets and stars. *Mugus* were aliens. I was an astronaut.

I made the mistake of sharing these thoughts with Augustine and he said, "You see? Totally ignorant. I told you. When you won't read."

The internet was a network of computers, he said, stationed all over in America, in buildings.

"So Muslims can burn it down?" I asked.

Muslims wouldn't stand a chance, he said. George W. Bush meant business. He was like Clint Eastwood in *Dirty Harry*. He would blow up any Muslim before they reached the doors.

I didn't trust him and he got on my nerves, but he gave me reasons to continue to listen to him. In a way, he was better educated than me. He had been to the Central Library, the National Museum, and National Theater to see the Chinese acrobats.

Mrs. Savage had taken an interest in his educational progress. Her name was Libby. She was a psychologist by training and she had worked with children who had learning disabilities before she married. She wasn't like the other expatriate wives who were either so miserable that their husbands had been posted to a godforsaken country like Nigeria, or so delighted that they could afford to employ servants for the first time in their lives. Those were the bossiest women, Augustine said. They would scream their houseboys' names and ring bells. Mrs. Savage never did. She would walk to the boys' quarters, sometimes barefoot. She didn't care much for shoes, except for the ones she had to wear to play golf. She would find her way through the laundry lines of bedsheets in the backyard and call out in a soft voice, "Enoch? Enoch?"

She sounded very much like a woman in need of sex, but I didn't comment on that.

American women washed their hair almost every day, he said, and they did not beat their children. Americans favored foods mixed with milk and cheese. They ate too much, yet they wasted food. I was learning more from him than I had from Koilywoily and other teachers. I didn't think we were a couple of juvenile delinquents who were letting our country down, nor did I spare a thought for the "majority of Nigerians who were enterprising and law-abiding." Good luck to them. Their rewards were waiting for them in Heaven. I wanted mine now, now. There were no guarantees.

We finished eating and left Tantalizers. On our way out, we saw a billboard for a Nigerian comedian that read *Comedy is not a laughing matter*.

Augustine found that funny. He followed the comedians, Basket Mouth, Ali Baba, Julius Agwu and others. He had been to Fantasyland to see them perform and had the DVD of *Nite of a Thousand Laughs*. Comedians were commanding big bucks, he said.

"You should be one," he said. "You're funny and with a name like ID Salami, I know you can make it. I don't know why you want to be a journalist. Journalists don't make money in this country, and if they are any good they get shot in the ass."

He began to limp. He ought to be the comedian, I thought, and I couldn't imagine why anyone would be amused by anything I had to say. I was a serious person, really. He promised to show me the Savages' stash of videos with funny men I had never heard of like Peter Sellers, Mel Brooks, Richard Pryor and Roberto Benigni. I could pass for a young Nigerian version of the Benigni bobo, he said.

"*Life Is Beautiful.* You have to see it. Classic stuff."

He was very OK. Seriously. Not rotten to the core. I couldn't explain, but he didn't think too deeply about moral issues. He was sort of completely without a conscience. He also cared about educating himself. He wasn't totally delinquent. He was going to the bookshop to borrow more books.

I raised my fist to him. "Augustine of Africa!"

He raised his. "ID of Lagos!"

My next step was to find out how to get myself a bank account. I couldn't hide that much money under my mattress, even if I wanted to. Once I converted the dollars to naira, there would be bundles of it, stacks. Enough to fill a suitcase. I didn't even own a suitcase, but I could afford to buy myself one, soon.

School was not yet over so I walked around. Victoria Island was the banking hub, after all. If the Atlantic were to submerge the island, the whole economy might collapse.

I got to a bank. The car park was crammed with cars, jam-packed with them. They were pulling over from the street and reversing out. One almost reversed over my foot. A security guard shouted, "Come on, move away from there! Can't you see?"

He was shouting at me and the driver didn't even say sorry.

"*Omo komo,*" he said and hissed.

I was already frustrated and I hadn't even reached the entrance. There were two more security guards behind the main door, which was made of glass. I didn't make eye contact with either of them and stood behind a woman in a black skirt suit, who was waiting to walk into a transparent kind of cylinder. There were two of these cylinders, side by side. A man walked out of one. The woman in front of me pressed a button and the cylinder opened. She walked in and the cylinder shut. A moment later, it opened on the other side. The new-generation banks were like James Bond. Seriously.

I did exactly as the woman had done. The banking hall was on the other side. The place was not that advanced compared to the olden-day banks, but there was a marble slab here, a rubber plant there and the workers had tags showing their first names. None of the usual "Mr." or "Mrs."

A teller behind the counter called a customer by his first name and the customer hurried over. I sat in a chair by the customer-service desk, which was manned by a clerk. He was attending to customers while, at the same time, checking his computer screen. All the time, his colleagues in cash and teller disturbed him with questions.

The cash and teller line almost reached the cylinders. The customers didn't seem satisfied. They looked as if their mouths were dried up from waiting, and one teller was pregnant. She paused between customers, for at least a minute, as if to annoy them even more.

It was my turn at the customer-service desk. I got up and two men who had been hovering around the rubber plant walked over as if they were escorting me. One of them was wearing a traditional tunic and trousers; the other was an army officer, in khaki. He sat on the chair before I could. The man in the tunic stood by my side. He stank and, not to be disrespectful, but when Nigerians stank, we really did. The smell was beyond normal. It was spiritual. Of another realm.

The customer-service clerk was confused, meanwhile.

"Are you all together?" he asked.

"No," I said.

The army officer had a complaint. The bank had not given him the correct information. He was Hausa and mixed up his P's and F's.

"Fleas," he kept saying, while raising his hand. "Fleas. Let me talk."

I was furious with him for taking my place. Perhaps he thought this was a time of military dictatorship. Perhaps he'd forgotten this was a time of democracy. The other man, who stank, moved closer to me and mumbled about his accumulated interest.

"Accumulatedinterest."

"Fleas."

"Incorrectcalculation."

"Fleas."

"One at a time, please," the clerk pleaded.

I had to wait until he had attended to them. It took him about ten minutes and the stinking man left shaking his head, while the army officer stood up in disgust.

Nigerians, I thought. Why couldn't we just wait for our turn? It was the same in school. "Fall in line," and students fell out. "Queue for oranges," and we scrambled for them, falling over the baskets, and the worst part was that we took offense and got into fights because we were not first.

"Yes?" the customer-service clerk said.

No "please" for me. He was taking advantage because of my youth. He looked about Augustine's age and he was wearing a shirt and tie. His nametag read *Bola*.

I was not intimidated. Bola was a girl's name. I asked how I could open a bank account.

"What type of account?" he asked, smiling. His expression said, Yet another idiot.

"Any," I said.

"For you or… ?"

"Yes."

"Are you eighteen plus?"

"No."

He shrugged. "Then."

"Sorry," I said, slapping my head as if I'd forgotten. "It's for my father. I'm finding out for my father."

He looked at his computer, as if he couldn't handle human beings anymore. I didn't mind that. I could relate.

"Current account or savings account?" he asked.

"Savings." Savings sounded more sensible. Something Popsi would approve of.

All the "please"s came out as he told me what he would need to open one: a passport photo with Popsi's full face forward, please, indicating his full name and duly signed by him at the bank; an identification document, please, like a driver's license; a customer mandate.

"A mandate?"

"It is a form, please, and we will need specimen signatures."

"Specimen signatures?"

"Yes, please."

"But why?"

"Why what, please?"

"Why all the… hoo-ha."

"Hoo-ha?"

"Yes. Hoo-ha. Specimen signature, mandate, this and that."

Wasn't "hoo-ha" a proper word? Government officials used it a lot. They never seemed to know what the hoo-ha was about.

He sighed. "It is standard banking practice, please."

"But I'm giving you money."

He raised his hand. "Please. It is checks and balances. It is for your own protection. There is a lot of crime around."

That was all I needed to hear. I got up.

"Don't you want the forms?" he asked.

"I will come back."

Cross that bridge, as Popsi would say.

Bola told me to have a nice day. As he greeted the next customer, a Lebanese woman broke away from the cash and teller line. She was on a cell phone. She leaned over the desk and extended the phone to the customer-service clerk.

"My husband wants to talk to you," she said.

Bola nodded. "I'm sorry, madam, but as you can see I'm busy…"

She raised her voice. "My husband wants to talk to you!"

"Just a moment, please," he said. "I can't do two things at a time."

"My husband wants to talk to you, right now!" she shouted and then continued to talk to her husband on the phone, in her language: yallah this, yallah that.

Her white trousers were so low I could see her thong. Perhaps it wasn't just Nigerians, and the bank deserved her tantrum. They had too many stipulations. I spoiled the air in that cubicle of theirs and watched to see how the man who went in after me would react. He stood still. He did not wrinkle his nose. It was like a science experiment. It proved Nigerians were immune to bad odors.

It was late in the afternoon. I was sweating and my bowels were beginning to act up. The nearest toilet I could use was at home. I could have hopped on a *danfo* but there was so much traffic, it was faster to walk. There were mostly banks and boutique hotels down the street. I passed a goat grazing in burned refuse, a house with a sign saying *This house is not for sale. Beware of 419*. I took the Ozumba Mbadiwe Avenue route where hawkers were selling *Ovation* and *True Love* magazines. Across the street was a helicopter pad. Our president and his state governors used that. I didn't know why. I would never get into any helicopter in Nigeria. On my side of the street was Lagos Law School and, on a high-rise of flats, I noticed an advert for Virgin Atlantic.

Augustine was saving up for Virgin Atlantic tickets. Virgin Atlantic was decent to Nigerians, he'd said. But why wouldn't they be when Nigerians were always scrambling to get on their planes? I asked. At the rate we were going, that Richard Branson bobo would soon be able to buy up our whole country and he would have change. Augustine said we scrambled for British Airways as well and British Airways staff were rude to Nigerians, and at least Virgin Atlantic flights were safe. Safer than our local airlines. Loyola Jesuit in the capital had lost some of its students in a local crash the year before. It was one of the top schools, and what did those poor bobos get? Obituaries, condolences to their parents and a week of national mourning.

I got to Falomo Bridge and the sun had set. I passed those Rotary Club signs on the pedestrian walkway saying *Do not urinate*, *Do not defecate*, *Do not dump refuse*, *Keep Lagos clean*. There were missing protective bars on the bridge. Normally, I would be afraid of falling into the lagoon. It had strong undercurrents and was polluted with plastics. I imagined jumping in and committing suicide as Okonkwo had in *Things Fall Apart*. I focused on the mansions along the waterfront and ducked under an almond tree at the end of the bridge that had grown so tall I could reach out and touch its leaves.

A stray mongrel sometimes showed up in the barracks. I had christened him Aja. He chewed on the leftover bones he found in our rubbish piles and I had tried to train him many times before, but Aja was the dumbest and laziest dog ever. Sit, he couldn't. Fetch, he wouldn't. Half of his tail was missing and he had a slight bias when he walked. One of his legs was a little shorter than the others, so if he stood still for too long he just fell over on his side. He once fell over like that in the Mammy Market and he looked as if he was trying to hump a bundle of yams. "Abomination," the stall owner said and stoned him.

Aja was a mess. You had to see him, yet he had these eyes, so composed, as if he knew all the answers. He was back in the compound. He patted a cow-foot bone with his muddy paw and stared at me as if I was the wretch. He never returned my affection and I was the only one in the compound who showed him any.

"Aja," I said.

He turned his face away as if to say we were not on a first-name basis and walked diagonally towards the staircase. I hadn't seen him in a while. I was getting worried that he had been captured by a Hausa *suya* hawker and was being skewered somewhere in Obalende.

Popsi was in the sitting room when I got to our flat. He was wearing mufti—an ankara tunic and trousers—and underneath, a white singlet.

"You're back?" he asked, as if I had returned from years of traveling.

He was listening to juju music on a cassette player. His feet were propped up on the leather poof. I prostrated only halfway down. After school, I, too, was inclined to behave as if I had been on an expedition. My uniform was damp with sweat and my shoes were covered in sand.

In my bedroom, I threw my schoolbag on the mattress. I was late, but I had an excuse. Sometimes, I stayed at school to play football. Popsi might not even have noticed I was late. He had already heated up the beans in the kitchen. I scraped the burned layer at the bottom of the pot and served myself less than I would normally—not to be greedy—and sprinkled a handful of *garri* over the beans.

"So how was school today?" he asked, as I walked back to the sitting room.

"Fine, sir," I said.

I sat under the poster of Jesus that Brother had sent us and mixed the *garri* and beans together with my spoon. He was watching the television, which was off. I couldn't stand juju music. The singers were nasal and their lyrics were full of traditional proverbs. He called my hip-hop "yo yo" music.

"You're facing your studies?" he asked.

"Yes, sir."

The beans were saltier than I remembered, but the pepper had mellowed. That usually happened after the third heating.

"Good," he said.

Popsi could sit with me for hours without talking. If I got up, he would immediately ask, "Where are you going?" I thought it showed his appreciation that I wasn't rambling on, as Momsi would, about her day and prompting him with an "Are you hearing me?" every five seconds. Our conversations after school were a routine. His questions never changed, nor did my answers, but he was listening. I couldn't, for instance, say, "I missed school," and get away with it.

I wanted to talk about crime, but I didn't know how, so I brought up the subject of the inspector general instead. Popsi had to be approached subtly. You couldn't generally come out with whatever was on your mind or surprise him. He preferred routines at home. You had to ease in your out-of-the-ordinary requests, maneuver around the heart of the matter and gauge his reaction. I'd learned that by watching Momsi.

"What's the latest about the IG?" I asked him.

His head went up. "Who?"

"The IG," I said and spooned more beans into my mouth.

He slumped back. "Um… the EFCC is after him."

The head of the Economic and Financial Crimes Commission was like the Jet Li of Nigeria. There was no criminal he wouldn't take on and he wasn't afraid of being killed.

"Thank God," I said with my mouth full and a false air of maturity. "I mean, if the IG could do that, then the whole country has gone haywire."

He nodded as I heaped up the remainder of the beans.

"That's right. Let us see how they will launder this. This one done pass Sunlight soap and bleach."

"You must have heard of Yahoo Yahoos…"

"Ya?" He glanced at me.

"Yahoo Yahoo boys."

He nodded again. "Them? Oh, yes. They are all over Festac Town. The EFCC are after them, too."

My heartbeat quickened. What if I ended up being arrested by the EFCC? How would he ever recover from that? He would be wrecked. Only his career would survive the scandal.

Festac Town was a prime example of what could happen to a Lagos hub. It was now the capital of Yahoo Yahoos. It was built in the 1970s for a Festival of Arts and Culture, hence the name. The Yahoo Yahoos of Festac were prolific with their letters. Experts.

"But it will be difficult to catch them. How will the EFCC manage that?"

"Um…" He scratched his chin. "I don't know. I don't know."

"What can they do if they catch them?"

"The system will take um… care of them."

What system? The system he had said was trash? The motto of the Nigeria Police was "To serve and protect with integrity." Popsi was one policeman who did, which was why Momsi called him Mr. Esprit de Corps.

"How?" I asked.

He lifted his hand. "The world is spinning. Whatever you create will come back to you. The internet only makes for immediate consequences."

He pronounced the word "hinter net," and I didn't say more about that. You did wrong and you faced repercussions. Wasn't that how the law worked? How the world ought to work, according to him?

At first, he claimed he didn't talk about his cases because they were confidential. Then when Momsi said come on, Nigerian doctors and lawyers broadcast details about their own cases all over the place, he claimed he didn't talk about his cases because he didn't want to desensitize me to crime. Nigerians were desensitized to crime, he said, and that was our main problem. As soon as I found out what the word "desensitized" meant, I realized that was an excuse. Where did he think my eyes were when the newspaper headlines said that banks like United Bank of Africa and Société Générale were being investigated, or that state governors had been sacked? Where did he think my ears were when he complained about the government officials making millions by privatizing our electricity supply? They might end up privatizing the police, he said. That could happen in a country like Nigeria. The civilians were completely corrupt. He wished the military would take over again.

I asked after Momsi, to throw off suspicion. He searched the room as if she were hiding somewhere. Under her sewing machine table, perhaps.

"Um... she's... she's looking for fabrics."

"Fabrics?"

"Yes. Fabrics. She is looking for fabrics."

"For whom?"

"For bridesmaids, with Florence. That is your mother for you. I don't know what she is doing with that woman. She doesn't even like her. She says she interferes. Now they are gallivanting around. I have warned her. 'Look. If she says something to upset you, as she normally does, don't come back crying to me.'"

He scratched his armpit. They were in the city center, then. I finished what was left in my bowl and licked my spoon.

Everyone knew Auntie Florence's husband took bribes. Wasn't that how he had got his family a bungalow? He knew how to play the game, Popsi said. His name was Zebrudiah. She was forever talking about her "Zebby" and how he had bought her cloth or taken her to O'Jez nightclub to see a live highlife band. The worst part was that I wanted to kiss her. Popsi couldn't stand her either. I finally understood her relationship with Momsi. It used to unnerve me how much Momsi abused her in private, calling her husband a rogue and saying she was pretentious and thought her children were perfect when they were not. Now, Auntie Florence was her ally, but Auntie Florence couldn't have influenced her. She had made up her own mind. She had agreed to keep the wedding dress out of the sitting room, though. It was now in her room.

"What did Auntie Florence do this time?" I asked, as if I didn't know.

He sighed. "She is supporting your mother, and your mother says if I don't give your sister away, then she will go ahead and marry her off. I have told her my position. The man is supposed to send his family here to ask for her hand. There will be no union until he can show me that simple courtesy. If your sister cannot say yes to that, then she should stay where she is. No child of mine can be ashamed of this family."

Sister was not ashamed. She was furious with him for standing in her way. She had written him a letter stating that she wasn't a chattel. He had torn up her letter and written back to say she was acting as if she was coming from nowhere. Sister then wrote another letter saying she would not come home. Momsi had told me the whole story. Sister was Popsi's daughter, she said. They were both just as stubborn and strongheaded.

"I don't think she is ashamed."

"She is! And stupid! Very. You g-go and get p-pregnant for a man who doesn't want to ask for your h-hand? Isn't that a c-clear indication he doesn't w-want you? And even if you force him to marry you, do you think he will treat you well? She's telling me a woman has a right to choose. To choose what? To be foolish?"

I wasn't concerned. Sister had been through her own radical phase, as Brother had, and apparently, she had not yet come out of hers. Suddenly, it was women's rights this and that when she got the NGO job. Momsi said she would never find a husband carrying on that way. Popsi said she was spreading whatever propaganda she was being paid to. He disliked the NGO's patron, the American actress. He said she was single and lonely, so she flew all the way to Nigeria to make other women single and lonely. As for me, I lumped Sister in the same category with Brother. They came from that strange generation. They were both into rights and causes. All talk, sometimes action, but never any results.

"What does Brother say?" I asked.

"That one?" Popsi said. "His own is to follow his church family. He would rather have your sister a polygamous mother than an unwed mother. He says he will officiate at the blessing. What can I say to him? He calls himself 'Pastor' these days. They pay him well and send him all over the globe to preach."

Popsi had never been overseas. Perhaps he was a little envious. As a Muslim, he wasn't against polygamy, and as a policeman, he prayed only once a day and said his hours did not permit him to go to the mosque every Friday. I thought he was relieved that Momsi had at least given me some religious guidance, but he thought the born-agains could weaken a man. Make him effeminate, actually. He as much as suggested that was why Brother's wife hadn't yet given birth to any children, and Momsi said, no, the real cause was all the hemp Brother had smoked in his teens.

Brother was very OK. Super cool. He was not your typical born-again. He had never tried to testify to me. Same way he had never admitted to smoking Indian hemp. He had just told me, "Look, stay away from weed. It's the only leaf with five fingers, you hear me? Like a human being. There's a spiritual reason for that. Each finger means something. Emotions, you know. It can make you sad, angry, very creative, but it can also drive you crazy." He said Our Lord was wonderful to give up His life for people who denied Him. People who crucified Him. People who didn't even believe in Him, even today. Yes, I thought. Jesus had to be a wonderful bobo. He had to be amazing. Why the hell would I die for a bunch of people like that?

"Brother cannot command you," I said to appease Popsi. "Nobody can command you."

"Sometimes, I don't know," he said.

His face was like a worn-out sack holding in rotten onions. His nostrils frightened me. I saw my future in them. It was easier to look at the poster of Jesus. Yes, he was a policeman, but he wasn't one of those who had lost all sense of humanity. I could have wept. Truly. I wondered what he would say if I broke down and told him it was the best day of my educational life.

I went to the toilet and cried there as Brother had when he was a senior and Momsi locked him up. We had since lost the door handle when it dropped off. The chain for flushing had also dropped off and our toilet seat was cracked. We had running water, but the place always stank of stale pee. Still, it was the safest room to be in. My room had no door. I heard Popsi clearing his throat and clanging in the kitchen. His spoon clicked his teeth while he ate and he grunted. There were days those noises drove me crazy.

He knocked after a while.

"ID," he said.

I sat up and wiped my face. "Yes, sir?"

"Are you still in there?"

"Yes."

"What is the matter with you? Are you sick again?"

"Yes."

"You see? I told your mother to go easy on the beans. 'Go easy on the beans.' She says they are nutritious. They just run through you, these beans, and she uses too much pepper. I keep telling her, 'Use less pepper.' She says the pepper makes her food sweet. 'Let me cook.' She won't let me. She says it's her duty. As if I never fed myself between the time I left my father's house and married her."

He sounded exactly like her. They were like twins. Telepathic ones. Momsi no longer talked about the twins. There was a time that she would. She would say that had they survived, we would have money in the family. Twins brought prosperity, she said. How, I didn't know. They seemed more like extra mouths to feed. Other people must have thought the same because it wasn't that long ago they were strangling them at birth. The twins died because Momsi delayed their treatments. She couldn't afford to take them to the hospital until it was too late. Rather than waste her money, she kept hoping their temperatures would come down. Popsi stood by and was busy looking.

"It's not the beans," I said.

"Eh? What is it then? Malaria? You have to be... um, very careful with that. Have you taken any medicine?"

"No, sir."

"Why not?"

"There's none."

"That woman. Don't tell me she's been making her concoction for you, instead. I've told her before, 'These concoctions you keep brewing, do you know what they consist of?' She says they're effective. 'You're just playing with people's lives,' I said, 'practicing witchcraft.'"

I was rubbing my beads. Her malaria concoction was vile, but it worked for chest colds. I was a tough nut, or whatever they were called. Truly, I was. I was not crying out of weakness, but because I had to go all the way to that extreme: Yahoo Yahoo. I didn't drink beer because it tasted bitter, never took a drug because I was scared I might go crazy. Sex I'd never had, so no one was carrying my child. I was sure Popsi would beat the shit out of me with his *koboko* if he ever found out. He'd used it to discipline hardened criminals like murderers and rapists and said it peeled off their skins and they pissed on themselves and begged.

"I will bring some Lonart back for you tonight," he said.

"Thank you," I said.

He was going to his palm-wine parlor again, then. The difference between him and Momsi was that she would not go out if I were sick. She would stay at home and fuss so much I would wish her gone. Perhaps he did drink too much. The fact that he didn't stagger around or sing songs wasn't an indication.

I finished my math exercises and I told him I was going downstairs to buy groundnuts from a hawker by the gates. He was sitting with his foot up on the leather poof and listening to his juju music. Not to be rude, but he had more pride than sense. All he ever did was complain about corruption in the higher echelons and the lack of discipline among the rank and file. My phone was in my pocket. I ran down the stairs and ended up behind our block, by the leaking septic tank. The sun had set. Chickens were strutting around. Two girls were playing some skipping and clapping game. They were making so much noise. One was particularly annoying. Her voice was as deep as Popsi's and she was insisting that she was winning.

"No!" she said. "I no go 'gree! I no go 'gree today! We must play another round!"

She charged at her friend and her friend pushed her. In no time at all, they had each other by their bra straps and they were wrestling.

I watched them as Aja buried his head. Perhaps a dog like him did have the answers. He learned nothing, expected nothing, ate what he could and showed up whenever he pleased. God only knew how many puppies he had fathered along the way. Maybe that level of ambition was all a man needed.

It took me a while to figure out how to call Augustine to tell him I could not work for him. I wanted to. I really did, but it would complicate my life. Seriously.

ACKNOWLEDGMENTS

Many thanks to Michel Moushabeck, my ever diligent publisher, to Mrs. Phebean Ogundipe, Markeda Wade, Bridget Gevaux, Sue Tyley, Sarah Seewoester, Miranda Dennis and Hilary Plum, for your invaluable editorial support, and to Rick Barthelme of the University of Southern Mississippi, and Reg Gibbons of Northwestern University, for giving me opportunities to teach between rewrites.